SOMEPLACE
Familiar

Teresa Tysinger

FOR ERIC
My number one encourager. I would never
have made it this far without you.

FOR EMMA
Because you were watching, I kept working hard.
If you want it, make it happen, baby doll.

FOR MOM AND DAD
I'm a writer today because you let me be a writer
back then. Thank you for always reading.

I do not at all understand
the mystery of grace –
only that it meets us where we are
but does not leave us where it found us.

Anne Lamott

CHAPTER
One

Not much had changed about Laurel Cove, North Carolina in the ten years since Livy Johnson had last visited. Driving down Main Street, it was every bit as charming and picturesque as she remembered. American flags blew in the breeze in old store fronts. Two old men in overalls leaned lazily on the back end of a rusty pick-up, probably shooting the breeze.

A red traffic light.

Livy's foot slammed against the brake pad, lurching the car to a stop about a foot into the quiet intersection. The cracking of wood behind her seat could only mean one thing. Her easel had broken. How was she going to get back into painting without the easel she'd used since art school? What a great start to her new beginning.

With no traffic waiting, Livy steered the car left as the light turned. She needed no GPS to find the Laurel Cove Inn, a short, steep climb off Main Street. The car came to a much gentler stop in front of the grand white building sitting at one edge of the town square. Livy's muscles ached from the five-hour drive from Raleigh as she stepped from the car and stretched her arms toward a cloudless sky. The building was every bit as beautiful as she remembered.

The sight of a man looking down from a second-story window of the inn pricked at her insecurities. A gasp of cold, crisp mountain air stung her throat as her hand rubbed at the heat rising up her neck. Her eyes cut to the hood of her car, its engine still pinging as it cooled. The uneasiness of being watched eclipsed the serenity of her surroundings. She'd come to Laurel Cove to hide from her problems, yet someone had already found her.

Don't be ridiculous. It wasn't like she was hiding. Plus, everything, and everyone, she remembered of Laurel Cove was good. Curiosity pulled her eyes back to the window. The man's tall figure filled most of the space between the frame. Flat palm facing out, he nodded in her direction.

Her heart skipped in her chest. Who was he? A tenant or maybe the owner? And why was he watching her so intently? She returned an awkward wave but not a smile, a tingling electricity traveling from her neck to her fingertips. Apparently satisfied, the man disappeared from the window.

Hiding had been effortless in New York City. Getting lost in a sea of people was as easy as stepping onto a crowded Subway car. Sweet Laurel Cove would be very different. Generations of families filled its church pews, ran its farms, and schooled its children. Anonymity was as rare as lightning bugs in wintertime—as her Gram would say. Being new in town and keeping a low profile might prove tough. Yet, the memory of feeling so safe and loved during summers here with her grandmother made it seem like just the place she was meant to be.

A cool breeze whipped at the few loose strands of hair around Livy's face and pulled her away from her thoughts. She turned to gather her things from the backseat of the car. The easel fell apart as she removed a suitcase that had been holding it in place behind her seat. Ruined. But no time to dwell on more broken things. She straightened and retrieved the folded paper she'd carried in her purse the past two months, opened it, and scanned the contents. She refolded it with care and slid it back in for safekeeping.

Armed with a few bags and one large rolling suitcase, Livy took in the entirety of the picturesque inn. This would be home—at least for now. With its large pillars, wraparound porch, and grand hanging ferns, it epitomized southern charm. Her eyes wandered along the lines of the white siding, to cornices adorned with carved ornaments, and finally up to a red tin roof. It had been well maintained over the years.

As Livy took the uneven stone walkway toward the front steps, she dared to revisit the window. Empty. The encounter with the man had been harmless, yet something inside her stirred. Would she make friends easily here? Would they treat her differently once they found out she'd been living up north? Southerners may be known for their hospitality, but some could be wary of outsiders. Her future here was anything but clear. Yet she'd made it this far. With a deep breath, Livy opened the door.

Jack Bowdon stepped back from the window. When the woman standing in the parking lot had returned his wave, the soft lines of her face had stirred something deep inside. Absurd, of course. Laurel Cove may be the small town where he'd been born and bred, but that didn't mean he knew everyone. Visitors came and went from all over. One thing was for sure, though. She didn't look the least bit happy when he'd waved. Some folks just weren't keen on strangers—no matter how friendly.

Jack closed the white lace curtains and lifted his tool bag from the floor. With that stubborn latch fixed, he had only a running toilet in Room 10 to check before being finished for the day.

Old wooden floorboards creaked underfoot, the only noise on the second floor. Since the crowd of skiers had departed a few weeks earlier, it was so quiet he could practically hear dust settling. The last of the early spring snow had melted, and it would likely be this quiet until the summer vacation season began in June.

At the door to the guest room, Jack paused at the sound of voices downstairs. Thank goodness it was almost time to go home. Besides seeing his friends, he preferred to keep to himself these days. Even after a year, his divorce continued to be fodder for talk around town, and he'd rather avoid the looks of sympathy tonight.

Jack twisted his master key in the door to Room 10. A relaxing night alone at the cabin sounded perfect, even though he'd built the house for two.

Livy squinted to adjust to the lobby's dim lighting. A short, rotund woman standing next to a large wooden desk waved her over. The woman—maybe in her sixties—wore a crisp, white apron over a light-blue collared dress with little yellow flowers. Her grey-white hair, secured neatly at the sides with simple bobby pins, reminded Livy of her own Gram.

Livy smiled at the woman and the memory. "I'm checking in."

"Well, we're so glad you're here, honey. You must be that gal coming all the way from the Northeast—New York City, was it?"

When Livy had called to make her open-ended reservation, the inn keeper had had a few questions—curiosity surely getting the best of her. "Yes, that's right."

"I'm Beatrice Hall, but most people call me Aunt Bea. Not to be confused with that Mayberry character." She stepped behind the desk, shuffling some papers.

A chuckle teased in Livy's throat.

Before she could respond with her southern-trained *yes, ma'am*, Aunt Bea continued. "I bet you're tired. You didn't drive your pretty little self all the way today, did you?"

Livy let the duffle bag fall from her shoulder and rested her arms on the high counter. "No, ma'am. I drove from Raleigh today after staying with my mama a few weeks."

"Well, we've been ready. I personally spruced up Room 12 for you. Since the outdoorsy folks skiing over in Boone left a few weeks ago, things have been as quiet as a sleeping cat around here." Aunt Bea put a check next to Livy's name on a blackboard behind the desk, retrieved a key from an ornate pegboard, and pulled out some brochures. The way the woman darted forward, Livy half expected to be hugged, but instead Aunt Bea reached for the duffle bag and started for the staircase.

"You're just up this way." Aunt Bea paused to look over her shoulder. With her other things in tow, Livy took slow steps behind Aunt Bea as they climbed the wooden staircase. The woman's smile was warm and inviting. "This inn was the first in Laurel Cove. Built in 1833. Except for the years it was used as a Civil War hospital, it's stayed open for business. Our family wasn't the original owners, but we sure love the old place an awful lot."

"It's lovely."

Livy ran her fingers along the rail's flawless craftsmanship and admired antique frosted glass sconces adorning the wall. The warmth of this traditional inn was a stark contrast from her New York apartment's sleek white walls and expansive windows. The moment she'd seen the apartment, she imagined how perfect that natural light would be for painting. The city had lured her almost ten years ago with promises of adventure and realized ambition. She'd found neither. Instead, heartache, disappointment, and uncertainty marred her memories. At the top of the stairs, golden sunlight pierced through a window, a choreographed dance of particles interrupted into chaos as Aunt Bea led them down a narrow hall. That swirling chaos was all too familiar.

They stopped at the second door on the right down a narrow hallway. Room 12.

"This room is my favorite." Aunt Bea turned an old key in the knob and motioned for Livy to enter. It mirrored the charm of the town itself with a four-poster bed, dresser, side table, and desk all made of matching dark wood. With its white cotton curtains and quilted bedspread, Livy could have been in the guest room at her parents' house.

"This will do just fine. Thank you very much." Livy couldn't wait to kick off her shoes and lie down.

The woman giggled as she patted Livy's arm. "Oh, honey. We're just thrilled to have a guest. You're the only one scheduled for weeks."

Aunt Bea opened a small door on the side of the room. "Your bathroom is just in here. The toilets in this old place have a mind of their own, so let me know if yours keeps running and I'll have my handyman take a look."

Livy nodded as a yawn escaped.

"I'll let you get settled now. You holler if you need anything."

"I will. Thank you, again." Livy grinned, watching the sweet woman scurry toward the staircase.

It took no time to unpack. Most of her things were in storage at her mother's place. After sliding the empty suitcase into the closet, Livy reached in her purse and unfolded the worn paper again. She scanned the text circled in red from a listing in a Yancey County Real Estate book. Her grandmother's cottage.

"Oh, Gram. Am I crazy?" Her words mingled with the light scratching of branches on the window.

With creaking floorboards underfoot, she went to the window and admired the outline of gentle peaks and valleys of western North Carolina that rose and fell along the darkening horizon like a sleeping giant. Life had changed so much in the last six weeks. The breakup with Sam after years of emotional abuse was long overdue, and honestly, New York City had never really become home.

Chilly air pressed into the old seams of the window with a strong gust of wind. Livy wrapped her arms around her middle. Would she find the fresh start she needed here in Laurel Cove? Could fixing up her grandmother's rundown home—bought with a small inheritance from her father, now gone too—also repair her broken life? So many questions, uncertainties. Maybe she was just running, hiding from the still palpable pain and disappointment.

A long sigh escaped, and she turned from the beautiful springtime scene starting to turn golden as the sun sank lower. The bed looked so inviting, but her stomach growled in protest. A quick walk down to

Main Street for some dinner would feed her hunger and stretch her legs.

Locking the door behind her, Livy fixed her purse across her shoulder and turned for the stairs. *Wham!* She crashed into a figure that came from nowhere. Large hands grabbed her by the shoulders. She braced herself against soft flannel fabric covering the wide chest of a rather tall man.

"Whoa, there. You all right?" Jack released his hold on the woman he'd just collided with. The woman from the parking lot. He leaned to catch a glimpse of her face, but dark flowing hair hid her features as she bent to pick up her keys.

"I'm … I'm so sorry," she stammered.

"No, please, it's my fault. I wasn't watching where I was going." She didn't speak and seemed to be avoiding his gaze. "You pulled up a few minutes ago, right?"

She straightened and looked up at him. *Good gracious.* She had the most piercing green eyes, the color of freshly cut grass. He'd only seen eyes that color once before, a long time ago.

"Um, yes. I just checked in."

Jack readjusted the tool bag on his shoulder. He didn't want to be rude and stare, but he had to be sure. Could it be her? Same freckles across the bridge of her nose—though lighter now—delicate features, and full round lips. Adrenaline surged through him. She shifted her weight and looked toward the staircase as if searching for an escape.

"I'm Jack Bowdon." Slender, cold fingers slid into his outstretched hand. "And you are?"

She offered a timid smile. "Oh, sorry. I'm Olivia Johnson. But most people call me Livy."

His heart soared to heights it hadn't known in a long time. *It is her.*

The tightness in the pit of Livy's stomach knotted like gnarly roots, cementing her to the hallway floor. She didn't have it in her to make acquaintance with some tall-dark-and-handsome southern gentleman who made habit of staring at strangers. But, my goodness, he *was* handsome. Clear blue eyes, hair the color of chocolate, and a thick layer of stubble that covered dimpled cheeks. She guessed him to be a few inches over six feet. He studied her, too, eyes dancing as if working to catalog her features. Then something surprising.

His eyes locked on hers—and the tightness in her stomach found subtle relief, the knots of anxiety loosening enough to let Livy breathe deeply again. What should she make of it—and that look of his?

"So, where's home?" His velvety voice matched the friendliness of his smile. He twisted sideways and motioned for her to go ahead of him toward the staircase.

Where was home? She didn't know. Certainly not New York. And though her parents' farm would always be a welcoming respite and safe haven, it had lost something magical the day her father died. Livy prayed for a place to call her own. Maybe Gram's cottage would be the place she desperately needed.

"I drove in today from Raleigh where I grew up, but I'm moving from New York City." Her teeth pressed into her bottom lip. She usually didn't share much with strangers, so why was opening up to a man she'd just met so easy?

"New York City, huh?" Jack's calm and casual demeanor struck her as almost foreign. She'd grown accustomed to New Yorkers who, on the whole, were more closed-off and rigid.

His mouth parted as if he were about to say something, when Aunt Bea's voice bellowed from the bottom of the stairs.

"Jack, you still up there, honey? I'd love to show you that fencepost out back before I head home to feed Floyd his supper."

Jack nudged Livy's shoulder playfully. "She'll keep yelling if I don't come right down. I'd better go."

With a smile, Jack let Livy start down the stairs ahead of him. She'd missed the impeccable manners of southern men.

They were met at the foot of the stairs by a grinning Aunt Bea.

"How nice. You've met my nephew. I may let everyone call me Aunt Bea, but he actually has to." The woman's loud belly laugh triggered a giggle from Livy too.

Jack pulled his aunt close. "I don't just have to. I want to, silly old lady."

She swatted his arm before turning to Livy. "Something missing from the room, honey?"

"No, the room is fine. Thank you. I thought I'd walk down to Main Street for some dinner. I passed a café coming through town that looked to still be open."

"That's Brewed, the town's coffee shop. They stay open until eight on weekdays and serve soup and sandwiches." Jack slid on a pair of work gloves.

Coffee. The bittersweet aroma that permeated the cafe near her apartment was the one thing she missed about New York. She'd satisfy more than just her hunger with a trip down to Main Street.

"If you can hold off just a few minutes, I bet Jack wouldn't mind showing you the way." Aunt Bea looked with anticipation from Jack to Livy, then back to Jack. "Isn't that right, Jack?"

"Sure. I'd be happy to." His tone remained casual, but Livy couldn't shake the sense that he was studying her as he had upstairs.

Their eyes locked. Again, heat rose to Livy's cheeks. He needed to stop looking at her that way. She never should have noticed the captivating hue of his sky-blue eyes. When was the last time a man had flustered her like this? Not Sam. And she was finally done with him. Her fingers found the tassel hanging from her purse and worked it over.

"Thank you, but no. I'm sure you're ready to get home, and I need to start reminding myself how to get around here." A to-do list ran through Livy's head like a ticker tape, an effective distraction from Jack's eyes. *Open a local bank account, get a library card, and locate the grocery store, gas station, realtor ...*

Jack turned toward a door behind the check-in desk. "No trouble at all. Just let me see about that fence, wash my hands, and I'll be right …"

"I said no. Really. Please, Mr. Bowdon. I'd very much prefer to be left alone." The curtness of her own voice caught Livy off guard. She pressed her eyes closed and willed the threatening tears to stay in place. Where did they come from? When she opened her eyes, she found Jack and Aunt Bea watching her with concern.

She raised her chin slightly to protect her weakened pride. "I'm sorry. It's very kind of you to offer, but I'm not up for company this evening. Maybe some other time."

Jack cleared his throat. "Of course." The words were soft and somehow soothing.

"Thank you." Turning to Aunt Bea, Livy continued. "Does the front door lock at a certain hour, ma'am?"

"Oh, yes, dear. After 8:30 p.m. you can use the larger key there next to your room key to open the front door." The innkeeper's voice was soft, too. "I really was just trying to …"

"Yes. And I do appreciate it." The pain in Aunt Bea's eyes tore at Livy's conscience. But there was too much to explain. Too much she just wanted to put behind her. "Have a good evening."

Livy crossed the lobby, the creaking floorboards the only sound until the unmistakable crack of a screen door behind her. A glance over her shoulder revealed an empty lobby, the flat door behind the desk swaying back and forth.

There was no excuse for snapping like she did. A heavy sigh passed a lump in her throat as she made her way to the front porch, now illuminated by the yellow glow of an antique lamp hanging over the entrance. The early evening ombre sky boasted brilliant purples and pinks. Livy sunk into a rocking chair and watched streetlamps flicker on around the edges of the town square. She hadn't imagined her fresh start in Laurel Cove beginning this way. Maybe fresh starts weren't really possible—even in Laurel Cove. Maybe Sam was right and she'd never fit in anywhere.

"I'm afraid I meddled too much just now." Aunt Bea fiddled with the latch on the back door of the dimly lit kitchen. "She seems like a sweet one, though."

"I imagine she's tired and just needs time to adjust. It's mighty different here than up in New York City, I reckon." Jack stood behind her. He had most certainly noticed—remembered—Livy. Her sweetness as well as the quick shift in her demeanor when he'd offered to walk her to the coffee shop. But did she remember him?

"Did her name ring a bell, Aunt Bea?" Jack waited for his aunt to make the same connection he had. He followed her through the screen door, down the stone steps, and into the inn's backyard.

She turned, nose scrunched in confusion. "Whatever do you mean?"

"Johnson. Olivia Johnson?" He let the name linger in the cool, evening air.

"Well, I'll declare." The woman let out a long, lazy whistle. "You don't mean Audria's granddaughter? That freckle-nosed, lanky, pig-tailed girl?"

"Yes, one and the same." Jack laughed at her description of the girl he'd played with all those summers ago. Pretty spot on, actually. But Jack would also describe her as soft and sweet and enchanting.

After their first summer running through her grandmother's gardens, chasing frogs along the creek, and swinging on the tree swing near the barn, he couldn't wait for her to return the next year. Livy Johnson was his first crush.

"What a small world." Aunt Bea made her way over to a section of fence and gave one of the posts a tap. "What do you figure she's doing back up here after all these years? I bet I've not seen her since Audria's funeral."

Jack knelt beside the post, the soft ground cool beneath a steadying hand. "I guess we'll find out. I don't think she remembers me, though." He shook the post and inspected the nails. One had rusted through. He reached for a nail and hammer from his bag.

"What woman in her right mind could forget your handsome face?" Aunt Bea's giggle tugged at the corners of Jack's mouth.

"You know as well as I do that I had many awkward years growing up, Aunt Bea. I'm not sure I'd recognize myself." In his youth, he'd been rather gangly, gap-toothed, and stuttered when he got excited. Nothing like he was today.

"Well, I'll have to be sure to catch up with her, if she'll let me. Maybe by morning she'll feel rested and more like chatting." Aunt Bea gave his shoulder a squeeze. "I've got to head out now and get the roast out of the slow cooker. Mr. Smith is on tonight." With mention of the night manager, she turned and started for the kitchen door. "Love you, dear."

"Goodnight. Love you, too." Jack called back as he hammered into the rickety post. Alone in the dark yard, all he could think about was Livy. He hadn't given a woman a second thought in well over a year. Not since Claire. He'd had no interest after their marriage fell apart quicker than it began. Yet, he couldn't deny the powerful shift in his heart the moment he held Livy in his arms upstairs, nor his concern after she passionately refused his company. What brought her here? Could he possibly care about her after all these years? Despite the swirling questions, Livy Johnson being back in Laurel Cove might just change everything.

CHAPTER
Two

inutes turned into the better part of a half hour. Livy's hunger melted away in the lazy motion of the rocker on the inn's front porch. The place reminded her of a refined lady, full of subtle beauty and without any entitlement or pride of position.

From where the inn sat on one edge of the town square, Livy had a great view. Rows of old storefronts brought back memories of leisurely Saturday strolls with Gram. Large terracotta pots full of multi-colored blooms, maybe pansies or geraniums—Gram would know for sure—adorned each corner. What a stark difference from the concrete jungle of the city. She'd returned to Raleigh for visits on several occasions, but it had been maybe ten years since she'd had the pleasure of witnessing springtime in the mountains.

She closed her eyes and rolled her head from side to side. The tension stretched and gave way to looser muscles. Somewhere unseen, crickets chirped. Sweetness of honeysuckle and freshly cut grass tickled her nose. The corners of her mouth pulled up as the faint mountain mist kissed her face.

These mountains enlivened her every sense. This was the magical place of the summers of her youth. This was what she'd come for.

The jarring ring of her phone made her jump and stole her breath. She looked at the illuminated screen. Sam? What did he want? The heaviness of dread pushed down on her shoulders. They hadn't spoken since the night he came by her apartment to get his few things. Nothing good would come from talking to him now. But what if it was important? What if something tragic had happened? She pushed the green circle to accept the call, but let a long moment pass before speaking.

"Hello?"

"I hear you're moving south." No greeting. Straight to the point. That was Sam.

"Um, hi, Sam." Her stomach knotted at the sound of his voice. "Yeah. I've, uh, bought a house in the mountains and I'm going to fix it up. It was time for a change." The confidence in her voice surprised her. Would Sam buy it?

"So ... you finally gave up trying to be a city girl, huh? I'm not at all surprised."

She stiffened and stopped the rocker's gentle motion, feet planted on the planked porch floor. She should have trusted her gut.

"What do you want, Sam?"

"I wanted to see if it was true." His voice became softer, quieter. If she didn't know better—and she did—she'd allow herself to believe it was regret.

"It's true." One leg bounced furiously. *Hold it together.* The other end of the call fell silent for a long moment. The porch light flickered as a moth flitted around the bulb. "Sam?"

"I'm here."

"Listen, I'm not sure why you are calling. You said yourself New York wasn't for me. I've moved on. Unless you need something, I've got to go." With eyes pinched shut, she swallowed past the lump in her throat. "I wish you all the best, Sam."

A familiar huff sounded through the receiver.

"You wish *me* all the best? Well, I wish *you* the best in finding another man to help you figure it all out like I did. But I doubt you will. You won't amount to anything there, either. Do you hear me?" The call disconnected. Sam's words were a punch to Livy's gut. Her hand holding the phone fell to her lap.

The creak of a porch plank startled Livy. Jack closed the front door behind him. Had he overheard her phone call?

His frown told her he had. "Everything okay?"

"Uh, yeah." Livy stood and wiped the tears away before facing him. "I sat for a minute before heading out and guess I lost track of time." Her legs wobbled a bit underneath her.

"That's easy to do out here." The kindness in Jack's eyes reflected an understanding Livy could not explain, which only called forth bigger, stronger tears. She bit at the inside of her lip to try to stop them from falling. "I just finished up with that stubborn fence post and figured I'd head down to the café for a quick bite before calling it a night. Laurel Cove is as safe as it gets, but my daddy would come back from the grave if I didn't at least offer to walk a lady in the dark. Are you sure you won't let me?"

Sam's biting words echoed in Livy's mind. Years of such treatment had left her feeling small and insignificant. But that was now her past. And she didn't come all this way to look back. She had to start living again. But how? She found Jack's eyes and whispered, "Okay."

"Okay," Jack echoed, a wide smile lighting up his face. "It's a bit chilly. Would you like to head up and grab a jacket?"

"Yes, thank you." Livy stepped inside as Jack held the door for her. She patted at the tears trailing down her cheeks as she climbed the stairs, pain and faint hope wrestling inside her. At the door of Room 12, she fumbled with her key and pushed through the door just in time for the dam to break. The darkness of the space embraced her like the blanket she used to hide under during a threatening storm. Silent sobs shook her tired body and exhausted soul. What was this power Sam's words had over her? He baited her with hints of regret then struck her exposed underbelly. *You'll never amount to anything.* The words echoed in her ears and flooded her heart. Breath became hard to find. She frantically searched the room for—for what? What was she doing here? Why had she agreed to go with Jack?

Illuminated by the soft yellow glow of an outside street lamp, Livy found a framed cross stitch hanging beside the dresser. She hadn't noticed it before. Wiping her face with the backs of her hands, Livy crossed the small room. The linen fabric pulled taut between what looked to be a hand-cut wooden frame dotted with multi-colored threads. *The joy of the Lord is my strength. – Nehemiah 8:10.*

A full, life-giving breath filled Livy's lungs. As she exhaled, peace ever so gently replaced her panic. Through a lingering sniffle, she felt the corner of her mouth pull up.

"Okay, God. I hear you." She would need this reminder daily, no doubt about that. And there it hung, in plain view. "Thank you," she whispered.

Her gaze fell on the bed. Livy had spent too many days and nights hiding in bed letting the layers of Sam's painful words weigh her down. But Jack waited downstairs. Her new beginning wasn't going to happen sitting alone in a dark room. She smoothed her hair, splashed a little cold water on her face, and grabbed her jacket, concentrating on taking deep breaths down the stairs. *Please continue to show me the way.*

"Sorry about that." The chilly night air brought goosebumps to Livy's arms as she joined Jack on the porch. She pulled on her jacket as he stood from the rocker.

"Are you up for walking? Or we could drive if you'd rather. My truck is right there." He pointed to an old, red Ford parked on the side of the inn.

"The fresh air will do me good. Let's walk."

They started down the walkway, steps falling into rhythm. Thank goodness the dark sky hid her puffy eyes.

"I need to remember to touch up the paint on this sign." Jack tapped the inn's wooden sign as he held the gate door open, sending it swaying on its post.

"So, you work for your aunt? A handyman?" Livy buttoned her jacket as they strolled toward Main Street.

"When she needs me. I come about one Saturday a month or when she has a special need. I also own the supply store in town with my brother."

"Well, then you and I would have met sooner or later. Bowdon's Supplies, right? I saw it as I drove in to town. I just purchased my grandmother's house and plan to fix it up. I'm sure I'll be in your store pretty often."

"Well, that's great." There it was again. The same warm smile Jack had offered when they'd first run into one another.

Livy didn't know what to make of that smile. Her father once told her to trust her gut about people, and her gut told her Jack was a nice guy. She just couldn't shake the feeling that he wanted to say something more to her. What a strange inkling with someone she'd just met. They rounded the corner onto Main Street in less than five minutes of comfortable silence and approached the coffee shop.

"Would you mind some company?" Jack shoved his hands in his jeans pockets. "It doesn't seem right to let a new guest in town eat all alone. Plus I'm hungry."

What could it hurt? Even still, Livy swallowed past a lump. "Sure. Be my guest."

Jack opened the door for her, but not with grand gesture. Such manners seemed a way of life for him— never missing an opportunity to be a gentleman. He probably did the same for everyone.

Jack chose a table by the window, which was fine with Livy. Across the street, a couple held hands while strolling a few steps behind a boy who was pulling a red wagon. Livy smiled.

"What do you suggest?" She surveyed the quaint restaurant. A short dinner menu written in colorful chalk hung next to a window looking into the kitchen. The clanking of utensils sounded from somewhere past the menu. Two old men in faded overalls and deep wrinkles sipped coffee from thick white mugs at the counter near the register. Besides the men, Livy and Jack were the only customers.

"Everything is good here, but the chili is my favorite." Jack crossed his arms along the edge of the table.

"Sounds great. I never did find a great chili up in New York."

"Chili it is." Jack made his way to the counter and placed their order with a middle-aged woman who looked a little like Ms. Gulch from *The Wizard of Oz*. Her features were harsh but not altogether unfriendly with an angled jawline that led to a pointy chin. She glanced at Livy with curiosity before smiling at Jack and submitting a paper ticket on the turnstile in the window to the kitchen. Livy was like the new exhibit at the local zoo.

"Shouldn't be long." Jack settled in his chair. "Dorothy said they've been slow all night." Livy chuckled to herself at the irony of the waitress's name. Jack leaned back and their eyes connected. It was no small feat to look away. She noted more of her surroundings to avoid his gaze. Mason jars full of what looked like wildflowers adorned each table.

"So what brings you to our little town?" Jack pulled Livy's attention back to the table.

She pressed her lips together. *Escaping an unfulfilling life and a broken heart.* She wasn't ready to explain. It was too heavy for casual conversation with someone she'd just met. "New York was nice for a while, but it was time for a change."

"How long were you there?"

"Several years—probably a few too many. The city has a way of holding you hostage." She laughed. If she made a joke of it, perhaps Jack wouldn't pick up on the truth. He reciprocated a chuckle as Dorothy approached with two steaming bowls of chili and a plate of cornbread.

The tall, rail-thin waitress jutted her pointy chin and eyed Livy before addressing Jack. "Butter's next to the salt and pepper. Let me know if you need anything else, darlin'." She walked away.

"Dorothy won't ever head the town's welcoming committee, but she's sweet in her own way." Jack winked and reached for a square of butter. For the second time that evening, the back of Livy's neck heated when Jack winked at her.

"Do you mind if I say a quick prayer over the meal?" The request surprised Livy, his directness somehow comforting without being overconfident. It had been years since Livy had attended church on a regular basis, but she turned to God for strength and comfort daily. In fact, prayer had surely helped get her through these last several weeks. Still, Jack's request to pray with her—someone he'd just met—caught her off guard.

"Of course." She returned her spoon to the table.

Jack closed his eyes. "Lord, today I'm thankful Livy made it safely to town. Bless this food and the hands that prepared it. In Your name we pray. Amen."

"Amen," Livy echoed. Her eyes didn't leave Jack's face while he prayed. Why did she feel like she'd known this man her whole life? Was there a reason he had been the first person she saw when she arrived in town?

Thankfully, the rest of the conversation remained casual. Jack told Livy about the harsh weather the mountains had experienced that winter and how everyone seemed relieved when the earth began to thaw, especially the farmers. She shared anecdotes about metropolitan life and some interesting characters she'd met in the city. He didn't ask about the phone call with Sam that he may have overheard. Didn't ask anything too personal. How nice to set aside her shield for at least a short time.

They were the last ones to leave about an hour later. Dorothy, busy wiping down tables, gave a flippant backward wave as Jack said goodnight and held the door open for Livy.

"I forgot how many stars you can see outside of the city. I used to love watching for shooting stars." Livy broke the comfortable silence between them as they started uphill toward the inn.

"I remember." His voice was just above a whisper. What did he remember?

The loud muffler of a truck slowly climbing the hill pulled her hands to her ears. Jack's shoulders shook with laughter, a lamppost revealing lines of amusement around his eyes.

"Bet you didn't hear that too often in the big city," he said once the truck had finally crested the hill.

"Horns and diesel engines, sure—but nothing quite like these big pick-ups." How quickly she'd detoxed her senses from the noisy metropolis.

Just a few minutes later, they reached Jack's truck parked near the inn. "You be sure and stop in the store anytime."

"You can count on that. Like I said, I have a feeling I'll need lots of supplies. Thanks for being so friendly. I'm not used to such courtesy." Why did she suddenly feel nervous standing here with Jack?

"Obliged, ma'am." Jack tipped an invisible hat and gave a grand bow.

"Well, my goodness." Out of habit, she stifled a loud laugh with a hand over her mouth. Sam had told her once she sounded like a fool when she belly laughed. *Not anymore, Livy. Not here. Laugh if you want, whenever you want.*

"Have a great night, Livy." Jack's smile was warm and genuine.

"Same to you, Jack." She followed the uneven flat stones back to the inn's front door and waved when she looked back and found him waiting for her to go inside.

Back in her room, Livy stood at the curved bay window. A bright white moon cast just enough silver light over the mountain range. The rise and fall was so much gentler than New York's jagged skyline. Livy hadn't anticipated meeting anyone and wasn't ready to explain why the last few years of her life had worn her so much, leaving her searching for home. Surely, Jack didn't care to hear a sob story from a perfect stranger. Actually, Livy wasn't sure she believed that. Something whispered inside her soul that Jack was just the person she needed to tell.

After a warm bath in the antique claw-foot tub, Livy finally settled in to the creaky, comfortable bed in Room 12. She had plenty of time to figure it out.

"That ought to do it." Jack stood, brushed his hands off on his jeans, and patted Rex on the head.

Even though spring was slowly creeping into Laurel Cove, on most evenings the chilled air still begged for extra warmth. He picked up the store's sales reports from the coffee table, fell back onto the soft couch, and let the heat from the fireplace begin to radiate over his body. The sharp crackling of the wood on the growing fire was interrupted only by Rex's tags as he circled the rug before settling. This spot, here in front of the fire at his home in the woods, was where Jack did his best work—and his best thinking.

Livy Johnson. He still couldn't believe she had suddenly reappeared in Laurel Cove. His first childhood crush all grown up. And beautiful. All these years, he'd never forgotten that enchanting girl with a wild imagination, adventurous spirit, and laugh that had resonated in his head for years. Earlier at dinner, Jack had hoped she would laugh like that again. But as a grown woman, her laughter was more subdued.

The fire danced before him, sales reports lying in his lap. It wasn't looking promising to get much work done this evening. His mother would ask, *Where does your mind wander off to when you stare into the fire like that, JB?* Did Livy not remember him because he now used his full name?

Or did she? If she did, she never said anything. He wasn't really sure why he didn't bring it up. He probably didn't mean as much to her as she had meant to him. It was only one summer, after all.

Jack jumped when Rex barked at some phantom annoyance outside the sliding glass door that led to the porch. Rex looked over his shoulder at Jack with his tail wagging furiously. "Okay, boy, okay." The chilly air blasted Jack's face when he pulled the door open. Less than a minute later, Rex sauntered back through the door and reclaimed his spot near the fire. "Took care of it, did you buddy?"

Surrendering the reports back to the coffee table, Jack leaned into the couch cushion and propped his feet up. The orange flames shifted to memories of the last time Jack had seen Livy. It was the summer after the one they'd spent playing together. She'd come for just one week that year. He'd caught sight of her, wearing a light blue sundress and a thick braid hanging over her shoulder, sitting across the small church sanctuary. She'd smiled and waved. When the preacher finished and the organ's last note hung in the thick summer air, they had met at the tree stump out front and shared an awkward moment filled with *hey* and *what's up*? When Livy's grandmother called for her to go, she had darted through the tall grass with a quick goodbye and was gone.

It was the last time he saw Livy—until today. He hadn't thought much about her since that last summer and their encounter in the church. But just like tuning the radio to the exact song you needed to hear, Livy was in Laurel Cove right when Jack needed something. He just wasn't sure what.

A log shifted, sending a burst of glowing embers up the chimney. Rex lifted his head, nose hunting the sweet and savory scent of the maturing fire. Jack stretched a foot and scratched the dog's side.

"It's just you and me, huh?" Rex let out a big sigh and returned his head to rest on his front paws. *For now.* The two words echoed in his head, resembling something like hope. Something he hadn't felt in a long time.

In the span of two short years, Jack had lost both parents—his mother from cancer and his father from a sudden heart attack—and his wife. Claire hadn't died, but there had been a death. The life of their marriage had been short, ending before it really began. He was grateful for the loyal companionship of Rex amid all the changes life had thrown him. Though almost a year had passed since the divorce, and he started to feel back to his old self, something was still missing.

He'd never expected to see Livy again, yet here she was, bringing Jack happy memories instead of heartbreak. While he had no idea what God's plan held for the future, his spirit lifted to have a new, old friend.

CHAPTER
Three

Hand me that crescent wrench, will you, Aunt Bea?" Jack reached from underneath the old leaky sink in the inn's kitchen.

"Sure, darlin'. Which one is that again?" Heavy footsteps followed the sound of a kitchen chair scraping the floor. Soft fabric from her dress brushed Jack's arm.

"The one that looks like a C at the end."

"Oh, right. If it were a snake it would've bit me. Here you go." Aunt Bea slapped the end of the wrench into Jack's hand. "Didn't expect you this early. It could have waited, you know."

"I wanted to see if the leak is from a worn washer or maybe the pipe itself before I head over to the store later today. I'll get what I need and be back this afternoon." Jack tightened a bolt then relaxed his arms. "Go ahead and turn the water on a little." He eyed the pipes from a few angles. A little water seeped from around the connection he'd just tightened. "Yeah, looks like the washer. Go ahead and turn it off." He shimmied out from under the sink and pushed to his feet.

He did, indeed, need to check the sink. But he also hoped to see Livy again.

"D'you hear me, honey?" Aunt Bea's twangy drawl refocused his attention.

"No, ma'am. My mind was elsewhere." He hadn't thought about another woman like this since Claire.

"I was just asking if you had any plans tonight. Maybe a date?" From anyone else, such a relentless interest in his love life would be bothersome. But his aunt only wanted to see him happy.

He leaned in and placed a gentle kiss on her cheek. She knew full well he wasn't seeing anyone.

A small hand rested on his back. "Well, you know, honey. You've got to get back out there sometime. An eligible bachelor like you can't leave all the single ladies this side of the mountain waiting forever." She gave him a gentle pat. "I really just want to see you happy. After all that mess. All the talk. It's just not right."

"Thanks, Aunt Bea. I'm just trusting in God's wisdom and timing." But she was right. Gossip in a small town spread like wildfire on a windy day. Even now, Jack was hard pressed to make it in and out of any establishment without someone suggesting a perfect match with their sister, cousin, teacher, or friend. But he was better off on his own.

Creaking floorboards sounded from the front of the inn.

"Oh, Miss Johnson must be up." Aunt Bea squealed, turning for the door that led from the kitchen. Jack straightened, something inside him warming. He quickly gathered the tools and smoothed his shirt, reminding himself to take a deep breath on his way to the lobby.

"Thanks, Landry." Aunt Bea waved a stack of mail in the direction of the departing postman. "He missed these few yesterday, so he stopped by before starting his morning route." *Well, shoot.*

He gazed up the empty staircase across the lobby, remembering the look on Livy's face just before she'd gone in to get her coat. He'd stepped onto the porch just in time to see her staring at her cell phone, mouth gaping, eyes wide. Though the night had ended on a higher note, maybe he should check on her. He lifted a hand to the back of his neck and rubbed away the urge.

"Time to head out if I'm going to have time for coffee before work. I'll see ya." He met Aunt Bea in the middle of the lobby on his way out, bending to place a kiss on her cheek.

"You enjoy your day, darlin'."

"Yes, ma'am. You, too." He loved that old woman. "Come on, boy."

Rex ran from the opposite end of the porch where he'd found a spot of sun. They climbed in the truck and rode the short distance to the shop. The town was still sleepy, with few people out. Jack tipped the rim of his baseball cap toward old Mr. Dexter, who sat on a bench outside the drugstore waiting on the day's paper delivery as he did every morning. The long-retired mayor of Laurel Cove and self-appointed watchdog waved a crooked hand then fixed his eyes back down the street.

Jack paused at the town's one traffic light that blinked a cautionary red until eight o'clock when most folks were up and about. With the all clear, he steered his truck into the parking lot behind Bowdon's Supplies.

The windy morning air bit at Jack's ears and nose, cold for mid-March. Rex pushed past him as he unlocked the back door and rubbed his nose in the dog bed that sat outside Jack's office. After dropping his bag and turning up the heater, Jack and Rex walked to Brewed, heads low against the wind. As he opened the door, Jack inhaled the familiar aroma of freshly-brewed coffee, ducking to miss the low-hanging antique bell that hung overhead.

"Well, hey there, buddy," Meredith greeted him from behind the counter as he hung his coat up. To Meredith, everyone was buddy, from little boys with baseballs to grandmothers with crochet needles.

"Morning, Mer. Pretty chilly out there." He rubbed his hands together and breathed warmth into his fingers.

"Greg's just pulled some fresh blueberry muffins out in the back. Want one?"

Jack never would have guessed that his two best childhood friends would one day be married, much less work down the street from him. "No, thanks." He sat at the short counter and reached for the day's paper. "A hot cup of that coffee will do just fine."

She poured Jack a to-go cup from the stacks behind the bakery display case. Her back to him, she asked, "So who was that girl in here with you last night?"

"How did you know about that?" Secrets didn't keep well in Laurel Cove.

"Dorothy mentioned it but said she didn't recognize her." Meredith delivered a sly smile with the coffee.

Greg emerged from the kitchen and slid a tray of oversized muffins into display case. "Yeah, let's hear it. Who is she?"

"Well, first of all, you can both put away the looks." Jack smiled back before they could tell him for the millionth time to get back out there. "Her name is Livy Johnson. She just arrived in town yesterday and is staying at the inn for a while. She bought Mrs. Johnson's old house outside of town and plans to fix it up. Livy's her granddaughter and used to visit during the summers." Jack paused while Meredith helped Greg place some of the freshly-baked goods in the case.

"Yeah, so?" Greg leaned against the case, munching on a scone.

"Well, we bumped into each other, literally, after she checked in. When she told me her name, I realized we played together almost every day one summer. But I don't think she remembers."

"Doesn't surprise me," Greg said. "You were pretty scrawny until after college. None of us recognized you when you came all bulked up from playing baseball at State."

Jack explained how they ended up at dinner together and that it was nice to catch up. End of story. Or was it?

"Well, well. Maybe I can finally hang up my matchmaker hat." Meredith poked Greg with her elbow, flashing a toothy grin.

"And the single folk of Laurel Cove breathe a collective sigh of relief." Greg cocked his head to one side and leaned against the back counter.

"Oh, hush, you." Meredith's vibrant laugh filled the café.

"Let's not get ahead of ourselves. It's just good to have someone new in town, don't you think?" Jack asked as he started toward the door with his coffee. Rex, who'd been lying by a heating vent under the front bay window, followed Jack. "About time we got the day started. Bye, guys."

"Bye, Laurel Cove's most eligible bachelor!" Meredith hollered after him.

Jack and Rex made it back to the store in plenty of time for Jack to set out some sales signs and stock the register before his regular contractor customers arrived. He looked at the clock on the wall. "Time to open shop, boy." He tossed Rex a treat from the glass jar on the counter and made his way over to the original wooden door. He released the latches at the floor and ceiling then turned the lock and flipped the sign to *Open*.

For a Monday morning, things picked up pretty fast. Jack had helped about ten customers by the time his brother came in. The midday shift was their busiest time, so Jasper worked for those few hours to help out and make sure Jack had time for a lunch. Around eleven o'clock, Jasper maneuvered through the congested store to the front register where Jack checked out a customer.

"Hey, it's my backup." Jack reached for a high-five. Jasper just grumbled under his breath and kept walking. The wilder of the two brothers and considerably younger at twenty-three, Jasper often came in nursing the effects of a late night out. While he was sometimes moody in the mornings, it wasn't like him to be downright negative.

Jasper handed the customer her bags then began reviewing the morning's receipts. When they were alone, Jack pressed. "What's up, man?"

"Charlotte's at it again." He grunted about his on-again-off-again girlfriend.

"What is it this time?"

"We were standing outside just now before she headed to her mom's. She started in on me about staring at some woman who walked past us and went into Greg and Mer's."

"Well, were you?" Jack used his big-brother tone.

"Listen, you live here all your life and you know who everyone is. I'd just never seen this girl before. And, I'm not gonna lie, she's cute enough to get anyone's attention with those green eyes."

Jack perked up. A stranger to town—a cute woman with green eyes. His brother had seen Livy. He smiled. "Well then, I guess you can't be blamed, can you?"

"Yeah … Charlotte didn't see it that way." Jasper sighed. "But you know her." He picked up a box of work gloves and crossed the store to restock them.

The crowd of customers had thinned out. Could he catch Livy? Jack called over to Jasper. "I think I'll go grab an early lunch if you think you've got it here."

"Oh, yeah. Sure." Jasper didn't even turn around.

Jack shook his head with a chuckle. When would his brother stop wasting time with complicated girls?

Outside, the rising sun had burned off the early-morning mountain fog and had warmed the air considerably. He was rushing. *Slow down, man. Deep breaths.* Why was he so anxious to see Livy again? Inside the coffee shop, he spotted her sitting at the same table they'd shared last night, reading a book and sipping from a teacup.

"Fancy seeing you here again so soon." Jack stood across from her.

She looked up from her book and smiled. His heart jumped. "Oh, hey! Yeah, the chilly morning called for some hot tea. But your aunt insisted on feeding me a home-cooked breakfast this morning. She sure knows how to welcome someone into town." She sat back and patted her belly, grinning. "I'm not sure I'll eat again all day after those pancakes!"

She seemed so much more relaxed than the night before. A sparkle in her eye danced in the midday sunlight.

"Not everyone gets her cooking on a Monday. She must really like you." Jack shook his head in awe. Aunt Bea was known for her fluffy buttermilk pancakes. No doubt, she showed off in grand form for her only guest.

"Where are my manners?" Livy waved at the empty seat across from her.

"You've not been back south for too long. I'll forgive it." His eyes scanned the place for Meredith so he could introduce them. But the midday crew had already taken over. He approached the counter to order lunch then took the seat opposite Livy.

"Reading anything good?" he asked.

"Well, I'm not really sure." She turned it to glance at the cover. *Remodeling Your Home for Beginners* showcased a young woman on the cover donning safety goggles and holding a hammer with a cheesy smile and gorgeous home behind her.

"I'm getting ready to drive up to the house for the first time since I've been back and see what I've gotten myself into." She let out a tentative laugh. "I bought this book in New York after the sale was final in hopes of having a game plan when I arrived. But after reading a lot of it, I have to remind myself it's just a house and won't hurt me."

Jack could help her—wanted to. But was it just being a nice guy, or was something else encouraging him to seize the chance to spend more time with her? A jolt of energy surged through his arms, standing the hairs on end, as if he were a schoolboy about to ask a girl to the prom. Ridiculous, of course, but Livy did that to him. It was undeniable.

"I'd be happy to drive up with you to the house, if you'd like." Jasper could manage at the store without him. Besides, when Jack brought Livy to the store, Jasper would probably be incapable of arguing anything.

"Oh, I wouldn't want to put you out. I bet you're working today, right?" Was that a subtle hopefulness in her eyes?

"My brother can handle things for a while. Best to get started on the right foot with such a big project. I don't mind at all."

"Thanks so much, Jack. Really." The smile that lit her whole face left Jack no choice but to smile back. He released a breath he only then realized he'd been holding. Being in her presence relaxed him. Like coming home.

As they stood to leave, Jack pointed to her University of North Carolina Tar Heels sweatshirt and cocked his head. "I won't help a Tar Heel. Deal's off!"

"Don't tell me you're part of the Wolfpack. I guess nobody's perfect."

What a night and day difference from the reserved woman he'd dined with last night—reserved one moment and cracking jokes the next. She'd keep him on his toes, for sure.

The two headed down the street, laughing about the rivalry of their former schools. Inside the mostly empty supply store, they found Jasper flipping through product catalogs behind the register. "Hey, man." Jack rapped his knuckles on the counter.

"Good lunch today?" Jasper glanced up. "Oh, uh, hi there." His eyes darted to Jack, eyebrows wrinkled with confusion. Jack winked. This was fun.

"Hi, I'm Livy." She extended her hand to Jasper, who took it while looking around the store as if he expected to see Charlotte waiting to catch him talking to the beautiful woman. Poor guy. Jack couldn't hold back a hearty laugh any longer, which only seemed to confuse both Jasper and Livy.

Jack formally introduced the two and gave Jasper the rundown of how they'd met at the inn. He totally deserved the side smile and narrowed eyes from Jasper as the three made their way toward the store's front door. Oh, how his brother amused him. Jack patted Jasper on the shoulder. "We should get going, Livy, if you're ready."

Like a slow-motion movie scene, Livy brushed the hair off her shoulder. Sun shining through the door's glass window painted her brown hair with streaks of intoxicating gold. "Sure thing. I'll drive since you're doing me the favor."

Lord, help me. "Oh, no need. I know the way." Then his breath caught as the words left his mouth.

"You do? How's that?" Surprise flickered in her eyes as they left the store and rounded the street corner toward the back lot where Jack's truck was parked.

In some way, he had hoped she'd remember him on her own. "You really don't remember, do you?"

"Did I mention the address yesterday? I keep forgetting it's such a small town."

No such luck. It was time to step in. "Well, yeah, it is small, but there's another reason I remember your grandmother's house, Livy." Jack opened the passenger door for her then climbed in the driver's side. He started the truck and let it idle. "Do you remember the summer you were about nine or ten years old? You came to stay with your grandmother and played almost every day with a boy from the house down the road?"

Livy's brows furrowed, her mouth pinched. Then her eyes widened, and her hand went to her mouth. "JB." She squinted a little as if searching for something in his face. "His name was JB."

"Yeah." Jack watched the memories come to life for her. It awakened something more in him, too. "Folks called me that for years, until I started sixth grade and didn't want to sound like a little kid anymore."

"Oh my goodness." Livy sat still, quiet for a long moment, before she suddenly gave his arm a shove. "I just don't believe it! Why didn't you say something sooner? Can you believe this?"

She remembered him. Jack swelled with satisfaction.

"Wow." Livy shook her head slowly, still bearing a goofy grin. "That was the best summer, wasn't it?" Her breathless, faraway tone told Jack she'd gone back in her mind.

"Yeah, it really was. I saw you arrive at the inn yesterday, and you looked so familiar. When you told me your name, I remembered why. I couldn't believe it."

"Seriously, though. Why didn't you say anything in the hallway, Jack?"

Jack shifted the transmission and pulled the truck onto the road. "I'm not really sure. Aunt Bea called me right after, and I guess the moment that seemed natural passed. So I waited."

"Well, I'm glad to know and remember now. I'm not sure I would have recognized you on my own. You've changed so much. You're so tall and...and grown up." She blushed at the clumsy attempt to find an appropriate word. "Well, you know what I mean. We both are."

"You're right. I used to be so scrawny. And, yes, you've grown up, too." Jack stared into her bright green eyes, silence filling the space between them.

Livy straightened in the seat beside him. "I should be paying attention to where we're going if I want to find this place on my own next time."

They were a few miles outside of town, driving alongside a creek on a two-lane highway. Jack turned the truck down a short lane lined with thick trees on both sides. Soon the trees thinned to the right and revealed sprawling farmland. Fresh dirt had been turned in rows in preparation for planting summer crops.

"Corn is probably going in pretty soon," he said. "Rob will start soybeans in May."

After another quarter-mile or so, they began to see a few small homes. Did Livy recognize the area, even if only a subconscious familiarity? They passed a small, white church with a tall steeple and several steps leading to its double doors. The church where Jack and Livy last saw each other as kids.

Livy broke the silence. "That's the church my grandmother went to."

"I know." Jack let quiet return to the cab and imagined the memories flooding over her.

"I can't believe how little things have changed." If the wonderful night's sleep hadn't done such a good job of reviving Livy's spirit, this drive through the countryside with her old friend sure would have. So many years had passed between them—a lifetime really. She caught her reflection in the truck window, head slowly shaking over the unexpected reunion. But it shed light on the unexplainable comfort she'd experienced with Jack last night. She knew him. He knew her. There was a familiarity between them, even though she hadn't been able to name it. Until now.

Tall grass bending to the wind at the roadside gapped at a wide driveway. The old white church at the end of the long lane, now paved, brought a rush of memories. The old minister of the church with hair like wispy cotton who preached sermons she could actually understand in a voice as slow as dripping honey and sang hymns at the end of each message. The musty smell inside the small building next to the sanctuary and how excited she and the other kids got when the teacher announced they would have Sunday school outside under the tree on warmer days.

She saw her younger self, standing on the church's steep front steps to have her photo taken by a friend of her grandmother's. Gram had pressed Livy's white cotton dress flat and adjusted her woven hat before standing behind her with a hand on each shoulder. "Smile sweetly, my sweet girl." Her grandmother's old hand in hers on their walk home from church— wrinkled, of course, but soft as silk. Her nails were always filed and painted, even though it was sometimes hard for her to do when her arthritis acted up. About fifty yards from the little house, Livy would smell the inviting aroma of the pot roast waiting for them inside. To Audria Johnson, roast was simply what you had on Sunday. Sundays and any time she was expecting company. No matter what time of day they arrived or what the temperature was outside, Audria's guests were greeted with a full roast meal.

The truck turned off the road and jolted up a steep bumpy driveway, pulling Livy back to the present. They stopped in front of an old house.

"Oh my goodness." Livy let out a small gasp and pressed a hand to her mouth, her stomach sinking. The small photo in the realtor's guide did not prepare her for this. While the exterior frame of the small, white home looked to be intact, a few windows were broken, awnings were rusted and tattered, and weeds crept up the walls, engulfing the once-charming cottage from the bottom up.

"How did this happen?" Livy turned to Jack sitting next to her on the bench seat of the truck. His eyes were kind, almost sad.

"After he bought it from your grandma, Mr. Charles took pretty good care of the place. Not like she did, of course, but it was still well-kept. Then several years ago, he passed away and his children sold it to someone who rented it out to a lot of different folks. After sitting empty a while, it just became neglected. I think the bank took it about a year ago."

His words hung in the air. How could this be?

You can't do this. It's too hard. You'll fail just like Sam said you would. Her head shook hard, her face falling into her hands. What was she going to do? Why did she think she could undertake such a big project? Now, here she was, life savings and inheritance spent on this home she loved just to be faced with the impossible. Defeated before she even started.

Her eyes stung, throat ached. She looked again to the dilapidated cottage. Her mind's eye resurrected colorful flowerbeds, musical chimes swaying in the wind, and the vision of Gram standing on the porch in her housecoat waving her white handkerchief and calling Livy to supper. She drew in a deep breath that fanned the ember into a flame of determination. It wasn't the end, but rather the beginning. It had to be.

"Well, looks like I've got a lot of work on my hands." She reached for the door handle, pausing to fuel her determination with another deep breath, then stepped from the truck and walked to the house. She stopped about fifteen feet short of the front steps.

Tears blurred the scene before her, threatening to extinguish her building confidence. Where was the home she loved? How could she have let this happen to this once magical place? If she had paid more attention years ago, could she have done more?

On the left side of the porch roof, she saw the hooks, now rusted, where baskets of bright pink bougainvillea had always hung. The bright white siding was gray with dust. Bricks at the base were splashed with mud. The light pink paint on the concrete porch steps was badly chipped, exposing deep cracks. They'd probably break if she climbed them. Were her cracks that deep, too? Maybe that's why it hurt so much to see such disrepair.

"I'll fix this, Gram. I promise," she whispered toward the sky.

"We'll fix it." Just a step behind her, Jack placed a warm and comforting hand on her shoulder. Might this house and the memories of an easier time be just the thing God had in mind to mend her hurting heart?

CHAPTER
Four

W e don't have to do much today, if you're not ready." Jack swallowed the lump in his throat. His arms twitched with the instinct to hold and protect Livy, but he resisted. They sat on the concrete steps, a yard full of high weeds in front of them.

Livy had been quiet for several minutes, her elbows resting on her bent knees.

"No. I'm ready. Things aren't going to get fixed just sitting here." Her voice wavered, but her spirit remained tenacious. A memory sprung to life, of a time that first summer they biked down to the part of Lawson's Creek that ran behind the old mill at the end of the lane. Although he was sure she'd been scared,

Livy had taken his hand and led him across the slippery, moss-covered tree trunk lying across the rushing water. Her words then, in her matter-of-fact tone, echoed hers today. "We're not going to get to that abandoned barn by staying over here where it's safe and easy." Together they had made it across and spent much of the remaining days of that summer playing in and around the old barn.

Livy gripped Jack's hand and pulled him up from the steps, bringing him back to the present. "You just call out things you see that need to be done and I'll make notes." She pulled out a small red spiral notebook from her pocket and looked to Jack. He couldn't help but reciprocate her wide smile.

"Yes, ma'am. Let's get started." They began walking the exterior of the home to prioritize repairs.

Jack tapped at the frame of a few windows. Warped wood gave way in several places. "The windows look to be original. Most will need to be replaced, even some that aren't broken." He paused as Livy scribbled in her notebook, then reached above one window and gave the white awning a tug. Fairly sturdy. "These metal awnings aren't a total loss. I bet most just need to be taken down for a good cleaning. But let's keep an eye out for any that may be rusted through in spots. And a few will need to be pounded back into shape."

Continuing to the left side of the house, Jack pulled away several vines grown up almost all the way up to the roof. Chunks of decayed siding crumbled into his hand at the slightest pull. "You're gonna need new siding, for sure."

Just a few paces behind him, Livy sighed. When he turned to face her, she had two fingers pressed against her temple. Deep wrinkles formed between her furrowed brows.

"Are you okay, Livy?"

"Oh, sure. It's just a lot to take in. I think my brain isn't catching up as quickly as my heart. My heart is committed to this project, but my brain is doing the math and calculating the time and money." She offered Jack a half-smile. "Let's keep going."

"I know it's probably more than you expected. But, as I see it, there's no rush to get this just right. Is there? The house didn't get this way overnight. There's no pressure to fix it in a day."

"You're right." Livy stood a bit straighter and shook her head as if to also shake the stress she'd begun to feel.

"But it will get there. I promise." Jack's chest tightened in an unexpected ache to fix things for Livy. He'd always been the sympathetic type, but it overwhelmed him how much he wanted to see Livy unburdened by the project set before her.

After another half hour, their to-do list had grown to include minor masonry work around the chimney, clearing debris from the gutters, repairing the broken railing on the front porch, pressure washing the stone base of the house to remove the quarter inch of mud and whatever else clung to it, and lots of fresh paint. Even to Jack, who had a lot of experience, it was daunting—and this was just the exterior of the house.

After the inspection, they returned to the front steps and sipped water from the cooler in the back of the truck.

"I know you own the supply store, but you seem to know an awful lot about home repair." Livy drew circles in the dirt with a stick.

"You're right." Jack leaned back, resting his elbows on the step behind him, his feet stretched onto the grass. "My degree from NC State is in architecture. For a while I designed homes, but enjoyed being out on the build site much more."

She sat up straighter and tapped him on the knee with the stick. "Hey, how fun to design people's homes."

"It was a real joy. I worked for several years as a contractor with a large company out of Boone before moving back to Laurel Cove."

"What brought you back here?" Livy spoke through a big yawn. With arms reached high over her head, her elongated torso revealed gentle curves. The loose ponytail that held her dark-brown hair off her neck exposed a gracefulness that stole Jack's breath. As she glanced out at the yard, he moved from her neck to the soft features of her cheeks and lips. *Mercy.*

"Uh, well..." He looked away to clear the distraction. "Dad had a heart attack. I came back to help run the store while he recovered, but he never got better. Soon after that, Mom was diagnosed with cancer. She died less than a year later. Before I knew it, it was just Jasper and me. Neither of us could bear selling the store, so we decided to keep it going ourselves."

"Jack, I'm so sorry." Her hand rested on his forearm, calling the fine hairs to attention despite the afternoon warmth. When their eyes met, he saw sincere sympathy. She somehow excited and calmed him at the same time.

Several moments passed before Livy stood and took a few steps into the front yard, hands on her hips. "This yard is going to need a lot of attention, too. Better add landscaping to the list."

Was she feeling uneasy? There was a lot they didn't know about each other. For instance, Jack not only enjoyed the hands-on work, but did it as a hobby, flipping two houses so far in Laurel Cove in his spare time. Some guys sat at the bar after a hard day, but as long as Jack had a hammer in his hand, all was right in the world. But he still harbored some resentment over the topic. His ex-wife had never understood his interest in building for fun, and her incessant nagging had sucked a lot of the joy out of the experience. He had no intention of bringing up anything negative today.

From the porch, Jack followed Livy's steps along the edge of the front yard. She leaned over every now and then to inspect a flower. Her interest to be part of restoring the house was admirable. Hiring someone to do it for her would certainly be easier. Claire, on the other hand, never had interest in Jack's houses. He'd tried to get her to join him on several of the easier projects, like painting or landscaping, but she refused. Jasper, Owen, and Greg had suggested Jack find a house to work on after the divorce, but he couldn't find the motivation to begin—much less finish—another one. Until Livy came back into his life.

He rose from the porch steps and faced the old house that held dear memories for them both. The run down place offered a new sense of purpose, of hope. He longed to see the house brought back to its full potential. Maybe Jack wanted that for his life, too. To discover what was possible in life after so much change and heartache. To feel the joy he'd felt as young boy playing with Livy that summer long ago.

"Well, you ready to go inside?"

To Livy's surprise, Jack jumped as she spoke right behind him on the porch. Maybe he had been lost in thought—that was easy to do. Her short walk around the yard and back had allowed her mind to fill with thoughts of the day and the months that had led her here.

"Guess there's no use putting it off. Can't be any worse than what we've seen out here, right?" He stood and brushed off the back of his jeans.

"You've got that right!" They shared a laugh as they approached the wooden front door. Upon close examination, the simple semi-circle stained-glass window at the top of the door was still intact. The colors were muted with layers of dirt and dust, but it was otherwise fine.

Jack unlocked and opened the door with ease. "Well, what do you know." They were met with a musty, damp odor.

"It reminds me of the inside of my father's work shed on the farm and mildewed bath towels." The sound of their chuckles echoed in the lonely space. A small but strong ray of sunlight shone across the otherwise dark room from a gap in the plywood that covered one of the windows. Specks of dust danced in its path. Jack switched on his heavy-duty flashlight and panned the room.

"The living room is there." Livy pointed to the right of the entry.

Thick, dark drapes heavy with dust flanked the boarded window that looked out over the porch. The only furniture left in the room was a thrift-store couch with its cushions askew, a floor lamp, and a small coffee table that still held beer bottles and a full ashtray. Turning away, Livy moved through a doorway to the kitchen. An old white iron stove anchored the room.

"Gram's stove." Livy ran a hand over the metal edge. Her gaze followed her steps past the stove to a deep porcelain sink, full of dirty and broken dishes. A rogue vine had taken root inside the sink and trailed to the floor.

"It reminds me of a fairytale my mother told me as a young boy about the jungle taking over a cottage in the woods." Jack spoke in a hushed voice as they surveyed the room. Livy looked over her shoulder at him and grinned. What a sweet memory to share with her.

Across from the stove and sink sat a card table in front of double windows that were boarded-up like the living room window. Two of the three chairs, high-backed and upholstered in a 70s, mustard-yellow vinyl, were overturned and lying on the floor. Jack reached to set them on their feet.

"She loved this kitchen." Livy pointed to where the table used to be. "She'd sit right there and sip on a cold glass of iced tea after she'd come in from gardening. The bed in front of these windows held her pansies and other small flowers. She had pink, white, purple, yellow—you name it. She asked me once if I could see their faces." Livy looked back at Jack, who leaned against the stove listening. "If you look at a pansy, the dark centers do look like little faces. I was six or seven when she told me that, and I remember thinking she grew magical flowers with eyes and smiles. She said that's why she talked to them when she watered them. She was waiting for them to talk back."

"That's a great story," Jack said. "I remember her garden was prettier than any I'd ever seen." He paused, and the room fell silent again.

"My dad used to say she could get a rock to grow." Livy could almost hear her father's words in her head. She turned away from the window and pulled herself back into the moment.

At the opposite end of the small kitchen was a door she remembered that led to a mudroom. It proved more stubborn than the front door, not giving at all when Jack pulled at it. The original iron knob had once been painted black but was now chipping so badly that when Jack tried turning it with more force, paint broke into his hands in large pieces.

"I think it's locked." He grunted as he pulled harder.

"Looks like the same knob that was here when I was a kid," Livy said. "Gram had a master skeleton key that went to all the doors." She looked around the room.

The front door was the only one whose lock had been replaced with a modern set.

"Oh, wait!" Livy darted out of the kitchen. Jack followed her out of the house and over to the truck. "The realtor gave me a packet of information earlier this morning when I stopped by to pick up the final paperwork."

Jack took the notebook she handed to him. She opened the passenger door and reached on her tiptoes for the packet. "Yes!" She faced Jack, holding up an old skeleton key. "I think this is the key to the pantry door!" She handed it to Jack, and he turned it over in his hand.

"It's in great shape. Not rusted at all." His eyes were wide, eyebrows arched.

Livy placed her hand over the key in his, squeezed, and looked up with excitement. His warm fingers closed around hers. He held her gaze, returning a warm smile. For a lingering moment, Livy got lost in his eyes.

"You coming?" She pulled her hand away, took the key, and walked back to the house. *What am I doing?* What was it about Jack that suddenly made her heart flutter? She had to keep her head clear.

"Yeah, right behind you." Jack lingered several moments at the truck before joining her.

Had she spooked him getting so caught up in the moment? Had he even noticed? It was so nice to have her hand in his. But she hadn't moved to Laurel Cove to find another boyfriend.

Back in the kitchen, Livy brushed away some cobwebs and fitted the key inside the lock. She turned it and heard the mechanism give way. Pausing, she shot

Jack a hopeful look then turned the knob and pulled. The key had done its job, but the door itself stuck. "Well, what now?"

Jack stepped forward and examined the doorframe. "Looks to me like the door may have warped a little, swelling from moisture inside the house. We'll likely have to shave it down a bit or replace the whole door." He gave the knob a hard pull, then another. On the third try, it gave way and flew open, almost knocking Jack to the floor. He caught himself against the side of the sink.

Livy laughed under her breath. "Graceful, you are not."

"Oh, don't let my lack of moves fool you," he said with a twinkle in his eyes. "I'm full of grace." He wiped his dirty hands on his jeans and wrinkled his nose. "The sludge on this sink is disgusting."

"Yeah, we'll have to draw straws to see who gets that project." Hopefully, he'd keep helping past today.

"I didn't know we were already divvying up chores," Jack joked with ease, swatting at her arm with the back of his hand. "In that case, I'll do the sink if you deal with the rats." He pointed down to the floor past Livy, making her think one of the vermin was right out in the open.

"What?" She screamed and flew toward Jack, her hands around his waist as if ready to shove him toward the rat as an offering to save herself. There was nothing she hated more than rats. He gave a big belly laugh and tried to pull her from behind him. But she kept her face planted against his back, fingers digging into his sides.

If she'd actually seen the rat, she may have climbed into his arms.

"Livy, it's okay." He no longer laughed and spoke in whispered tones. "It was just a joke. I didn't see a rat. I promise."

Her head shook with uncertainty.

He turned to face her, her head now resting on his chest and her arms hugging his middle. For a minute, he held her. Oh, how she missed the feel of a man holding her. The strength, the security, the invitation to linger. She took a few deep breaths before looking up.

"I'm so, so sorry," Livy stammered as she backed away a few steps and rubbed her flushed cheeks, which were hot to the touch. What was she doing? "You must think I'm such a silly girl, afraid of rats. The small mice on Dad's farm didn't bother me growing up. But rats in New York City are like small, untamed cats." She headed out of the kitchen, through the living room, and into the larger of the two bedrooms at the back of the house. She'd seen enough of the kitchen, rats or not. Jack's heavy footsteps followed a few steps behind.

"The first night I was in the city I stayed in a cheap hotel." Livy stood at the window, looking out at the overgrown backyard as Jack came up beside her. "I woke up to scratching sounds, turned on the light and found a huge rat gnawing on my toothbrush. I packed up my stuff that minute, minus my toothbrush of course, and left. Ever since, me and rats just don't mix."

"I'm sorry, Livy." Jack spoke with a soft sensitivity that was foreign to her. Sam rarely showed this type of kindness, so it had become second nature to not share such things with him. Yet, talking and laughing with

Jack came so easily. It pricked her heart with a pinpoint of hope, illuminating for a brief moment the possibility of being both vulnerable and safe with a man. What a strange realization. She had love and trust with men her whole life before Sam. A wonderful father, grandfather, friends. Then Sam came along and single-handedly erected an invisible but strong-as-steel cage around her heart. It was tempting to doubt a budding affection for Jack was possible, but even more tempting to believe in a miracle that freed her.

"Please don't apologize. It's really okay." With her acceptance of his apology, a smile returned to his face.

During the next hour or so, Jack and Livy finished inspecting the house, adding to Livy's long to-do list. The two bedrooms needed only major cleaning and fresh paint; the bathroom, however, needed fixture upgrades, a new floor from water damage, and a new door to the linen closet that had cracked up the middle.

Outside, they walked across the overgrown backyard, bending under the double clothesline that still stood, and made their way through a few thorny brambles to Gram's large shed. Without a doubt, it had suffered most from the years of neglect.

"I don't know how this is still standing, Livy. One intense storm and it might not survive." Jack tugged at the slatted wall of the shed. It broke off into his hand without a fight. Livy leaned her entire body weight against the barn-style door to coax it open.

"Let me—there may be rats," Jack offered with a teasing smile.

"Be my guest." Her hands went up in surrender.

Before he could get it more than halfway open, the rusty handle broke off in his hand.

"Well, add that to the list, too." Jack tossed aside the handle and pushed the creaking door until it would open no further. He propped it with an old cinderblock. With his flashlight, he panned the space.

Just as Livy had suspected, it was set up for a garage with a rickety wooden bench for tools on one side, rusty discarded car parts in a pile on the other, pictures of old cars tacked to a wall, and a bunch of junk in the back.

"Gram had that baby-blue Oldsmobile, remember?" They used to take trips into town with the windows rolled down, Gram's hair blowing in the wind, their skin sticking to the hot vinyl upholstery.

"Yeah, I do. No one else in town had one that color. It was easy to spot her coming." Jack kicked at the pile of parts, creating a racket that hopefully scared away any nearby rodents.

"I think it's safe," he said over his shoulder. He swatted at a string hanging from a simple overhead light in the middle of the shed.

"I'll come over, but first scurry I hear, I'll leave you to fend for yourself!" Livy joined him at the back near the pile of junk. "Some of this looks familiar," she said, pointing to an old wood-handled rake. "Pretty sure I used that to help out as a kid." A rusty roll of gardening wire for vegetables and a few weathered boxes looked old enough to have belonged to her Gram.

Jack moved around a few larger pieces. "I love old stuff like this."

"I didn't think I did, but now that I'm here, it is pretty amazing to see some of this." Livy walked to the other side of Jack as they followed the trail of his flashlight with their eyes. Then she saw it: the outline of an old washer tub.

"Well, look at that!" She bent and rubbed her fingers over its iron ridges. "I would come out here in the early morning when Gram liked to wash the laundry so it could be on the line to dry when the sun was hottest. My favorite job was to sit on the side and turn the crank as she fed the clothes through to wring them out." Livy narrated the memory just as much for herself as to tell Jack. It had been so long since she'd recalled the sweet times.

"It's funny how things come back to you in layers." Jack sifted through odd tools and cast-off machine parts sitting in the tub.

Uncovering the layers of her memories as she and Jack stripped dirt and dust and paint off the charming old house might just be enjoyable. The work, and maybe even the company, would be good for her.

Late that afternoon, Jack turned his truck onto the paved lane in front of Livy's grandmother's house. They left with a long list of jobs to be done to restore the old home. For Jack, it had been a day full of both excitement and uncertainty.

"What was I thinking, Jack? I can't do this." Livy set the notebook down in the space between them on the seat of the truck, the end of it hitting Jack's seatbelt buckle.

"What do you mean? Sure you can." He hoped his voice sounded energetic and full of optimism. He knew the day had overwhelmed her. "Plus, like I said earlier, you won't have to do it all alone. I'm around to help if you'd like. For the bigger projects, I can even bring my brother and a few friends along."

"I can't ask you to do that," Livy objected with a firm shake of her head. "We're not just talking about helping a friend paint a dining room. You saw it."

"Didn't I mention my lengthy résumé? Designer? Contractor? I can envision it *and* build it." Jack flashed her a playful smile while steering them onto the main road to town.

"Yes, you did mention all that. And I suppose it would be crazy not to take your help, but"—she paused, pointing a finger at him—"I insist on paying you and paying full price on any supplies from your store. No special favors."

"Now, Livy, don't be stubborn. I'll agree to no discounts at the store, but there's no way I'll accept money for helping a friend."

Livy's lips turned up as her eyes softened. "We are friends, aren't we?"

It took real effort to return his focus to the road. "I'd like to think twenty years later we can still pass as friends." Was his casual manner convincing? She was alarmingly charming. "And I don't know about you, but I sure could use a friend these days."

"Me, too, Jack." Her soft and simple reply brought an easy smile.

The ride back to town took little to no time. Before Jack knew it, they were pulling into the back lot of Bowdon's Supplies. He promised to look over the list that evening and make notes about the supplies Livy needed to get started on the first few projects.

"Want to meet for breakfast at Brewed around seven? We can go over the list, then you can start shopping as soon as I open the store." Jack held his breath. Was he pushing it, asking to spend more time with her so soon?

"That sounds perfect." Livy threw her bag over her shoulder and put a hand as a visor over her eyes. "Thanks so much for today, Jack. I don't know what I would have done without you, and that's before we're even really getting started."

She took a small step toward him. Was she going to hug him? Instead, she rocked back on her heels and hugged her arms to herself. Jack let breath return to his lungs as the anticipation of holding her close again evaporated.

"No need to thank me, just remember a home-cooked meal goes a long way for us small-town mountain men." Jack winked, looking down at Livy. She was so pretty, her green eyes gleaming against her dark hair in the late-day sun. He cleared his throat. "After we get this house back up and running, just save me a seat across from that old stove."

"You got it, but I can't promise cooking like my gram's. I'm sure we won't find that in the rubble." The two shared a laugh, followed by a long pause. "See you in the morning." Livy turned on her feet with a wave.

"Have a good night, Livy." Jack walked toward the store, turning to catch another glimpse of her making her way up the inn's sidewalk. Its windows were just beginning to glow in the dusky sky. It was Jack's favorite time, when the sky couldn't seem to make up its mind between day and night. Already a deep, enveloping dark blue to the east, Jack tracked the sky up and westward, watching the blues brighten into purples and pinks, then brilliant oranges and yellows. His eyes settled due west and gazed through the silhouetted, leaf-bare branches to the now-black rolling hills of the mountains he called home. The sun was setting on another day in Laurel Cove, though he couldn't help but wonder what was coming on the horizon.

The back door of the store closed hard behind Jack. His eyes took a moment to adjust to the dim light through the stockroom. In the storefront, Jasper locked the front door. "Just in time to go home, I see," Jack called to his little brother.

"Hey, man. Have yourself a good time, I guess?"

"Yeah, it was a good day. Lots of work to do up at that house." Jack didn't take the bait on his brother's joking. "I'm going to help her when I can. There's no way she'll be able to pull it all off on her own. I might need you to come up with me a few Saturdays. The plumbing is going to need a good once-over."

Jasper tossed the keys from one hand to the other and grinned. "So, what is it about this girl? I mean, she's gorgeous, but you haven't given any girl a second look for months."

"How about I buy you dinner and we'll talk?" Despite their difference in age, Jack and his baby brother told each other just about everything—nothing was off limits. Although Jack could stand to hear less about his brother's dating drama.

"Sounds about right." Jasper started for the back door. "That's the least you owe me for running out all afternoon."

They finished closing up and walked down Main Street to The Garage, Laurel Cove's only bar and grill. A crowd of construction workers returning from a long day out on work sites filled the joint. Taking the only two empty stools at the far end of the long bar, Jack filled Jasper in on the history between him and Livy. How he'd secretly pined for her all year after that one summer, looked for her for summers to come, then lost track of her—and how she'd reappeared out of the blue.

"So sentimental." Jasper's shoulders shook from a silent chuckle as he finished his last bite of burger. "But, in all seriousness, if this girl excites you at all after Claire, then you've got my support."

"That's pretty serious coming from you." Jack studied his brother across the table. Sure, he knew Jasper wanted him to be happy, but the mature reaction reassured him. "But, thanks, man. That means a lot." No need to count chickens before they hatched, as Aunt Bea would say. Fact was, two days ago Jack would never have believed he could be interested in anyone. He tipped his glass and Jasper clinked his bottle against the rim.

"Guess it's just nice to have a little hope."

And it was.

CHAPTER
Five

"Have a good first day in town, honey?" Aunt Bea looked up from behind bright pink bifocals. She sat at the front desk reading a magazine as Livy walked through the lobby of the inn.

"Yes, ma'am. Jack helped me up at my gram's house to decide what all needs to be done. I'm afraid I've really got my hands full."

The woman let out a high-pitched squeal. "Oh, Jack is helping you? How *wonderful*. You be sure to tell that boy that if he needs to put some projects on hold around here, I'd be happy to lend him out to you on Saturdays."

It certainly was no mystery what the woman's intentions were with her nephew. Livy couldn't stop the smile from breaking out across her face. "That's awfully nice of you. Thank you. We'll have to see how things go."

"Well, it's my pleasure, honey. And you're welcome here as long as it takes to get that house all ready for you. 'Night, now." Aunt Bea pushed her glasses back up from where they'd slipped to the tip of her nose and returned to her reading.

"Goodnight, Aunt Bea." A warmth filled Livy as she made her way upstairs. Though beautiful and cozy, the inn would not be as charming without its sweet keeper.

At her room door, the night manager passed Livy. "Need anything, miss?"

"No, I'm all set, Mr. Smith. Goodnight."

He nodded at her, tipping an invisible hat, and headed back down the steps. Inside the room, Livy released a heavy sigh. There were infinitely more people in New York City, yet she had spoken to more people in Laurel Cove in the last few days than she had over the course of a whole week in the city. What a different culture. Though a lovely change of pace, it was an adjustment to be noticed so often.

After a quick snack of crackers and a banana, Livy slipped into her pajamas and slippers. The soft fabric of the large armchair welcomed her as she slid into its overstuffed cushion, grabbing the television remote from the side table. TV had always been her guilty pleasure to unwind. Landing on a rerun of some old sitcom, the dancing glow blurred, and her thoughts refocused on the events of the day—and to Jack.

A lump swelled in Livy's throat at the thought of that first look at Gram's house. It would have been foolish to expect to see the cottage of her childhood.

No, that home was gone. What remained was a house. Walls, window casings, rusty nails. God willing, they'd be able to fix it, she and Jack. *Jack.* As his name whispered inside her thoughts, she allowed her eyes to close.

The kindness he showed to listen as she reminisced hadn't been lost on her. When was the last time she'd felt truly heard? He'd cared for her feelings, but also her safety—going before her when the house's integrity was uncertain, and understanding when she'd been frightened at the threat of rats. She should be embarrassed over that childish display of fear over small, furry creatures, but he hadn't judged her. With a sigh so deep she sunk further into the cushioned chair, she imagined his arms around her again as they stood in the kitchen. So warm and inviting.

Her eyes flew open. She didn't need to be thinking about a man at this time, with so much heartache behind her and so much work in front of her. It had only been two months since she split with Sam. She hadn't come to Laurel Cove to give in to her loneliness with the first man who came along.

Resolute, her body relaxed against the chair's back.

It had been so long since a man had held her, even Sam. But from the moment she saw him, there was something different—special—about Jack Bowdon. Pulling the afghan over her exposed arms, Livy drifted to sleep, unable to get him off her mind. Her waking thoughts carried over to her dreams.

Gram was there. They sat at the table in her pristine kitchen, looking out over the smiling pansies as a gentle breeze blew delicate, gauzy white curtains away from the screen.

"He makes me feel special and cherished. How could that be after such a short time, Gram?"

"Love is a funny thing, my darling Olivia." Gram's wrinkled hands tenderly held Livy's.

"It's too early for love. I pulled away from his hand and his embrace. I'm scared, Gram." Livy's eyes filled with tears, and she turned them toward her lap.

The old woman's fingers held Livy's chin, turning her granddaughter's eyes toward her again. "My dear, love isn't something to be feared. Jesus loved us the moment we became ourselves. We pull away from Him in our mistakes and in our imperfection. Yet He loves us still. It's never too early, or too late, for love. Do you understand?"

"I understand. I miss you, Gram. I miss gardening with you, wringing laundry with you, holding your hand on walks." She gazed down at her young, smooth hands inside the weathered old ones of the woman who'd taught her so much. But when she looked up again, she was alone at the table. The table was again old and cracked. Livy frantically looked around the kitchen to find the sink covered in vines, the floor tiles faded, and the windows bare of the delicate drapes. It was once again in the state Livy and Jack had discovered it earlier that day.

Livy sat up with a start, short of breath, Room 12 lit only by the glow of the television. Settling in bed, sleep didn't come again easy. She reflected on the dream and the words of her grandmother. *It's never too early, or too late, for love.*

Did she believe that? Could she?

Livy rolled onto her hip, facing the window. A distant mountainside glowed under a bright moon. The color was not unlike the blue glow from the television, yet softer. Her eyes wandered around the sky, her thoughts drifting to Sam. A few weeks into their relationship, he had begun correcting her. At first in small ways, then less subtle and harsher.

"New Yorkers don't order their coffee like that."

"You can't leave your windows open all night."

"Didn't I tell you last time to take the A train so you wouldn't be late?"

They were barks, commands, and subtle insults at her intelligence and worth. Looking back now, Livy could see they were red flags, warnings she'd chosen to ignore for fear of being alone. She'd been raised to believe in herself, and Sam had single-handedly ruined that part of her.

She blinked, and the moon-kissed mountains swirled as a flood of tears cascaded across the bridge of her nose. If only sleep would come again and rescue her from these memories.

Over time, the comments had grown worse, so gradually Livy couldn't even see it. One day, after selling a painting, Livy called Sam at his office to tell him the great news. Instead of congratulating her, he scolded her for accepting too little for it. And just a year ago, in front of a few of their friends at dinner, he told her she should order the salad because she was getting "thick like all the other southern *gals*," emphasizing the last word in a way that hit Livy like a four-letter curse word. That's when things started going downhill for her. Fast.

Livy began to realize how much she had let Sam's opinion control her self-worth. She dressed as he preferred. They only ate at restaurants he liked. Her "friends" were really his friends that she inherited because they never went out with anyone else. She painted less and less, avoiding it altogether the last few months she was in the city. All thanks to Sam's constant criticism.

He could be a nice enough guy by some standards. He never forgot a birthday or anniversary. He took her on weekend trips away from the city. He helped with errands. But he'd never traveled with her to North Carolina, not even for her father's funeral. For a long time, Livy held onto the relationship because she didn't know what to do without him. She saw that now. They'd been together almost the whole time she lived in the city. Without him she would have had to, in a sense, start over.

Livy turned several times in bed, unable to get comfortable. She finally settled on her back, staring at the ceiling. Outside in the distance, she heard what sounded like a gunshot. The last fight she had with Sam raced to the front of her mind. They had been arguing about something trivial, the kind of fight that, when a relationship was strained, could turn into a fight about everything and a fight about nothing all at the same time. They were both unhappy.

"If I'm wrong all the time, then why are you with me?" Livy's throat had threatened to choke her as she tried to keep tears at bay.

Sam bit back, "Because I'm the only right thing in your life. Without me, you'd be a huge mess in this city!" Though stung by his words, a sudden moment of clarity had washed over her. While he thought he advanced her sad life, he was just the thing holding her back from being her best self.

"You need to pack your things and not come back." Though they didn't live together, signs of him littered her place. He'd narrowed his eyes and stepped so close that his breath warmed her face—then left without saying a word.

It's funny how moments that are catalyst to positive change can be so painful. Livy had scribbled the statement in her journal after Sam left the apartment. The concept still bewildered her. After that night, every time she saw Sam, it took all she had not to take back what she'd said and just let things be. More than being undermined and undervalued, Livy was most scared of change, of the unknown. That hadn't been the case when she'd come to the city as a young adult, ready to take on the world after leaving home and everything she'd known. Sam left Livy jaded and empty of the spunk she'd once had.

It was for that reason, when she acted fast after seeing the ad for Gram's house, that it had to be God giving her a newfound determination. God had a plan for her life. She just knew it.

Words her father once told her floated through the sleepy fog of her mind. *When you feel peaceful about something you would usually fear or doubt, it is God giving you a nudge to walk along the path he has set for you.*

81

Livy did have peace about moving to Laurel Cove. At least for tonight, while lying in the cozy bed, the haunting memories were no match for the possibility that Jack could very well be part of God's plan for her life.

CHAPTER

Six

So? How'd it go?" Meredith's eyebrows arched high, her smile mischievous.

"How'd what go?" Jack waved his empty coffee mug impatiently.

She held the full pot back, taking his morning caffeine hostage. "Jasper was in here yesterday and said you spent the day with Livy. How was it?"

Jack rolled his eyes and laughed. Even his own brother rode the gossip train.

"Oh, that. I just spent a few hours inspecting her grandma's cottage with her. She doesn't know a whole lot about remodeling, so I offered to help out. No big deal."

"I think that's great. It's been a long time since we've seen you pick up a hammer other than to stock shelves."

"Yeah, it felt good to have my contractor hat on again. I think it'll be fun. But there's a ton of work to do." He straightened his arm so his mug was just inches from her face. "May I please have some coffee now?"

Meredith laughed and finally obliged. "Greg is in a creative mood this morning, so we've got French toast on the griddle."

"Sure, that sounds good." The mug warmed his hands on the way to the table that he and Livy had already shared twice. He chose the seat facing the street. As if on cue, she turned the corner at his store and headed toward him.

She moved swiftly in the brisk morning mountain air. With a skip, she narrowly missed a small puddle across a dip in the sidewalk just before making it to the shop's door. The corners of Jack's lips turned up as he watched her display of youthful energy. The bell over the door clattered loudly as she stepped through and let out an audible shiver.

"There's something about these mountain mornings that feel colder than up in the city." Livy discarded her gloves, scarf, and coat onto the chair opposite Jack before sitting. "I thought you said it was starting to thaw."

He smiled at her and sipped his coffee. Inside, though, his heart raced like a schoolboy in front of his crush.

"Don't worry. Soon you'll be wondering where the heat wave came from." Meredith approached the table with a mug and the pot. "This'll help. Coffee?"

"Oh, yes. Thank you."

Meredith shot Jack a full, toothy grin. Good grief, his friends were relentless about him starting to date again. "Livy, this is Meredith. She and her husband Greg are two of my closest friends. They own the shop. Meredith, this is Livy."

"It's so nice to meet you, Livy. We're glad to have you here in our little town." Meredith offered Livy a fresh mug of coffee, which she took and wrapped her hands around.

"It's good to be back. Though it won't be a vacation with all the work to do up at my grandmother's house. That's where Jack comes in." Livy looked to Jack, her smile warm and thankful. He couldn't look away. "We're starting to become predictable meeting here every day since I've arrived."

"You're welcome anytime. Jack's practically a fixture." Meredith squeezed Jack's shoulder, winking at him. "How 'bout some French toast, Livy."

"No, thank you. I'll have a bagel with cream cheese and some coffee. There's still a little New Yorker in me." Livy followed Meredith over to the counter with a small brown wallet in hand.

As she pulled open her wallet, something fell onto the counter. Meredith picked it up.

"Who's this handsome fella?" The small, quiet shop carried her words.

"Oh, I didn't know that was still in there." Livy spoke under her breath and stood a little straighter. "Just someone I used to know." Taking the photo back and handing Meredith the proper payment, Livy took her coffee to the small table opposite the counter to add cream and sugar. Jack met Meredith's gaze as she shrugged her shoulders. She must have hit a nerve.

Livy returned to the table, quiet for a long moment with her hands warming around her coffee mug, eyes fixed out the window. She'd gone somewhere far away. When she finally turned toward Jack, it was a few seconds before she refocused on him.

"Sleep well?" she asked.

Jack took her lead, not wanting to pry. "Yeah, not too bad. Rex, my dog, was restless this morning, so we were up extra early. How about you?"

"I laid in bed for a long time thinking about yesterday. The house, the memories, the huge list I'm sure you're going to give me in a minute. And how I got here. But once I fell asleep, I was out like a light."

"How *did* you get here?" Jack took a risk by going a little deeper, but he couldn't help himself now.

Before Livy had the chance to respond, Greg came over with their breakfast orders. He wore a black apron dusted with flour and a red Asheville Tourists baseball hat turned backwards.

"Okay, man. Let's have it. Take a bite and give it to me straight." His tone was earnest and to the point, but Jack was used to it. Every time Greg tried a new recipe, he used either Meredith or Jack as his guinea pig.

Jack winked at Livy before putting on his game face. Jack made a slow, dramatic production of cutting off a bite and easing it into his mouth. Greg shifted his weight and gnawed on a fingernail while waiting for the verdict. An otherwise laid-back guy, he took his food very seriously.

"Really, really good, man. I think you nailed it." Jack offered an outstretched hand.

"Ha!" Greg shook his hand hard. He turned to leave abruptly, calling out, "Sorry for the interruption. Good review means it's on the house, buddy!"

Jack and Livy laughed.

"So, where were we?" Jack went for another bite.

"You asked how I got here." Livy looked at her hands, turning over the spoon she'd used to stir her coffee.

Jack's breath caught as her bright eyes, a little dimmer as her laugh faded, met his gaze. Was she unsure how to proceed? "Listen, let's make a deal." Jack wanted her to feel safe with him. "I've got a little more than half an hour until the store opens. We'll only need a few minutes to go over my list, so you give me a quick version of your story, and I'll give you a quick version of mine. We all have a story, right?"

"That sounds fair." A strand of dark, lustrous hair danced across her face as an overhead vent kicked on. Jack's urge to reach over and tuck it behind her ear surprised him. "To spare you a lot of boring details, the short version of my story goes like this: I moved from my parents' small-town farm to pursue a career as an artist—a painter—in New York City. I soon met a guy who swept me off my young, naive feet. Things were great for a while." She paused and took in a deep breath. "Until they weren't. The few paintings I had time to do in between real jobs weren't selling. Sam wasn't supportive at all. He thought painting was a silly hobby. It took several years of his constant undermining, but I eventually began to realize he didn't love me. Not in the way I think love should be, anyway. I started to wonder if he even liked me." She fixed her eyes out the window, probably on nothing particular. "I had become pretty dependent on what he thought of me, so the little pokes and jabs were real blows to my ego. It sounds cliché, but I lost myself. I don't know where I found the courage, but I finally told him we were over."

A large delivery truck pulled up across the street and Livy turned back to look Jack in the eye. How could someone treat her—anyone—like that? No wonder she was sometimes more reserved. She was recovering. Like those long months after his divorce when he trusted no one. Maybe she'd learn to trust him.

"The morning after Sam left, I picked up a paper my mom had sent me from North Carolina, found the house for sale—much to my surprise—and decided to buy the place. Just like that. I guess you could say I came here hoping God was trying to tell me to look for myself in a place with some of the happiest memories I can recall." She searched Jack's eyes. "So, here I am."

"Is Sam the guy in the picture?" Jack nodded toward the counter telling he'd overheard the exchange with Meredith.

"Yes. I didn't know that was still in there."

"I'm sorry you've been through that. I think you're extremely brave coming all the way here. Seems to me you haven't lost yourself as much as you think you have."

Yes, this indeed explained some of Livy's hesitation at the house yesterday. And he could relate. The hurt of a breakup was fresh in his memory, too.

"Thank you for saying that, Jack." She tucked the wisp of hair behind her ear. "Truth is, I came here with the intention of throwing myself into the house as a way to hide. In my mind, I never considered that I'd meet people, new friends...old friends. Isn't that silly?" She smiled at Jack. Another long pause hung over the table. Livy's sparking eyes held his for a lingering moment, then continued. "Okay, spill it, mister. Fair's fair. What's your story?"

Jack released a chuckle at her obvious relief at being finished. Since everyone in Laurel Cove somehow knew his business, as small towns tended to be, actually getting to tell his story was a rare opportunity. He pushed his plate away and leaned across the edge of the table. He looked down at his hands and his bare ring finger.

"My ex-wife Claire and I dated in high school, your typical football quarterback and cheerleader couple. I went off to State and she stayed here to attend the community college a few towns over, so we headed separate directions. Several years later, my dad got sick and I needed to come home, which I think I mentioned yesterday. Claire was newly divorced, and not long after being back in town, we began seeing each other again. After Dad died, Claire was there for me when I needed someone. I loved her for it. We were married a few short months later." Livy listened with a few fingers curled up around her mouth, resting on one elbow.

"As kind as she was during that time, Claire was always a little wild." An all too familiar anxiety twisted into a knot inside him. "She wanted to go out every weekend to Boone or Asheville and really live it up. I just looked forward to settling down in the evenings in front of the fire. She complained a lot about how busy I was at the store or working on houses. Maybe I was too busy." Jack rubbed at the scruff on his cheek. "So, I found myself missing my dad terribly and in a marriage not at all like what I had expected. When Claire and I weren't fighting, things were pretty good. Our families got along. We joined a bowling league together. Then one day"—he looked down at his hands—"I ran home to grab some paperwork I'd forgotten that morning and saw a silver pickup parked behind Claire's car in the driveway. I went in and found her in bed with some guy."

"Oh, Jack." Livy's hand went to her mouth as her eyes closed.

"Yeah. So, that was that. She wouldn't even talk to me about it. Before we were married even six months, it was over. Our divorce was final about a year ago." Looking across the table at Livy, Jack was amazed how easy it was to tell her what he'd been through. It would never be an easy time to recall, but the hurt had receded. "It's in the past and I've finally come out of it—thanks to the help of great friends like those two." He nodded toward Greg and Meredith, who were tending to a few customers. "And that's my story."

A comfortable silence joined them like a welcomed third person at the table. Livy offered him a tender smile full of compassion, not pity. Talking to her was not burdensome or awkward or forced like it often was with meddling townspeople. No, they were two broken hearts speaking the same language. Jack inched his hand across the table but stopped short of touching her slender fingers. *Be patient.* The friendship forming here needed time—like a concrete foundation setting up to be a formidable structure. If he'd wait and trust, something told Jack a relationship with Livy had the potential to be pure and strong and real. He pulled his hand back to his lap and let the tender grin stretch into a full-blown smile.

Jack and Livy spent the rest of their breakfast reviewing the list of projects. They ordered them by importance and practicality, also creating a list of materials she would need to purchase. Jack offered to bring tools from his house for big projects, but also suggested several essential tools she should purchase. Once they finished the last of their coffee, with the lists in hand, Livy followed Jack to Bowdon's Supplies.

The first time Jack took Livy to the store, she must've been more distracted. She hadn't really seen the quaint character of the old corner store before. The double wooden front door let out a weathered creak as Jack pushed it open and moved two bricks with his boot to hold them in place. Livy ran her fingers over the hand-painted yellow letters spelling *Bowdon's* on the glass door. Bags of potting soil and grass seed lined the front window overlooking the street. Her lungs filled with the musky smell of leather and lumber.

Jack was several paces ahead of her heading toward the check out counter. "The smell reminds me of my father's work shed." Her voice echoed through the quiet store as she called out to him. She dipped her hand into a bucket full of sunflower seeds sitting on an old potting table near the front window. Something cold and wet grazed the back of her free hand, and she jumped.

"Well, hello there. You must be Rex." She knelt to rub the neck of a black Labrador who seemed to be smiling at her, tail wagging fast.

"We've put him in charge of the welcoming committee since Watch Dog didn't seem to fit." Jack came to Livy's side with a clipboard, patting Rex on the head.

"Oh, I think he's so sweet, Jack."

"Yeah, he's sweet, all right. A regular ladies' man." As if on command, Rex leapt forward to lick Livy's chin, both front paws landing hard on her chest. Jack caught the back of her arm, pulling her to her feet before she fell backwards. Her hand instinctively landed on his opposite shoulder, and for a moment, they were separated by only an inch. He smelled of fresh laundry. His arm was strong under the soft, red flannel as her hand followed it down to his elbow before falling back to her side. She looked up and studied his face. His cheeks and chin were rugged with a few days' growth and his dark eyes were stranded with gold running through them like lightning as he looked at her. *My goodness, he's handsome.*

Rex excitedly stepped between them, breaking the moment.

"Uh, thanks. I'm so clumsy."

"No worries." Jack's warm smile heated her cheeks. "Do you mind flipping the sign over to Open?" He nodded past her shoulder to the front door.

"Oh, sure." She used the few steps back toward the door to compose herself.

Livy then followed Jack with a shopping cart up and down the aisles, list in hand.

"What do you think you'll start with?" Jack spoke over his shoulder, approaching a display of work gloves.

"I figure it'll be good for my morale to begin with a project I can see progress on by the end of the day." Livy eyed pairs of gray and yellow women's gloves Jack held up before taking the gray ones and tossing them in the cart. "I think I can make some real headway clearing out the kitchen. Or I may just start moving everything out of the way so we can get down to the bare rooms and really know what we're dealing with."

Jack hummed something, but she didn't think he was aware he was doing it. The words of "Stand By Me" by Ben E. King softly filled the store. She hadn't noticed the sounds of the radio coming from near the register until now.

"Sounds like a plan. But makes me think—" Jack's eyes widened as if an idea had struck. "I know a guy who rents large trash containers that he'll drop at construction sites for all the demolition and trash. I bet that'd be a great thing to have on site. You'll surely fill at least one."

"Great thinking." She would be lost without Jack's help.

"Awesome. I'll call and see if he can deliver one today. We're about done here." He set a heavy-duty rectangular broom on top of the stash that was now swelling in the cart. They made their way to the register as Jack sang under his breath the words of the popular chorus.

Livy couldn't ignore the heavy beating inside her chest. His deep, smooth voice was soothing and charming. Jack stopped singing and let a loud laugh escape when his eyes met hers. "Well, that's embarrassing! I sing to myself when the store's quiet and I can hear the radio. Guess I don't know when I'm doing it anymore. Don't mind me."

She joined his laughter. "Don't be embarrassed. You have a nice voice."

At the register, he plugged in the scanner they'd been using, and the total appeared in a matter of seconds.

"That's pretty impressive technology for a small-town business."

"Small-town charm with big-city conveniences, ma'am." Winking, Jack replied in a playful countrified accent. They both laughed. "Total comes to $285.65."

"Well, here we go. The project is officially underway." Livy handed him her credit card. *Thanks for that inheritance, Gram.* The inheritance, paired with her own savings left after the down payment on the house, should see her through about six months of remodeling. After that, would her painting sustain her? *Not if you don't start painting again.* But that worry was for another day.

With everything loaded in her SUV, there wasn't an inch of space to spare. Livy carefully closed the back hatch and turned to face Jack.

"I can't thank you enough for your help with all this, Jack. You've already done so much."

"Well, my weekday mornings are usually pretty quiet, so it worked out great."

She fiddled with her car keys so she wouldn't stare at his tall frame, kind eyes, and wide shoulders. *Get it together, Liv. You're not in high school.*

"Jasper doesn't come in today, so I'm here until we close at six. Wish I could stop by and help."

Livy couldn't be sure, but maybe he didn't want her to leave.

"But on Tuesdays several of us get together at The Garage—the small restaurant at the end of Main—for wings. Greg and Mer will be there. You're welcome to join us."

"That sounds fun." She couldn't resist meeting his eyes this time. "I'll have to see how today goes. I may be soaking in a hot tub by sundown. But I'll certainly be there if I'm up for it."

"Great. We usually meet up around six-thirty and don't head home until around nine or later." Jack shoved both hands in the back pockets of his jeans and shifted his feet, looking at the ground. Definitely stalling. She pressed her lips together to hide her amusement. He suddenly straightened and burst out with, "Hey, why don't you take my cell number? You know, just in case you need something up at the house."

How cute. "Sure, that'd be great." She pulled up a new contact form on her phone and handed it to him to input his number.

"Thanks, Jack. Really." Getting into the car, she wrinkled her nose then smiled. "I've said that a lot over these few days. I'm sure going to owe you big time!"

"Nah, I bet we'll be even before you know it." Jack closed the door behind her and rapped on the hood before stepping to the curb. As she pulled onto Main Street, she watched him wave through her rearview mirror. If only he were coming with her.

CHAPTER
Seven

She's cute."

Jack turned sharply from watching Livy's car pull out of town. It was Owen Barnett, one of his best friends and his pastor.

"You can't sneak up on a guy like that, Rev." Jack laughed, shaking his friend's hand and escorting him into the store. Owen came by to chat at least one morning a week, taking the short walk from the parsonage next door to the Methodist church a few streets over.

"Don't think I've ever seen her around. Just someone passing through?"

"No, she's Mrs. Johnson's granddaughter. She came to visit one summer when we lived over there as kids. I haven't seen her in years, but she's back in town for at least a good while." What *would* she do after the house was finished? Did she plan to live in the cottage? Or was she just here for the project, to clear her head and then move on with her life? He hadn't thought that far. He filled Owen in on Livy's plans to fix up the old home and that he planned to help. That much he knew, and it was enough for now.

"I'm glad to see you with another project, even if it's not one of your own. Feeling good about it?" Just like Jasper, Owen had expressed worry when Jack stopped his work on house projects after the divorce, knowing how much they were like therapy for him.

"Yeah, I am." Jack paused, unsure what else to tell. Many of his thoughts about Livy were still unclear. *I've really only known her a few days. He'll think I'm crazy if I tell him how often she's on my mind. We've both gone through a lot and become much different people since that summer all those years ago.* Because Owen was both his pastor and a faithful and kind friend, Jack usually tested his thoughts and feelings on him. He'd been the one to counsel Jack after he'd caught Claire being unfaithful and after the divorce. There wasn't much Owen didn't know about Jack.

"You know, it's strange," Jack started again, working to put together a birdhouse for a display. "The minute I saw Livy up at the inn, I just knew there was something about her. When she introduced herself, I remembered her from the summer we played together. After all these years, it was like finding fate standing right in front of me. She's been in town only two full days, and we've spent a good bit of that time together. At the coffee shop, up at her grandmother's house, here at the store. I'm telling you, Owen, as insane as it sounds, I really like this woman."

"Can I tell you something?" Owen shifted his weight, arms crossed and eyes piercing Jack's. Owen often started with this rhetorical question. Even the church members to whom he preached knew it was his polite way of announcing something especially worth telling. "Ever since the day you signed the divorce papers and told me you never wanted to love another woman, I've been praying that God would bring someone into your life who knocked you off your feet and made it impossible not to love her. I have no clue if Livy is that woman, but I consider this proof that God is at work in your life big time, brother. You're talking like the old Jack I know, the guy who swoons easily and loves hard." Owen's grin grew, his high dimples cresting at the top of his cheekbones above a thick, dark beard.

"That means a lot, Owen." Jack loved his friends deeply, and they loved him. He couldn't recall even one time that they weren't there when he needed them— during his parents' deaths, when things went sour with Claire, when the depths of his sorrow threatened to suffocate him. They were always there. And Owen, in particular, saw to it that Jack didn't succumb to hopelessness. Jack had lost count of how many times Owen called to make sure he'd be at the men's Bible study, came over to the cabin when he'd missed church, and prayed with him when the anger took over.

Jack rested a hand on Owen's shoulder. "Just keep those prayers coming, will you? And we'll see what God has in store."

The two friends talked for a few more minutes about the condition of Livy's house and how much work she had in front of her. As a few customers wandered in, Owen gathered his coat and readied to leave.

"Maybe we can rally the gang one weekend and have us an old-fashioned barn-raising to hammer out some of the heavy work up at Livy's place." Owen said, shaking Jack's hand.

"That's a great idea. I know she'd appreciate the help. Oh, I also invited Livy to join us tonight if she feels up to it." Jack and Owen made their way toward the front door as the clock in the town square chimed eleven o'clock. "Remind me to tell her your idea. She'll love it. And I'll bet she and Jen really hit it off." Jennifer was Owen's wife, and he was right. Jack would have to get the women together sometime. Jen was sweet, funny, and a wonderful, tender mother to their two children. Jack had no doubt Livy would love her as much as he did.

Owen said goodbye as another customer came in asking for a rare size lightbulb. For the rest of the day, business picked up, keeping Jack busy for several hours—though not quite busy enough to forget about Livy and her first day of work on the house.

Gravel crunched under her tires as Livy reached the top of the steep driveway. She pulled herself forward, staring over the steering wheel at the huge task in front of her.

"Well, Gram, I'm counting on you to be with me through this, okay?" A strange tingling of excitement and fear surged through her body. It was kind of like the feeling she'd had right before hitting big rapids on that wild river in West Virginia with her college sorority. The last time she'd experienced the sensation was when she moved away from home to New York as a young adult. Here, alone in front of the old house, came the same seesaw of emotions. Excitement won. She smiled, removed the key from the ignition, and stepped out of the car.

The handle of the passenger door felt hot in her hand despite the cool spring morning air. She reached in for the old coveralls she used to wear when she painted. They were perfect for today, as the house was her blank canvas. An ugly, dirty, covered-in-junk canvas.

Livy tugged the coveralls over her jeans, stretched her arms into the sleeves, and zipped them. Thankfully, they still allowed plenty of room for her thick sweater underneath. Knowing it wouldn't warm up until around lunchtime, she had dressed in layers. She slid on the new pair of work gloves she'd bought at Bowdon's and began unloading her supplies onto the front porch.

She walked the front yard, picking up discarded cans, a sun-faded pizza box, and the shredded remnants of a plastic grocery bag snagged on a low tree branch, and tossing them in a trashcan. The two she'd bought would fill fast today. Jack had suggested they open the packaged items back at the store to avoid having to do it at the house. *He knows what he's doing, that's for sure.*

She then moved inside to spend the cooler hours indoors working on de-cluttering as much junk as she could. The living room went fast. In less than an hour, only a large couch and an empty, but still heavy, old Army trunk remained. She'd need help to move those. Sweeping the floors stirred up clouds of dust and grit that sent Livy outside for a break. She used that time to remove the boards from several windows that were not broken, leaving the damaged ones for fear of rain. Inside again, she smiled at the huge difference some sunlight made to the small space. Even though it illuminated everything that needed fixing, she could also better see glimpses of the charming house she remembered.

Livy leaned against the wall at the edge of the entryway, her eyes set on the yellowed sheet covering the couch on the far side of the living room. On a rainy day one summer, she and Gram had built forts with old sheets in this very room. The storm had come out of the blue, as storms tended to do in the mountains, right when they were going to plant new flowers. The first fat drops fell from the swelling sky onto Livy's skin before they ran breathless from the garden to the house. She closed her eyes.

"Oh my gracious, no warning as usual." Setting the wicker laundry basket just inside the back porch door of the kitchen, the old woman giggled and patted at her damp white hair.

"What are we going to do now, Gram?" Young Livy *pouted as she stared at the steady streams of water falling outside the kitchen window. The ping of rain on the metal awnings reminded Livy of the faint sounds of her father working on his tractor back home on the farm.*

"Whatever our imaginations tell us, dear. What is your imagination telling you today?"

"Dunno. My imagination isn't talking. I wanted to plant those flowers."

"I know you did, honey. But it wasn't in God's plans, I suppose." *Gram sat down next to Livy, her weathered hands smoothing the checkered tablecloth.*

"Why didn't God want me to plant flowers? I've been waiting all week." *Livy turned from the window and wiggled closer to Gram, nestling under the soft pillow of the woman's tanned arm.*

"The way I see it, we shouldn't ask God why not?" *Even at six years old, Livy could hear the wisdom in her elder's voice. She peered into the woman's gentle eyes. "Instead, let's ask what now? The rain may keep us from planting those flowers, but the time inside is a gift as well, if we let it be. When life doesn't turn out quite as you hoped, take a deep breath and ask Him what now?"* *Gram gave Livy a tight squeeze under her arm and kissed the top of her head.*

Livy looked through the open door to the basket of sheets on the front porch. "We could make a fort! Dad showed me how, and I can show you!"

"What a wonderful idea, Olivia. I've always wanted to learn how to build a fort." *Gram nuzzled Livy's nose with hers.*

Gram attached the corners of sheets to the back of chairs and other furniture with clothespins. The two spent the rest of the afternoon in their fort. They read fairytales in funny voices, colored with crayons in coloring books, and munched on homemade oatmeal cookies.

When thunder struck with an unexpected rumble and the room darkened as another wave of ominous clouds rolled across the land, Livy scooted closer to Gram.

"Don't be afraid, my dear. Do you remember what thunder is?" Gram's quiet voice calmed Livy, covering her worries like the fresh sheets over their heads as they sat together against the heavy couch.

"The angels are bowling in heaven."

"That's right!" Gram laughed, shaking Livy's head in her lap. The old woman stroked her hair. As was usual, Gram began singing lines of old hymns, almost to herself but just loud enough for Livy to hear over the heavy rain. In that moment, like many others spent with her grandmother, Livy wanted for nothing. She fell asleep, safe and sound under the shadows of the sheet fort. On waking, she was welcomed by late-afternoon sunlight, the color of amber, and the smell of fried chicken on the stove.

Standing in the doorway of the same living room, some twenty years later, the memory gave Livy the same warm feeling. She missed her grandmother a great deal, yet also felt safe and at peace. There was a quiet protection in that old house from the still-clearing storm that had clouded her life. The advice she'd received as a child about weathering the storms of life hit home in a whole new way today.

Livy spent the rest of the day hauling what she could from the house into piles in the yard: one for trash, one for donations, and one for items she might be able to refurbish and use again. By four o'clock, she was tired, dirty, and ready to call it a day.

She stood under the open hatch, loading the last few tools into the trunk, when the sound of crunching gravel down the long driveway made her turn. An old man, maybe eighty-five years old, made his way toward her at a slow but steady clip. Although his frame bent slightly, the simple cane he balanced on seemed more preventative than necessary. Once he was about halfway up, she walked to meet him.

"Hi there." Livy pulled off the gloves and reached a bare hand out to her guest. "How are you, sir?"

His chuckle sounded like a hen's cluck, high-pitched and quick. "Sir? Ha, thanks for that, young lady." He eyed her, resting both hands on his cane's curved top, and broke into a friendly grin. "Thought I'd wander over and see what's going on. Have you bought the place?"

"I sure have." Livy brushed at her dusty coveralls, wishing she had already changed out of them. "My name is Olivia Johnson. Livy for short."

As he searched her through squinted eyes, his smile faded. "Johnson, you say?"

"Yes, sir."

"Any kin to the Johnsons who built the place?"

Livy kept forgetting how connected people were here. Still, her interest was certainly piqued. "Audria Johnson was my grandmother. My grandfather, Tobias Johnson, died before I had the chance to meet him."

The old man let out a high, long whistle, the kind that carried through the woods like a hunter calling for his retriever. "I'll declare. Her granddaughter. Mind if I ask what brings you here now?"

Excitement surged through her like electricity. "You knew my grandmother?"

"Sure did. Name's Pete Wilson. The little stone house down the way with the drive over the creek is my place. Your grandmother and I knew each other for over fifty years."

Livy stepped forward and grasped one of his arms. "My goodness! It's a pleasure to meet you, Mr. Wilson. I just happened, quite by accident, to see her home was for sale after all these years, and decided on a whim to buy it and fix it up the way Gram would have wanted."

"No such thing, dear." Pete shook his head with purpose.

"Beg your pardon?"

His intense stare fixated on Livy. "No such thing as *quite by accident*."

A warmth spread over her. "No, sir. I guess not. I am beginning to believe I'm right where I need to be."

"Well, I'm right down the way with nothing to do." He started back down the driveway. "I imagine you'll be up here a lot. If you need anything or just want a break, stop on by. And fair warning, our mail gets crossed a lot. Bert's been delivering here for twenty years and still can't keep it straight." With a wave of his hand over his shoulder, the old man turned toward his little stone house.

"Goodbye, Mr. Wilson!" Livy called out.

As she pulled out of the drive just a few minutes later, she still smiled over the encounter with her neighbor. *Her neighbor.* That had a nice ring to it. For the first time Livy thought of this place as her new home as much as Gram's old one. Fixing it up was therapy. A distraction. A welcome break. She hadn't planned the future for certain, but so far Laurel Cove had a great deal going for it. A great deal, indeed.

Whatever the future held, Livy knew one thing for sure: a hot shower and some wings sounded just about perfect.

CHAPTER
Eight

$\mathcal{T}$he Garage was busier than usual for a Tuesday night. From where Jack sat, it looked like all but a few tables were full. Thankfully, Owen and Jen had arrived early enough to snag two tables together. The owner often booked local musicians, mostly on Fridays and Saturdays. Tonight was a rare midweek night with live music to keep the crowd hanging around. Jack tapped the toe of his boot to the beat of a popular country song playing on the small stage.

"The food is still going to be a while. Kitchen's backed up." Owen approached the table with a pitcher of tea. "But they gave me this instead of having to wait for the waitress to get to refills."

"Oh my gosh. I'm starving." A shrill, dramatic whine sounded from the end of the table. Lane, without a doubt Jack's most opinionated friend, shifted in her seat, swollen feet propped on another chair. "Don't they know it's seriously risky keeping a seven-month pregnant woman who's taught rowdy kids all day waiting?"

Jack's chest shook beneath his folded arms. Lane's spunk had become one of her most endearing qualities.

"Let me go grab some peanuts, babe." Hank, Lane's husband, rubbed her back as he stood. He was like a palm tree—tall, lanky, and always swaying easily through life. He was the perfect match for Lane, which was part of what made them one of Jack's favorite couples.

"Thank you." Looking back at her husband, Lane's scowl faded to a tender smile. Jack and all his friends knew her soft spot for Hank was as deep and wide as the French Broad River.

Out of nowhere, Greg let out a loud belly laugh from the other end of the table.

"What's so funny?" Meredith linked her arm through her husband's, resting her chin on his shoulder. Couples sweet on each other surrounded Jack.

"Oh, just thinking of good ol' Barney Fife. He stopped by this morning on his rounds. Parked the squad car with a wheel up on the curb again. He went on and on for twenty minutes about some new donut flavor he saw on a cooking show."

"The man sure loves his donuts. Oh, a donut sounds good right about now." Lane shook her head. The table erupted in laughter.

Livy walked through the door, and Jack stopped listening to the conversation at the table.

He'd purposely chosen a chair facing the door so he could wave Livy over if she decided to join them. After the first hour passed, he'd figured she was spent from the long day of work at the house and had decided not to come out. Now, through the full house of patrons and waiters and musicians, Jack saw only her—and she took his breath away.

She paused a moment just inside the doorway to remove her jean jacket and yellow scarf. A loose, almost messy braid fell across one shoulder. Even from across the room, her emerald eyes popped from behind long, dark eyelashes. In her light blue, button-up shirt, fitted jeans, and tall brown boots, she looked casual and effortless. Stunning.

"Oh, there's Livy! Go get her, Jack." Meredith snapped him back to the moment. He stood and walked toward her, waving to get her attention. She spotted him and waved back with a smile that made him feel like the only other person in the place. He was a goner.

He made his way to her, the chilly wind brushing past him as another couple left. "You, uh, look amazing." It came out barely a whisper.

She leaned in close, gripping his elbow. "What was that? I didn't hear you." She smelled of lavender. Good grief. Adrenaline rushed through his veins. "Oh, I just figured you had turned in already, but so glad you made it out."

"Oh, thanks, Jack. Had the hot water not eventually run out in the shower, I'd probably still be standing there." She mesmerized him with those green eyes. "Are your friends still here?" She looked past his shoulder.

"Oh, yeah. Everyone is still here." He stepped aside, motioning for her to go ahead of him through the crowd. *Get it together, man.* He took a deep breath to focus.

"Livy! You made it!" Meredith jumped up, and the women exchanged a big hug. Greg nodded with a tip of his glass and smiled in her direction. Jack offered Livy the chair between Meredith and himself and introduced the rest of his friends.

"Jack told us you moved all the way from New York City, right? Us country bumpkins can't imagine what that was like." Lane gave a friendly wink in Livy's direction as she popped a few nuts in her mouth.

"It is pretty different from here, that's for sure," Livy replied. Jack felt her knee brush up against his under the table as she shifted in her seat. He made an effort not to turn and stare at her beautiful profile. Instead, he found Owen watching him from a few seats down with a big grin. He returned a quick smile and lowered his gaze to his drink.

"There are a lot of wonderful things about New York. The museums and art are unparalleled. The theater shows are great, if you can find a good deal. I didn't even mind the subways, though you do have to get used to the busy pace of all the people."

Hank chimed in. "I don't think I'd ever get used to that. I feel cramped when the pew at church is full." The group erupted in laughter.

"I did have one trick for unplugging, though," Livy continued. "About once a week, I'd wander down to Central Park. It took me a while to find it, but there's a spot off of one trail where big rocks shelter you from the view of the tall city buildings."

Jack tried to imagine her anywhere except here, but failed. She looked around the table from friend to friend, landing on Jack's gaze last.

"If I closed my eyes," she said, "I could picture myself back in North Carolina. On nice days, I could spend hours sitting there with a book, no need to talk to anyone or push my way through layers of people on the street. I'd even lie down sometimes and watch the clouds pass overhead. Funny how the sky looks the same everywhere, when you take the time to notice."

Her voice had a sweetness to it that Jack found intoxicating. Though she'd been gone from the South for some time, she had a drawl that seemed more pronounced now than just a few days before when they'd met. His look must have given him away, because just past Livy, Jen's eyebrows raised, and she smiled at him knowingly.

The table had grown quiet listening to her. Jen spoke up, "That's the first time anyone has made New York sound like a place worth visiting."

"Yeah," Lane chimed in, "and I don't like it." Again, laughter bellowed through the group.

Jack shook his head slightly at Jen's persistent grin. If she saw right through him, did everyone else? Did Livy?

"What's the church scene like up there?" Owen spoke up, redirecting his wife's attention. *Whew.*

Livy shifted in her seat and wrung her hands on the tabletop. "Well, honestly, I never became a regular member of any church up there. I guess you could say I was distracted for a while."

"Just what we suspected!" Greg blurted out. "All heathens up there past the Bible belt."

"Greg!" Meredith swatted at her husband.

"I'm just kidding. Anyone with one good eye can see she's about the farthest thing from a heathen." He winked in Livy's direction.

Livy perked up at his compliment. "You all sure do a lot of slick winking around here," she retorted.

The group once again joined in a round of laughter.

"Looks to me like she can hold her own, Jack." Greg shrugged his shoulders in mock defeat as he sipped on his beer.

"That, she can." Jack relaxed in his chair, grateful for the way his friends were doing their best to welcome Livy into their circle.

The attention turned to Lane as she updated the group on her doctor's appointment that morning. But the band's up-tempo song drowned out her voice.

Jack leaned in close to Livy. "I'm going to check on our order. Would you like something to drink other than tea?"

"No, tea's great, but I'll come with you." She turned toward him and spoke in his ear over the loud music.

Her breath on his neck left chills in its wake. He paused for a deep breath before pushing back from the table then fought the instinct to guide her through the crowd with a hand on her back, as his habit had been with Claire.

"I know you just met them, but this is the best group of people you'll ever know." The counter near the kitchen was quieter, taking away the excuse to lean in close to Livy again. A waitress came over and said she'd check on the table's food.

"Jen is so sweet and kind." Livy followed Jack's gaze back to the table of his friends. "Lane is fun and spunky. The guys seem just as genuine and nice as you are. Though I must say, Greg is a lot more laid back when not wearing his apron!"

Jack nodded in agreement.

"I'm so glad I came tonight," she said.

"Me too." Jack grinned.

Livy leaned back on the high top counter. She tapped a boot and nodded to the beat of "Friends in Low Places." Jack couldn't take his eyes off of her. She seemed relaxed, as if she had let go of some burdens she'd been carrying. Was she more confident about the decision to move? Maybe the city was gradually wearing off of the natural country girl in her. Whatever it was, she wore it well.

"I've always loved this song." She shifted her eyes from the band to Jack and held his gaze. She had to have noticed him watching her, but she didn't seem bothered or uncomfortable. He relaxed against the edge, too. They listened to the band for another minute before the bartender tapped Jack's shoulder and presented two large baskets of wings.

They brought the food back to the table, met with rousing cheers. The group engaged in more lively conversation and laughter over the food.

After a while, Jen turned to Livy. "Jack mentioned you bought your grandmother's old house. We all knew Mrs. Johnson and are happy to see the house restored."

"Yes, that's right. I needed a change, I guess. New York chewed me up and spit me out." Livy glanced at Jack and shrugged her shoulders. Her vague explanation was endearing.

"Whew, mercy." Hank let out a long whistle. "We've all been there." His head shook slowly as he bit into another wing.

"Felt chewed up and spit out, have you?" Lane shot a sharp look at him.

"Well, um, not by you, dear," he said sheepishly.

Lane let out a long, tired sigh and rubbed her round belly. "Oh, good grief, I'm too tired to even give you a hard time." She blew a kiss in Hank's direction. They may have bantered and poked, but his friends loved each other so well.

"Jack said you visited your grandmother one summer when you were young," Meredith spoke up. "Did you attend church with her?"

"I visited a few summers, but only played with Jack one summer. And yes, every Sunday I was here Gram and I went to church." Livy answered.

"I'm pretty sure I remember you being in our Sunday school class. Did you usually wear a white lace dress and a blue bow in your hair?" Meredith motioned above her head as if tying an invisible ribbon.

Livy's eyes widened and she swatted at Jack's arm in disbelief. Amusement lit up her face. "Yes, every Sunday."

"We were all in that same Sunday School class," Jen added. "Isn't it crazy to think we all have met before, even if years and years ago? And now, here you are again."

Jack found Livy staring back at him with a tenderness that both stole his breath and quickened his heart again.

"Here I am," she whispered.

Here she is.

An hour or so later, Greg and Meredith announced they were ready to leave. But Jack hoped Livy would stay a while longer.

"The rooster crows early and the coffee don't brew itself." Greg pulled out his wife's chair and helped her into her jacket.

"I've hit the end of my rope, too, darn it." Lane narrowed her eyes at Hank, who laughed.

"Ah, the night-owl has finally been tamed," Hank teased. "I'm doubling up on mail routes tomorrow, so I start early, too."

Hugs were shared between the women. Handshakes between the men.

"I'm going to walk them out. Will you be here when I get back?" Jack leaned in to ask Livy.

She answered with gentle eyes and a nod, making it easier to walk away from her.

Jack followed Hank and Lane to the parking lot to get a tool that Hank had borrowed.

"Jack, Livy seems great," Lane said as Hank helped her into their car. "I hope you'll bring her around more."

"I have a feeling we'll all see a lot more of her." A big smile stretched across Jack's face. Hank closed Lane's door, and the two men walked to the front of the car. Hank, the most cautious of the close-knit group when it came to serious matters, was also the only guy tall enough to meet Jack eye to eye. He placed a firm hand on each of Jack's shoulders.

"Listen. I want to see you come out of your *Claire funk* as much as everyone else, but there's no need to rush anything. I saw the way you looked at her when she came into the joint. What is it about *this* girl?"

Jack paused before answering. *I just know* would do no good with Hank. He was not the hopeless romantic type. He and Lane had dated for five years before he proposed, and that was after making practical lists and detailed plans to ensure he was ready. "I guess we'll see."

Hank shook his head, a rueful smile turning up the corners of his mouth, before he got in the car and pulled onto Main Street.

Back inside at the table with Livy, Jen, and Owen, Jack listened to the women talk about Jen's school. "You'll have to come to the school and give a painting demonstration to the kids."

"Oh, I don't know." Livy dismissed the invitation with a wave. "I've never taught before, and haven't been around kids a whole lot. They'd probably find it boring."

"You'd be surprised what kids find fascinating, actually," Jen said. Jack would have to thank Jen for being so encouraging. The two women shared the same sweet spirit. It was probably why they were hitting it off so well.

One summer when he and Livy were kids, they'd come across a baby bird that had fallen out of its nest and knelt over it together. Livy had been so distraught, crying and insisting they place it in an old shoebox and walk it to the veterinary clinic in town. It ended up being fine, and Livy had made Jack climb the tree to put the bird back into its nest. That kindness hadn't changed in the woman he watched sitting in front of him now.

Another full hour passed, and Livy noticed the band's numbers take on a slower pace. The foursome sat back and listened, sipping on their last drinks. Jack leaned over to her and whispered in a low voice, "Dance with me?"

She turned and stared at him for a long moment. Should she? Lord knows she wanted to. He smiled, eyes soft, and extended a hand to where hers rested in her lap.

What did she have to lose? Here with Jack nothing else existed—not her miserable failed relationship, not her insecurities, not even her uncertain plans for the future.

When she took Jack's hand, the feeling of his warm skin against hers sent tingles from her toes up her legs as he led them through a sea of tables and chairs.

The dance floor was a small area in front of the band where several tables had been moved out of the way. Only one other couple swayed to the slow ballad. Jack tightened his grip on her hand as he turned to face her and pulled her close. His other hand gingerly wrapped around her waist. Heart thumping against her chest, she needed to distract herself from the intoxicating proximity to him. Livy's gaze darted from the band, to the few folks laughing near the front door, and the waitress clearing a table. She breathed in the subtle scent of his cologne and felt her resolve weaken. *You're safe. It's okay.* She wasn't sure if it was her own resolve willing to calm the nerves, or God's still small voice. But with a deep breath, courage crept in. She tilted her head back and found a mix of tenderness and affection in his handsome face. He pulled their intertwined hands close, too, and they swayed together to the gentle cadence of the band's ballad.

A dizzying mix of natural familiarity and exhilaration swirled inside her. Could he sense her schoolgirl nerves?

As if trying to create an album of memories of the evening, Livy cataloged his every move. He wrapped his arm around her back a little tighter, pulling her even closer. She squeezed his hand and rubbed his back with her other hand. They moved so slow that the beat of the song no longer mattered. Jack's hand wandered under her hair and held her neck, silently asking her to look up at him.

There was an intense but gentle desire. His eyes trailed to her lips as their swaying steps stilled. But the last chords of the song faded, replaced with clinking glasses and chatter. *No, wait, please.* What she'd give for a few more bars to soundtrack the moment. They both looked toward the band, then back to each other. Livy managed a half-smile. Would he have indeed kissed her? She may never know. The band's lead singer thanked the crowd for coming out and announced they'd return on Saturday night.

Jack shrugged and rubbed her arm. "I wonder if they'd keep playing if I paid them."

"Thanks for the dance, Jack." Livy whispered, breathless. She smiled and gave his hand another little squeeze as they slowly made their way back to the table.

"Well, time for us to scoot." Jen gathered her purse and stood by the time Jack and Livy reached them. "My mom's got the kids, and it's getting late."

The two women embraced and agreed to get together sometime soon for coffee. From the corner of her eye, Livy watched Owen shake Jack's hand with an accompanying sly grin. "So glad we had the chance to meet Livy. She's really great."

The four walked out together, then Jack and Livy waved to Owen and Jen as they pulled out of the parking lot.

"Mind giving me a ride back to the inn?" Livy turned to Jack, rubbing her hands together in the chilly night air. "I walked here not thinking of the walk back.

Guess I was also counting on your chivalry." They both laughed at her honesty.

"Of course. My truck is right over there." They walked the short distance across the parking lot, lit only by the yellow glow of the bar's sign, in silence. Jack opened the passenger door and waited for Livy to settle on the seat before closing it. She stayed fixed on his tall frame as he circled to the driver's side and felt the cab rock slightly as he slid in behind the wheel.

"I can't tell you how much I enjoyed spending time with your friends, Jack."

"I don't know what I would do without them. I'm pretty sure you knocked their socks off, too, by the way." Jack said.

"Oh, *sure*." She chuckled.

At the town's one stoplight, Jack turned to look for crossing traffic. His broad shoulders filled the space of the cab. Her gaze wandered to the hand resting on the gearshift. His hands were gentle—the dance had proven that—but they also appeared strong and capable of taking care of her. She resisted the urge to reach out and hold his hand. Was she looking to be taken care of, protected in ways she'd not been in recent years? There was a fine line between being protected and controlled—if Sam was any indication.

Jack turned toward her, and their eyes met. She only saw desire staring back at her. The back of her neck warmed. Had he seen her concentrating on his hand? The traffic light turned green and cast a brighter hue over them.

Jack made the left-hand turn up the street, and a moment later, they pulled in front of the inn under the branches of a large tree. Bright moonlight shone on the truck's metallic hood. Jack shifted the truck into park and left it running, the heat continuing to blow toward their feet.

"I'm sure glad you decided to come out tonight." He looked at his hands now resting on the steering wheel, loosening and tightening his grip as he shifted in his seat. If she didn't know any better, she'd say he was nervous. How adorable was that? The corners of her mouth turned up.

"Me too. I really needed it after the long day I had."

"Oh!" She jumped as he smacked the steering wheel and turned in his seat. "I didn't even ask you how it went at the house."

She laughed. "It was fine. I got a lot of stuff cleared out from the front rooms, started several piles, and met a really sweet old neighbor who knew my gram. It was a good first day."

"Well, good." He let out a sigh, and the truck fell silent again. The windows began to fog up from the cooler air outside and the warmth of the truck's interior. "That dance was very nice." His voice lowered again, and he looked right into Livy's eyes. "It's been a long time since I've danced with anyone."

"Me too, Jack."

"I'd like to take you out sometime. I mean, I know we've spent a lot of time together since you've been in town, but I wonder if you'd let me take you out on a proper date?"

"I'd like that a lot." In that moment, the tentativeness she'd felt before faded to the background.

"Good." A big grin broke out across his face. "Friday night? There's a nice steakhouse up on the mountain in Spruce Pine about thirty minutes from here. I get off early that day and can head home to get dressed then pick you up here around six-thirty."

"Sounds perfect." Livy rested a hand on his arm.

The hint of passion that rekindled in his eyes made Livy believe that, when he loved, he loved fiercely.

"Good night, Jack." But something held her frozen in the truck.

He reached for her fingers resting on his arm and lifted them to his mouth, the heat of his breath warming her skin as his lips brushed the back of her hand. "It sure was." His husky, deep voice intensified the attraction pulling her closer still. But he let go of her hand and reached to open his door, breaking the quiet moment.

Livy released a long, exacerbated sigh as Jack walked around the truck to her side, opened the door, and reached for her other hand.

His shadow enveloped her as his tall frame obscured the yellow glow from the antique porch light. Even though they didn't touch, his nearness intoxicated her. His lips parted slowly as if about to say something. Instead, he reached for the doorknob, pushed it open, and nodded for her to enter.

"Coffee in the morning? Say around eight?" Hopefully her voice didn't give away the anticipation of seeing him again so soon.

He cleared his voice. "Yes, please."

What was he thinking? Was he as caught off guard by their obvious attraction? Was he also fighting urges?

The soft shifting of his boots brought her back to the moment as he scooted to let her by. She walked past close enough that her shoulder brushed his chest. *Good gracious, what it did to her to be this close.* A surge shot through her and she darted her eyes back to his.

"Goodnight, Olivia." She liked the sound of him using her full name. Very much.

"Goodnight, Jack." The heavy door shut behind her.

Livy floated up the stairs. With a flick of the switch just inside the door, Room 12 filled with a golden glow. She tossed her key onto the dresser, and the creak of the mattress filled the quiet room as she sat to remove her shoes. What a lovely evening, in such a lovely town, with such lovely company.

Maybe too lovely. From somewhere deep inside, an uncertainty welled up. It was all too good to be true. Something would go wrong, like it always did. People—maybe even Jack—would disappoint her.

No. Things could change. She came to Laurel Cove believing that. She shook away the momentary doubt.

One thing, however, was absolutely certain. There was quite possibly something very special about Jack Bowdon.

CHAPTER

Nine

Jack's watch read 7:56. His still-damp hair caught the chilly morning breeze, and he shuddered walking from his truck to the inn. He couldn't wait to see Livy again. So, when Jasper had called late the night before asking to swap his day off, Jack was all too eager to oblige. He'd surprise her by picking her up for breakfast.

Waiting in the lobby wasn't without its risks. He would likely see Aunt Bea, who'd run wild with any sign that something brewed between him and Livy. Truth was, he wanted to keep that close to his chest for now. Thankfully, he had the excuse of checking on a possible repair before coming in on Saturday to do routine maintenance.

"Morning, Aunt Bea." He found her watering the houseplants around the lobby, floorboards creaking under her feet.

"Jack! You're here early. It's so good to see you, honey." She stood in front of a large philodendron with a few pruned brown leaves in her hand. Her face beamed with genuine excitement.

"I'm just here to check the sink again so I can get a new part while I'm out today if I need to." He fingered through some mail on the front desk, forcing what he hoped looked like a casual smile.

Aunt Bea's eyes narrowed with a sideways glance. "Is that right? I thought you'd already done that." She set a hand on a hip that jutted out from her apron.

"Well, I'm also picking Livy up. We're going to head over to the Blue Bird for breakfast." He held his breath, waiting for her reaction. She said nothing, so he continued with more explanation. "She's not been anywhere but the coffee shop, and I thought it'd be a nice change of pace."

Aunt Bea failed to hide a smirk. "Well, that's neighborly of you. She's a nice girl, isn't she?"

That was a pretty subdued reaction compared to what he'd expected. "Yes, Aunt Bea, she's a very nice girl." Before she could pry any further, he excused himself to check on the leaky pipe under the kitchen sink.

Jack returned to the lobby a few minutes later, wiping his hands on an old rag, just in time to see Livy coming down the main staircase. It wasn't the first time the sight of her stopped him in his tracks. He'd have to get that under control if he didn't want to give away his feelings for her to everyone in town.

Livy was casual in a denim button-up over an old T-shirt as bright green as her eyes. *Those eyes.* Like last night, her hair was pulled back in a loose braid that fell forward over one shoulder. How different Livy and Claire were in this respect. Jack never understood the need for all that fuss.

Livy's beauty was simple and effortless. She wore a little bit of makeup, just enough to highlight a natural radiance about her, and she probably didn't even know it.

Aunt Bea kept her distance, busy dusting the bookcase across the lobby. Thank God for that, but Jack had no doubt she was paying attention.

"Good morning." He beamed as they met at the bottom of the stairs.

"Jack! What are you doing here?" Her cheeks blushed at the sight of him, making his breath catch.

"I unexpectedly found myself with the day off. Thought I'd chance it that you would be up for breakfast." He fidgeted with the truck key in his hands.

"That sounds wonderful. What a treat!" She touched his arm, her fingers as cool as the morning air on his skin. Together they made their way toward the front door.

"Sleep well last night?" Livy asked.

"It took a while to fall asleep." Was her mind as full as his after they'd said goodnight? "But yes, thanks. You?"

"Actually, I crashed right away." She paused and reached out her hand. "But I had wonderful dreams."

Jack's fingers wrapped around hers. They said goodbye to Aunt Bea, who gave them a quick wave and giggle.

Together in his truck again, Jack caught himself staring at Livy as she settled in the seat and buckled her seatbelt. The moment lingered only a second before he started the truck, but that's all it took for Jack's heart to respond.

"I couldn't wait to see you again." Stretching his arm along the back of the seat, his fingers found the end of her braid in short order and gave it a playful tug.

She sighed. "No complaints here."

After a short, meandering drive through the misty mountain morning on a few back roads, they pulled up to the rustic Blue Bird Café. An old wooden sign hanging from rusty chains over the porch swayed in a gentle breeze. The café was no bigger than a small family home, but the pebble-covered parking lot held at least two dozen cars.

"I hope we can get a table." Livy scrunched up her nose.

"It holds more folks than you'd think. This is actually a light crowd."

Together they walked up a rickety ramp to the screen door, which Jack held open for Livy.

"Be right with ya." A waitress with fiery red hair and a blue-checkered apron passed without looking at them, hands full of plates of food. *Oh, great.* Mary Sue, a friend of Claire's, had been quite vocal about siding with his ex-wife. He had no idea she worked here now. She tossed a rag into a plastic tub behind the waitress stand and stared.

"Well, look who's here. Mr. Perfect." Her hip jutted out, lips pursed and pencil-drawn eyebrows arched. Her cold, sable eyes took in Livy's entire body, head to toe.

"It'll just be the two of us today. A booth if you have it." Jack gritted his teeth. He had absolutely no intention of taking the bitter woman's bait.

Mary Sue yanked the menus from the waitress stand with a scraping sound that grated through his middle. Why did she even care that much? God only knew what Claire had told her. But he wasn't the one who had broken any wedding vows.

Jack and Livy followed the woman to a booth in the main dining room. The menus slapped as they hit the table, and Livy's wide green eyes met Jack's.

"I'll send someone else over to get your order." Mary Sue directed the statement to Livy with a fake, quick smile that clenched Jack's fist tight on top of the table. This wasn't even about her.

"Thanks very much," Livy responded with a genuine smile to the woman who'd been nothing but rude to them both. Jack chuckled to himself, looking back at Mary Sue. The waitress huffed loudly, turned sharply, and marched back toward the kitchen.

"Well, that was awkward. I'm so sorry." Jack rubbed his hand over a scruffy cheek.

"It's fine. But I'm guessing there's a story there."

"Pretty simple, really. Mary Sue is Claire's best friend. She never liked me, I don't think. She even used to tell me in front of Claire that I didn't deserve her. I'm not really sure where that came from, but we never got along. Then, when the divorce happened, Mary Sue made it perfectly clear that she blamed me for pushing Claire into someone else's arms. She and I have had strong words with each other a few times. I've not seen her in over a year, though."

"I'm sorry. It's a shame people take sides when they don't know the whole story." Jack sensed Livy spoke from experience from the way she shook her head while peering down at the menu.

"Exactly. But no need to let it stop us from enjoying the best breakfast in the county." Jack exhaled a deep breath, as if it could clear the negativity Mary Sue had left at their table. However, in the back of his mind, he had a feeling this unfortunate run-in with Claire's friend wouldn't end here.

About half an hour later, Livy sat back into the vinyl-cushioned booth, cupping her coffee mug with both hands. "Well, we've about covered everything under the sun." The pleasant woman who'd waited on them after Mary Sue had just cleared their empty plates. Over the scrumptious meal, Jack and Livy learned all sorts of tidbits about each other, such as her hatred for olives and his allergy to pineapple.

"Mind if I ask you a more serious question?" Jack searched Livy for any sign of discomfort, but her posture remained easy, her face relaxed.

"Sure. If it's too serious, I just won't answer." Her laugh pulled Jack from staying lost in her gaze—again.

"Fair enough." Jack sat up and rested his elbows on the table. "What are you most scared of?"

"Besides rats?" Livy's nose wrinkled, and they laughed. Her smile faded, and she searched the bottom of her coffee cup. "I think I'm most scared of not finding myself again." Her eyes had lost some of their brightness when she looked up.

Though Jack had heard the story of her relationship already, Livy's sense of being lost became even more clear. A feeling he knew all too well.

"What part is still missing?"

Livy sat up to the edge of the table, took the last sip, and set the cup down so slowly and gently that it made no sound. Everything else in the small café faded into the background as Jack focused on Livy's words.

"I moved to New York after graduating college as an artist with a hunger for independence and adventure. My parents supported me and told me I could do anything. I believed it without a doubt."

"They sound a lot like my folks." Had her parents struggled to watch their daughter lose the confidence they had worked hard to build? Jack hadn't known Livy nearly as long or as well, but he could see it, and it sure bothered him.

"Then I arrived and the city was so different from what I expected." Livy's eyes fixed on something out the window, like they had in the coffee shop when she'd told him about Sam. "It was harsh and unforgiving. It chewed me up and spit me out. Well, I don't know if it was the city itself, or maybe it was Sam preventing the city from being accessible to me."

Jack reached across the table and placed his hand over hers, giving it a gentle squeeze.

"Either way, before I knew it, I let other people and circumstances convince me I was someone other than that adventurous artist who knew she was destined for great things. I lost her." Livy's eyes brimmed with tears as she found Jack's face for just a moment. He handed her his handkerchief.

She took it and dabbed at the corners of her eyes. "It's like those dishes." She pointed to a table scattered with dishes topped with scraps of food, used silverware, and crumpled napkins from a large party that had just left. "There are traces of the whole meal that was originally neatly arranged on the plate. But now all you see are crumbs and smears and unfinished pieces of the whole." She straightened and turned to face the window. Her hardened expression mirrored his own outlook following his messy divorce. A long moment of silence filled the space between them.

Jack panned the room for Mary Sue, feeling tense about what the bitter woman might be up to. He found her near the front door talking to another waitress, her back turned to him. The other woman looked past Mary Sue's shoulder in Jack's direction. He and Livy were undoubtedly the topic of conversation. Anger rose up inside him. His jaw tensed, and he inhaled a deep breath to remain calm. Running into Mary Sue, of all people, wasn't going to do him any favors.

"Oh, Jack, I'm so sorry." As if she just realized how somber the mood had turned, she handed back his handkerchief. "I didn't mean to be so depressing. I really know how to show a guy a good time, huh?"

"As a matter of a fact, you do." Jack reached across the table and took her hand. "You can always tell me what you're feeling. I can relate more than you know. After the incident with Claire, I lost all faith in the decency of people. If someone I had chosen to spend my life with could be so different than I thought she was, how could I trust anyone? So, I guess I'm most afraid of trusting someone and getting hurt again." He squeezed her hand, and she squeezed back.

There was no need to label their new relationship, just budding like the early leaves of spring. It was nice, though, to share some of his deepest feelings. Maybe she could help him get over his fear of trusting. Maybe he could help her find a way back to herself, too.

"So, what's your favorite color?" Jack asked, looking back to Livy and pretending to be perfectly serious. Livy let out a loud belly laugh that was as uninhibited and joyful as when she was a child.

A few minutes later, after some lighter conversation, they decided to head out.

"I've got to warn you," Jack said as Livy pulled on her coat. "Mary Sue has been eyeing us the whole morning. She seems pretty worked up about us being together. She may say something on our way out. Try to ignore her and don't let it bother you, okay?"

"Small town folks, huh?" Her weary smile was crooked with worry.

Jack paid the check at the small counter near the door. He tipped the rim of his hat in Mary Sue's direction on the way out. Her rudeness would not prevent him from remaining a gentleman. Although his gesture was met with narrowed eyes and a loud *humph*, she thankfully didn't say anything else as they passed her out the door.

"Do you mind if we check out that small antique place we saw on our way in?" Livy's eyes sparkled with excitement. Holding his hand, she climbed into the passenger seat.

"Sure. That sounds fun." He closed her door and chuckled. It was so easy to make her happy.

After the short drive around the bend, Jack pulled the truck off the road into a narrow, grassy lot beside a renovated barn. They said nothing as they walked hand in hand toward the shop naturally, as if they'd done it for years.

Inside, antiques crowded the old barn so tightly that a narrow walkway only allowed for one person at a time. Jack guided Livy with a hand on the small of her back. They admired a section of old fixtures—drawer pulls, hooks, lights with beautifully shaped glass globes. There were rows of rusted iron décor, other small handcrafted furniture, collectible records, longneck Pepsi bottles, and even old metal gas station signs.

"I'll remember this place when it's time to decorate the house," Livy said once they had made their way to the back. She thumbed through a pile of weathered postcards of the Appalachian Mountains, Blue Ridge Parkway, Biltmore Estate, and other local attractions.

"I didn't even ask yesterday if you planned to work today." Jack eased up behind her, leaning in to talk softly. Another sigh escaped Livy before she answered. "Since it's my day off, I'd gladly come and help in any way I can."

"That'd be great, but the last thing you want to do on your day off is get all dirty."

Jack raised his eyebrows playfully, as if shocked by her accidental suggestiveness.

"Oh, you know what I mean, Jack!" Livy swatted at him.

He raised both hands, professing his innocence. "I'm hardly ever lazy when I'm off work. I actually prefer to have something to do. Plus, doing just about anything with you sounds great."

Jack's cell phone rang. He answered it, and after a moment, whispered to Livy, "It's the guy with the trash container. He wants to drop it off around noon. That okay?"

Livy nodded. Jack finished securing the plans and hung up.

"This is great! It's ten o'clock, so that gives us plenty of time," Livy exclaimed as they made their way to the front of the store. Jack thanked the owner, a wrinkled old man who hadn't moved from behind a newspaper at the front counter since they'd come in.

"Oh my goodness!"

Jack turned at the sound of Livy's excitement. She stood in front of an old artist's easel that held a tacky oil painting of an owl.

"Is the easel for sale?" Livy called back to the man behind the counter.

When the man didn't answer, Jack reached behind it and held up a price tag.

"This is perfect. I've been looking for one with a heavy wooden frame for years. They're hard to find." She ran her fingers over the wood covered in countless layers of paint. "Who knows how many paintings were done on this one easel…" Her voice trailed off. "I hope it's still here when the house is finished, and maybe it can be my reward to myself."

Jack placed a hand on her shoulder. He didn't know much about art, but it looked like a good and sturdy easel. Livy seemed to be in her true element as an artist. While he built with his hands, he never considered himself creative. He'd love to watch her paint. Why did that thought feel intimate? She reached up and patted his hand, making him realize just how close they stood.

They thanked the owner again. The man offered a silent wave from behind the paper, and they left.

"Want to go back to the inn and get anything before we head to the house?" Jack asked Livy, starting toward Main Street.

"Yeah, my tools and coveralls are in the back of the car."

"Coveralls? Mmm … very attractive." It was natural for Jack to be playful, and she brought it out in him.

"Hey, don't knock 'em! I used to wear them to paint and figured they'd be perfect to work in. They were great yesterday, Mr. Funny Man." She swatted his arm. "But I'll need to find a Laundromat in the next day or so because my other clothes won't last long without a good wash."

Why hadn't he thought of that sort of need before? He knew the inn didn't have laundry facilities. "You're welcome to use my washer and dryer. Why don't you grab whatever else you need to be washed and I'll bring you back to my place when we're done at the house? If you're up for changing plans a little, we can move our date to tonight and I can cook something for dinner." The thought of welcoming Livy into his home created a swirl of excitement and curiosity. In fact, he'd never invited a woman back to his home—besides friends, of course. Yet, the instinct was natural with Livy.

"Are you sure, Jack? You're doing so much for me already and that'll take up your whole evening off, too."

"Believe me," Jack replied, a little more serious this time. "There's nothing else I'd rather do than spend the whole day with you."

Livy let out a sigh as he held her gaze. "Then it's a date. A laundry and dinner date."

CHAPTER
Ten

The dresser mirror reflected a happy woman. For the first time in Livy's life, being vulnerable hadn't come with the price tag of weakness. *I'm safe with Jack.* Though their stories were different, he understood the struggle of overcoming a broken heart. And, mercy, the chemistry between them was like lightning crossing between two summer storm clouds. Electric. She smiled and tossed her perfume in her bag.

With her laundry bag and a dress for dinner in hand, Livy headed downstairs and back out to the porch. Jack leaned against the truck hood with eyes closed and arms folded across his chest, facing the warm sun. The strong lines of his jaw, muscular arms, slightly tapered waist, and long legs all screamed of strength. Livy let out a breathy sigh punctuated with an audible whimper. Her hand flew to her mouth.

"Ready to go?" With eyes still closed, Jack's cheeks dimpled and the corners of his eyes wrinkled.

"Uh, sure." *Smooth. Real smooth.*

"I do believe you were staring, Miss Johnson," he whispered when she approached. His drawl was thick, the way tea grew more potent the longer it steeped. He lazily pushed off the truck and reached for her laundry bag, effortlessly tossing it in the truck bed.

"Was not."

Standing face to face at the passenger door, he paused with a grip on the handle before opening it. His lips met her ear. "Was."

She melted into the seat. He could teach a class on how to flirt.

By the time Jack pulled up the driveway of Gram's house, their small talk had allowed Livy's heartbeat the chance to slow to a normal rate.

"What's your favorite memory of the house?" A strong floral scent welcomed them through the truck's open windows. Livy studied the house and thought back to her childhood.

"Time in the garden with Gram." Her throat tightened, although she wasn't sad. "I remember the rainbow of colors and fragrances. The red and white and pink roses. The bright hibiscus. The climbing vines with little white buds along the fence—honeysuckle, maybe? The tall bush on the side of the house with bright orange flowers. The multicolored pansies under the kitchen window. And all of that was just in the front and side yards."

In her mind's eye she could see the beautiful yard in its prime. All her senses enlivened by vibrant colors, velvet petals, and sweet scents. But now all that remained was a neglected, weed-infested space.

She turned to Jack. "Do you remember the row of tomato and pepper plants up against the house in the backyard?"

"Yeah, I sure do. She grew the best tomatoes."

"And the large garden bed lined with white stones across from that housed vegetables." She pointed to the left side of the house as she imagined it. "Her clothesline hung between the tomatoes and that other bed. I would follow her along the line, handing her clothespins as she hung up clothes or taking them from her as she pulled them down, usually right before a rainstorm. Gram always forgot she had clothes drying. Guess I get that from her." Livy chuckled.

Jack pointed to a large tree at the side of the house. "I remember the old wooden plank swing that hung there. Remember how that yellow nylon rope would burn our hands if we held too tight when we spun each other around?"

The rubber seal of the truck's window frame warmed Livy's forearm. "Yeah. Didn't you try to jump out of that swing one time and get hurt?"

"Got this scar to prove it." Jack leaned over, and she made out a small pink scar above his right eyebrow. "Fell face-first into some twigs on the ground."

She traced the scar with a finger. What a treasure that they shared these childhood memories. He turned over her hand and placed a tender kiss on her palm before casually stepping out of the truck. How did he do that—keep his composure so well? She breathed deep to regain her own wits—a common practice now—and stepped down from the truck, too.

Just as they finished unloading the tools onto the porch, the loud rattle of a diesel engine sounded from the road. The delivery of the trash container was a little early. After a few tries to back the truck up the steep driveway, the driver eased the big metal container down on the far left side of the yard. Livy signed for it, giving the inn as her address for the invoice as Aunt Bea said she could do.

Time to get to work.

Standing with the passenger door open, Livy rummaged through her bag for the coveralls. From the other side, Jack removed his long-sleeved pullover to reveal a dark blue Bowdon Supplies T-shirt—and strong, toned arms. Dancing in his arms the night before, she'd noticed his fit frame, but seeing his muscles flex as he pulled on work gloves left her a little breathless.

He smiled at her through the cab of the truck. *Get it together and stop staring.* Blushing, she grinned back, shimmied into her coveralls, and closed the door.

"You look like my middle school janitor. Where's your yellow bucket and mop?" Jack tugged at the arm of the baggy work clothes as they made their way to the porch.

Sure, the one-piece tan outfit wasn't the most flattering. "Well, let's see what tune you're whistling when we're done here and I can just whip this thing right off." Like back at the antique shop, Jack's eyebrows perked up again with a flirtatious grin. "Oh, Jack, you know what I mean! Stop flustering me!"

He laughed with her.

Why did she fight the urge to flirt? So what if he flustered her? And there was no shame in finding him attractive. She was a single woman and Jack was a single man. *Just enjoy the day for whatever it's meant to be.*

The next several hours, they worked hard to clear the remaining junk from the entire house. The large furniture made it into the trash container except for the couch, a set of old dresser drawers, and a floor lamp, which went into the back of Jack's truck for delivery to the local thrift store. Livy also filled a large box with random books to take to the community library, which held a book swap once a month. Around two o'clock, they took a snack break. Livy went to the truck and retrieved the apples, peanut butter, cheese and crackers, and water they'd thrown in the cooler in the backseat.

"Thanks. I'm starving." Jack caught an apple Livy tossed him. They walked to the back of the house and spread a drop cloth underneath a shade tree. Livy set the other items down and stretched her arms above her head.

"It's really warmed up this afternoon." She unzipped the coveralls, but the zipper stuck about a third of the way down. After struggling with it a minute, she let out an exasperated huff. "Would you please see if you can get it?"

"Sure." He set his apple down, rose to his knees from the spot he'd claimed on the drop cloth, and motioned her closer.

He tugged and pulled. Licking his bottom lip, he appeared to concentrate on the task, but Livy saw his lips quiver to hold back a laugh. A bead of sweat rolled down her back. She also needed to pee. With a nervous giggle, she placed her hands on her hips and shook her head.

He gave the zipper a forceful tug and it gave way. Livy tumbled into him, nearly knocking them both to the ground. His arms wrapped around her, helping keep their balance. Laughs faded, as their faces met, his cheek scruffy against hers. She sat back, putting some space between them again.

"I'm glad you're here, Jack."

"I wouldn't want to be anywhere else."

"That's nice." Livy smiled, lifting to her feet. "But I've got to go." She scurried off to the other side of the house to find a private spot to squat, his laugh floating on the air.

Once back, Livy claimed a spot on the cloth close enough that her knees touched Jack's.

"It's been kind of hard, you know?"

"Yeah, it's a big move." He nudged her knee before resting back on his elbows and looking up into the branches above. A strong breeze blew stray hairs across her face.

"We've accomplished a lot already today with your help, but it's more than that." She lay back with her arms behind her head. "You've kept me company. When I decided to move here, I had one objective: get away from the city and the person I'd become. I didn't think about not knowing anyone here. On the drive up here from my mom's, it hit me. I'd be away from certain people I no longer want to see, but I wouldn't have anyone at all here." She propped herself up on an elbow, facing Jack. "I prayed to God that He'd put a friend in my path. I think my exact words were, 'Lord, give me someone to keep me company.' As usual, He did so much more than that." Her hand found Jack's laying against his chest. Did her smile convey her affection?

Jack seemed to study the leaves high above. His hand closed over hers and squeezed. Had she shared too much and made him uncomfortable? She didn't think so, but doubting herself was a hard habit to break.

He twisted to face her, eyes damp. She held her breath.

"Livy, that is the *exact* prayer I've been praying for the last six months. Those very same words." His voice was deep and soft, breathy. "I have the most amazing friends, and I couldn't ask for a better brother. They've all been there for me through the divorce, encouraging me and supporting me as I've worked to heal. Once I moved past the shock and anger of the situation with Claire, they started to set me up on dates. I haven't been interested. Dating seemed so trivial, so risky after what I had been through. But I've been lonely." His voice cracked and he drew in a deep breath. An understanding she'd gladly give up flooded her as he continued. "About six months ago, sitting in church, I prayed that God would bring me someone to keep me company. And I believe He has."

Livy finally exhaled the breath she'd been keeping in, rolling onto her back. Her feelings were enough to process. Jack's both overwhelmed and scared her. This wasn't just a wink and flirty quip. She and Sam had become involved so quickly after meeting. She hadn't known him at all, really, when they'd begun dating. She'd been pulled in by the attention he offered—and look where that had gotten her.

Livy had to find a way to talk to Jack about her fears. Maybe tonight at his house they'd have a chance to talk some more over dinner. Here at Gram's house, in the middle of so much to do, wasn't the time or place.

The only sounds were of an occasional cricket, a songbird's serenade in the distance, and the rustling of leaves in the gentle breeze. Livy stood and offered Jack a hand. As she helped him up, her arms found their way around his middle. Her head rested against his chest for a long moment, and she noted its rhythmic rise and fall. She wasn't used to being held by a man again. The embrace was exciting and tender, just like on the dance floor the night before.

He kissed the top of her head. In that moment words like *treasured* and *safe* swirled in her heart. Had it really only been four days since they'd met? Could these feelings be real? *God, if it's Your will, help me be the woman Jack needs. And help us see where You're leading us.*

They spent the rest of the day scrubbing the kitchen, pulling up rugs in the two bedrooms—revealing original hardwood floors—and purging the shed. Jack checked the integrity of any walls that appeared to have water damage from a leaky roof and marked a few for new sheetrock and finishing.

"I'm going to talk to some of the guys and see if we can arrange a Saturday for us to come and bang out several of these bigger jobs." Jack loaded the larger tools in the truck.

She handed him her tool bag. "I think your contractor voice is pretty cute." *You look pretty cute, too.*

"Thanks, I think." He laughed, placing it inside and pulling up the hatch. "Tonight, we can talk more about the other big projects you want to do."

"Let's not worry about the house tonight. We've gotten a lot done today, and I feel really good about the progress. Shop talk can wait one night, don't you think?" She smiled at his raised eyebrows.

"Yes, ma'am. No arguments here."

As the truck meandered down the winding country road away from Gram's house, Livy caught a glimpse of herself in the side mirror. Just like the cottage, there was already a little more vibrancy in her face. Did it reflect a renewed hope? Next to her, Jack cleared his throat. She turned to him and watched him study the road, masterfully maneuvering the twists and turns. Would he be as careful with her heart?

CHAPTER

Eleven

Jack's truck made easy work of the steep, but gentle climb up the mountain to his house. Livy was curious to see where he lived. The tall, swaying pines along a winding private road were enchanting. Just when the trees grew thick enough to drown out most of the daylight, they came to a clearing.

"Well, this is it." Jack's truck rolled to a stop, and quiet filled the cab.

"Wow." Livy let the word linger. Before her stood a large, honey-colored log cabin and a simple but beautifully landscaped yard. Mature spruce trees that flanked the sides of the house reminded her of Christmas.

Up close, it was even more mesmerizing with a wraparound porch, natural stone chimney, and deep red tin roof. She wasn't sure what she had been expecting, but this was something special. Both impressive and somehow modest and inviting.

"Hey, buddy! Did you have a good day?" Rex bounded off the porch. Jack knelt and gave the dog a good scratch behind the ears. "Do you remember this pretty lady?"

Rex pushed his wet nose into her hand. "I remember you, too, boy." She turned to Jack. "He looks a lot like my daddy's dog, Molly. They were inseparable on the farm. I have a soft spot in my heart for men who love their dogs."

"Lucky us." Jack's eyes brightened as he patted the side of his leg, beckoning the dog to follow his lead. "Come on, boy. Let's show Livy around."

Jack grabbed Livy's duffle bag from the backseat, and Livy followed him inside. The spacious interior was stunning. Walled by the same wooden beams as the exterior of the house, it boasted tall, vaulted ceilings. She followed him through the main living space to the open kitchen.

"Jack, it's just beautiful. Doubt I can afford granite like this in Gram's house." He ran her hand over the cold, smooth flecked granite counter.

"Sure you can. I know the guy who runs a quarry just about an hour from here. I could get him to sell it to you wholesale."

He was even more handsome in his home, in his element.

In the living room, an oversized brown leather sofa and loveseat, antique wooden coffee table, and brick-red woven area rug were positioned in front of a large fireplace. She ran her hand along the mantle, made of the same natural stone she'd seen outside. The comfy throw pillows and blankets on the couch and seat made the place feel homey and lived-in. "It suits you very well."

The home was comfortable and sturdy, just like Jack. She walked over to a huge, floor-to-ceiling wall of windows past the living area. Outside was an expansive porch and balcony that framed a breathtaking, unobstructed 180-degree view of the valley below and misty mountain ranges in the distance.

"Thank you. I worked for a long time on this house. It was a real labor of love." He joined her at the window.

She turned and swatted his arm. "Get out! You *built* this?"

"Designed and built—with a great crew of guys, of course." Jack looked around his home, standing tall and beaming.

Livy shook her head. "You have an obvious eye for architecture. Do you miss designing houses now that you're running the store?"

Jack surveyed the expansive living room. "Well, I'd be lying if I said I didn't miss it at all. It's my passion, really. But I don't regret for a moment coming back here to help my family. Bowdon's is the only supply store Laurel Cove has ever had. I couldn't let the family legacy die with Dad. I always expected to take it over one day, just not quite this soon. But, as you know, life has a funny way of leading you right where you need to be." He smiled at Livy and brushed a strand of hair out of her face.

"Yes, I do know a little something about that." She leaned in to playfully bump his shoulder.

"Building this house kept me sane during Dad's illness. It was my therapy. I had intended to finish it in time for Claire and I to move in and celebrate our first anniversary, but that never happened. So it's just me and Rex." He patted the dog's head, who sat at his side looking out over the view. "Do you want the rest of the tour?"

"Would love it." She nodded and he grabbed her hand, sending electricity through her arm.

He pointed across the room. "That small spiral staircase leads up to a second floor loft, which is my office."

He then showed Livy the guestrooms and guest bathroom down a long hallway, his bedroom down a short hallway on the other side of the living room, and finally the laundry room. He set out the soap and fabric softener for her laundry then paused in the doorway. "Guess I'll leave you to it. Holler if you need anything."

"Thanks, Jack." He stood there a moment watching her before turning to go. She smiled and waved him away. Gushing water filled the washer but didn't drown out her thoughts. The craftsmanship of the home was immeasurable to anything she'd seen before. And the cozy style suited him nicely. But did it bother him to live in a house he'd intended for his now ex-wife? She added the detergent, closed the lid, and started toward the kitchen. The sun was below the horizon now, the large living room even cozier in dim light.

"Do you like shrimp?" Jack set items on the counter from the refrigerator.

"One of my favorites."

"Good." Jack maneuvered around the kitchen with little effort, in his element.

Being in his home filled Livy with a sense of comfort too. But she suspected that had more to do with Jack himself than the beautiful and cozy design. How did he do that? Put her so at ease?

"I think I'll get these marinating, then we can grab a shower." He shot her a wide-eyed look, face flushing.

Livy's hand flew to her mouth to stifle a laugh. It was Jack's turn to pull his foot out of his mouth.

"What I mean is, we can each take a shower." His hands flew up in defense. "Me in my bathroom, and you in the guest bath."

"Yeah, sure that's what you meant." Livy drew out her words and squinted her eyes at him.

He washed his hands, prepped a quick marinade for the shrimp, and placed the bowl in the fridge before showing Livy to the guest room. It was just as charming as the rest of the house, with a high four-poster bed covered with a colorful quilt and rocking chair in the corner facing broad windows. She smiled at a square pillow on the chair with "Cabin Fever" stitched across it in thick red thread. The grand view mimicked the one from the porch. If she lived here, she'd never tire of this view.

Jack pushed open another door that led to an attached bathroom.

"Watch out for the purple bubble bath in there." His tone was serious, but a smile played across his face.

"Owen and Jen's kids spent the night a few weeks ago when they went out to Asheville to celebrate their anniversary. They left their soap here." With a wink, he left her to clean up. As if she didn't already find him delightful, the thought of him caring for children was even more impressive. A known instinct jumped inside her. *One baby step at a time, Livy.* As she reached to turn on the shower, her own laugh at the pun echoed off the tiled walls.

Jack heard the rush of water sound through the pipes from the direction of the guest bathroom as he headed toward his bedroom. A longing tugged at him. He'd actually never been alone with a woman in his house. It had turned out to be a somewhat unexpected day with Livy. Breakfast had turned into shopping, which turned into helping at the house. Even despite the run-in with Mary Sue, having Livy here now—for an actual dinner date—made the day too good to be true. Could it really be this easy?

Jack showered and dressed in khakis and a lightweight black sweater before returning to the kitchen. He put on quiet music and lit a candle at a small table next to the bank of windows. The shrimp and vegetables were skewered for grilling, and he was preparing a small salad when Livy stepped into the kitchen.

His breath escaped at the sight of her in a long, black, flowing dress covered in a loose gray cardigan. Her hair, which he'd only seen pulled back in a ponytail or braid, now cascaded past her shoulders in thick, brown curls that framed her face. Her green eyes sparkled like emeralds. Beautiful before, she left him speechless.

As she walked toward him, Jack couldn't stop staring. He wasn't quite sure why, but her bare feet made her even more attractive. She was comfortable with him—in his house.

"You look..." Jack paused when she stood next to him. "Amazing."

Livy stepped close and inhaled near his neck. "So do you, and you smell great." Goosebumps scattered across his arms.

"Nah, that's the shrimp." He joked, attempting to clear his own head after having her so near him. "I've just got to throw these skewers on the grill back there." Jack pointed toward a built-in grill top on one side of the stove. "A few minutes and we'll be ready."

After Jack offered a quick blessing over their meal, Livy took the first bite of shrimp, closing her eyes and letting out a moan. "Jack, this is so delicious. I'm very impressed."

"I'm glad you like it. I really enjoy cooking."

"Well, besides my mama's spaghetti, I don't have many skills in the kitchen. I may have to start practicing." Livy devoured another bite of shrimp.

Jack wrinkled his nose. "I remember a rather, um, unfortunate treat you made one day when we were kids."

Livy shook her head and covered her mouth with a hand. "Oh, no. What was it? Back then, I watched Gram cook and thought I could do anything she could."

"Well, I'm not exactly sure what was in it, but you called it a cake." He nearly choked on a hearty laugh. "You made it for my birthday just after the Fourth of July, remember?"

Her eyes flew open. "Oh, I remember now! I slaved over that cake all morning after you'd told me at the parade that you were turning eleven. But you acted like you loved it. Was it very bad?" The way she bit her bottom lip, waiting for his answer, melted a hard space deep within him.

"Well, I imagine there's got to be someone out there who enjoys the flavors of raw orange peel and crushed cinnamon bark in their rubbery cakes. But to this day, I gag at the slightest hint of cinnamon." He waved his hand across the table in a matter-of-fact way, holding a straight face.

"Oh, Jack, honestly." Her arms lay crossed on the table, head cocking to one side. And her loud laughter traveled through the empty spaces of the house he'd been alone in all this time. That laugh. The same laugh from those summer days of tire swings and wading in cold creeks.

The rest of the conversation remained lively and easy. She told him about New York City, and he shared about designing nightmares for difficult homebuilders. They compared Livy's upbringing on the farm outside Raleigh to Jack's in Laurel Cove. Despite a few differences, they had a lot in common. They both grew up going to church, loved classic rock, yearned to travel, and preferred snow to the beach.

Jack stood to clear the table long after they'd finished. "I think I'll make a fire. I hope you'll stay a little longer."

"That sounds perfect. Plus, I need to dry my clothes." Livy giggled.

"Oh, right, that." He'd forgotten her laundry, but was glad for the reason.

After stepping away to tend to her clothing, she rejoined him on the couch, pulling her feet under her. "I've got a crazy question."

"What's that?" Jack poked the firewood as it caught the small starter flame.

She scrunched up her nose, which he'd come to recognize as a sign of embarrassment. "Would you care to loan me a pair of socks? My feet are freezing. I didn't even think about shoes with this outfit."

"Oh, of course." *That's adorable.* He grabbed a pair from his room.

"Thanks, Jack." She slid them on.

The comfortable couch faced the stone fireplace. His outstretched arm across the back cushion invited her to lean against him. Together they watched the growing, crackling fire for several moments in silence.

"You know, I had quite the crush on you all those years ago." Jack danced his fingers along the curve of her shoulder.

She turned to look at him and smiled. "You did?"

"Oh sure. My first real crush. After spending almost every day together that summer, then having to say goodbye, I realized I missed you. I couldn't stop thinking about you and wondering how you were and what you were doing. That whole year I waited, hoping you'd visit again."

"I never knew that, Jack. That's so sweet." Livy's hand rested on his right leg.

"Sweet, maybe, but tortured, too." He dropped his head against the cushion and let out a low chuckle. "I had myself so worked up when I heard your grandmother tell my mom at church that you'd only be visiting a few weeks the next summer. I tried real hard to figure out how I'd see you since we'd moved across town."

"That summer we first met and hung out was great." Livy's voice was soft and tender, almost melodious as she looked back at the now-full fire. "But I have to admit I'm surprised you have such long-lasting memories from that time. We were so young. I remember you happily, of course, but it seems to go deeper for you."

"Maybe so." Jack sat up straighter so he could look into her green eyes, which reflected the dancing flames. "But, to me, you were the most magical girl. You imagined things I couldn't see in my mind without your help. You saw the beauty in everything. You made me feel like I was the bravest kid you'd ever met when you would ask me to take you on an adventure through what you called *your mountain*. And you were the first girl I'd ever noticed to be cute. I loved the freckles on your nose that came out when we'd been in the sun too long." He traced the curve of her nose with a finger. "And the way your two front teeth had a little gap in between them, and the way you'd pretend to talk to the flowers like your grandma did."

"Jack, you really are too sweet." She looked away from him, her eyes fixed on the fire instead. Why was it so difficult for her to receive his compliments?

"Do you believe me?" Jack placed his hand over hers.

"Oh, sure."

Jack didn't buy it. He reached for her chin so she looked in his eyes. "I'm sorry it's been so long since you've been told how wonderful you are, Olivia." He traced the line of her jaw. "You were a cute, fun friend back then. And I hope you trust me when I tell you that you are funny, interesting, brave, and an incredibly beautiful woman now."

Her eyes softened as she listened to his words. It was hard for her to hear such direct admiration, but she was trying.

"I'm sorry." Her eyes closed as she drew in a deep breath. "The last several months we were together, my ex not only didn't compliment me, but he criticized everything I did. To be the woman he wanted me to be—more serious, less needy, more driven—I lost the ability to see who I really am."

Jack's body tensed. Hearing pain in her cracked voice just about undid him. He wrestled with the impulses to both comfort and defend her.

"But somehow," she continued, "when I'm around you I feel more like me than I've felt in so long. That girl you remember, carefree and imaginative, is what I feel when I paint, too. Full of life. Sam didn't see that. You make me feel relaxed, encouraged, and..." She paused and looked up, deep into his eyes. "And desired."

With the warm fire casting shadows on her face, Jack leaned in. The chemistry between them was electric. The moment their lips touched was like cutting through a bag of fine sugar—there was no containing it. Her arms wrapped around his neck, holding on tight.

Her lips tasted of sweet summer fruit. His hands slid down the subtle curve of her frame to her small waist, and his mouth moved to her neck. Livy wove her fingers through his hair, encouraging him. Their quickened breaths mixed with the snapping fire.

All of a sudden, Jack came to his senses. He needed a breather if there was any chance at keeping control. As much as he wanted to lose control with Livy—and boy, did he—she deserved to be pursued honorably. He pushed away and sat at the end of the couch with his head in his hands, leaving her panting.

She scooted next to him, placing her hand on his thigh. *Not helping.* "What happened?"

He took a deep breath, rubbed his face a few times with both hands to sober up, and looked at her.

"I was getting to that point of no return," he managed.

"Oh." Livy broke out in a wide grin.

"Yeah." He smiled back, letting out a long sigh. He took a few more deep breaths. "There is something special about you, Livy. I want to do this right. I don't want to rush into anything—for both our sakes. I've done that before and it didn't work. I'm not willing to risk that with you, even if it has only been a week. If God has plans for us together, I want to honor Him every step of the way."

She moved to the edge of the coffee table in front of him and looked him in the eyes. When she placed a hand on each of his knees, a pounding thundered in his chest.

"You are the gentlest, most decent man I know, Jack Bowdon. You are also the sexiest man I know."

"Livy." Jack's voice was low and gruff. "You're playing with fire."

She threw her hands up, claiming innocence. This confidence he saw through her teasing was only more attractive. It gave him a glimpse into what she was like without being held back by insecurities. And he liked it, very much.

After a long moment of studying one another, Livy spoke. "Take me on an adventure, Jack. Let's see where we end up."

This woman amazed him more and more every minute. He gave her one slow, sensual kiss. "You got it."

Livy floated up the stairs of the inn to her room, reveling in the sweet things Jack had said and the tender kisses they'd shared. And entering Room 12 was like coming home. She readied for bed and set out clothes for the next morning. Jack had invited her to attend church with him, and she couldn't wait. Soon, she laid her head on the pillow, drowsy with happy thoughts.

In the blink of an eye, she was standing on the street looking up at her New York City apartment. It towered above her, the top floors disappearing into stormy clouds. Behind her honking taxis raced by, passengers yelling things at her.

"You're no good for him."

"Better give up now, sweetheart."

"He's just like any other man."

When she spun around to argue, there was Sam, cell phone held up to an ear. "You'll never amount to anything, just like I've always told you." His words sounded crackled, as if spoken through a bad phone connection. She turned to retreat up the steps of the apartment, only to find Gram's cottage. Worse off than she'd found it a few weeks ago, it reeked of decay and moaned under the weight of thick vines overtaking every inch of the home. Hot tears streamed down Livy's face as the house imploded before her.

And there was Sam, next to her again with phone in hand. "You can't rebuild a life that's beyond repair. It doesn't work that way." Livy covered her ears with both hands, sobs wracking her body until she crumbled to the ground.

When she opened her eyes again, she was back in Room 12. Her pillow was damp from real tears, her chest still heaving with shallow pants. And in what seemed like the length of a single heartbeat, the still-tender wounds left by Sam's unkindness were ripped open. She ached with an unsettling doubt, her excitement from the lovely night with Jack crushed under the weight of renewed uncertainty.

She went to the bathroom for a drink of water and stared at her puffy face reflected in the mirror. *Is Jack really as nice as he seems? Can it be this easy? What if I let him in and he hurts me, too?* The whisperings of doubt continued as she climbed back into bed, nagging until sleep finally came in the earliest hours of a new day.

CHAPTER

Twelve

A radiant sun worked to burn off the remaining morning haze settled in the Blue Ridge valleys. Despite the rays of sunlight, Livy's heart was as heavy as the fog. Her car parted a dense patch of the mist with ease as she approached Laurel Cove Fellowship Church. Last night's dream and all the terrible things said left her shaky and vulnerable.

She spotted Jack and Jen on the front lawn, children running around them. He was dashing in navy blue pants, a crisp white button-up shirt, and light blue tie. Livy's stomach ached from the knots inside.

She steered the car into a vacant spot toward the back of the almost full church lot. Weary eyes stared back at her in the rearview mirror as she applied lipgloss. The forced, toothy smile she rehearsed before reaching for the door handle earned a half-hearted laugh. The moment of self-inflicted brevity lightened her mood. She knew one thing, she appreciated being at church. It'd been too long since she'd heard a sermon and studied God's word.

"Morning, Livy. We're so glad you're here." Jen's deep southern drawl was as welcoming as the organ music coming from the open doors of the quaint sanctuary.

"Thanks so much. It's good to be back." Livy kept a few feet between her and Jack, afraid that her doubt and worry might be contagious. She offered a tender smile to greet him good morning. Plus, how close was too close in the middle of the church crowd? He returned the smile and closed the gap between them in one long stride so his shoulder brushed hers. She drew in a sharp breath. Why? It's not like he was the one diseased by an inner turmoil.

"Well, I best run along and make sure Owen's tie isn't sticking up out of his robe again." Jen winked at Jack before excusing herself and heading up the front steps.

Jack turned to Livy and held her elbow. "You look nice. Blue really makes your eyes pop." The compliment sounded as sincere as the soft kiss on her cheek, his freshly-shaven face smoother than the night before. And yet, it didn't reconcile the raging battle between her worries and her hopes.

"Everything okay?" Jack's head cocked to one side, and his eyes narrowed.

Oh, how she both hated and savored his ability to see inside to the place that suffered. Church bells clanged from the steeple, signaling the start of the service. "Yes. I'm fine. Shall we find a seat?" Livy avoided holding his gaze for more than a second and nodded toward the sanctuary. But she wasn't fine. She was terrified that he'd see right through her and realize he wasn't interested in being with someone who was such an emotional mess. The lump in her throat burned, threatening to choke her with feelings that punched and scratched and wrestled inside. She held her purse so tight to her side she could feel the outline of her keys through the leather.

Thankfully, Jack didn't push any further, but led her inside to a pew halfway down the aisle. The old chapel smelled of wood polish and fresh flowers. The same as Livy remembered, its scent calmed her nerves enough that she was able to compose herself. There was also something very comforting being where her memories of Gram were so vivid. If she closed her eyes, she could almost feel Gram's polyester suit brush her arm.

Following Owen's brief welcome, the congregation stood for the first song. Jack held open a hymnal between them. Unable to find her voice, Livy listened for a verse then dared to lift her eyes from the page and watched Jack sing. His deep voice captivated her. On the last chord he looked over and winked, sending her heart soaring without permission. The simple gesture was a chisel to the hard exterior she'd erected. The song ended, and as they sat, Jack casually settled his arm along the edge of the pew behind her and gave her shoulder a small squeeze.

Following a few announcements and an adorable rendition of "Jesus Loves Me" by the small children's choir, Owen stepped to the front of the altar. He proceeded to deliver an encouraging message about the grace God extends to all of His people.

"Let's consider this passage from 2 Corinthians." He held up a burgundy Bible. "It says, 'Three times I pleaded with the Lord about this, that it should leave me. But he said to me, *My grace is sufficient for you, for my power is made perfect in weakness.* Therefore, I will boast all the more gladly for my weaknesses, so that the power of Christ may rest upon me.' Hiding our weaknesses only alienates us from the grace God can show us through the love of others. Don't limit God's perfect power by hiding." Owen was a gifted preacher and spoke without judgment. Livy let the scripture wash over her. It was as if the message was just for her.

My weakness is hard to be thankful for, Lord. It's really hard to see myself the way You see me. But I want You to be powerful in me. Be powerful in Jack, too, Lord. Heal any hurt he still feels and help me to be a good friend to him.

The old organ bellowed another familiar tune, the offering plates were passed, then Owen stood on the steps in front of his congregation and invited them to pray with him to close the service. Together, they recited the Lord's Prayer. Livy reached for Jack's hand and entwined her fingers with his. A smile spread across his face, his eyes still closed in prayer, and her soul swelled with a silent reassurance.

Outside, the sun was bright and high in the sky. Parishioners spilled onto the lawn after shaking the preacher's hand. Children scattered in delight, happy to stretch legs and lungs. Elderly couples leaned into each other on their way to their cars parked close to the ramp at the end of the sidewalk. Except for the newer vehicles, the scene was identical to years ago with Gram.

"Why don't y'all head over to our place for lunch?" Owen asked over his shoulder while he buckled a giggling girl into a car seat in the back of their minivan. Jack raised his eyebrows and shrugged his shoulders.

"We'd love to." *We.* It just slipped out. Did Jack even notice her use of the word? *I should have let him answer. Sam always hated that. But Jack is not Sam.* She closed her fist, nails digging into her palm. This roller coaster of emotions had to stop.

They parted ways with the Barnetts and headed toward the back of the lot where their cars were parked just a few spaces from each other.

"So, we're a *we*, are we?" Jack didn't waste any time. He'd noticed.

"I'm sorry I answered for you, Jack. I shouldn't have done that." Her cheeks grew warm.

"No, Livy. That's not what I mean." His furrowed brow replaced a smile. "I like being the other half of a duo with you. It was fine that you answered."

Her hand gripped the strap of her purse tightly, eyes closing tight as she turned to face her car. "Oh, okay." But the doubt nagged at her incessantly. *Go away, Sam!* Why couldn't she shake his reverberating voice?

"Livy, will you look at me, please?" Jack's voice was tender, pleading.

Tears threatened to fall. His hand enveloped hers. After a deep inhale, she turned and met his eyes.

He scooted closer to her. "What's going on? What's wrong?"

A deep breath helped regain control of her voice. "I'm sorry, Jack. It's hard, you know." Livy looked down at their hands.

"I know."

A tear rolled down her cheek, despite her attempt to keep it at bay. "You've been so kind. You've been a great friend, welcoming me to town and helping me at the house. And I like you so much." She looked into his soft eyes. "So very much. But I'm scared. You are so, completely, wonderfully different from my ex. But what if I'm not able to forget what's happened, what's been said to me, the doubt, and the insecurity? You've been through enough, Jack. You don't need a fixer-upper in your life." The words and tears spilled in tandem.

"Livy." Jack wrapped his arm around her shoulders as her face fell into her hands. "Aren't we all fixer-uppers? And just like Gram's house, maybe you can't do it alone. Listen, I'm overwhelmed, too. Meeting you was unexpected not to mention starting to..." He tipped her chin up so their eyes met. "Well, let's just say this is all unexpected." Through sniffles and watery eyes, Livy managed a smile.

"Being a *we* doesn't have to mean anything right now, other than enjoying each other's company. There's no hurry. But please be sure of one very important thing." Jack paused, his chest rising with a full breath. "You are worth so much more than any man can determine. Certainly not Sam—not even me. You have to believe your worth is established by God, more precious than anything here on Earth. I do hope I can make you feel special and important with my words and my time. But that won't matter unless you first trust in the grace God offers you."

Livy let Jack's words soak into her tired soul. It was naïve to think that after just a few short weeks she'd be able to separate from Sam and the disappointment of the last decade of her life. It was going to take time. "Thank you, Jack, for listening and not judging me. I guess I've got more of a wall built up than I realized. But I don't want to shut you out, I promise." She blew her nose into a handkerchief he offered.

"I know you don't. We've been spending an awful lot of time together since you've been here. I'm available whenever you want to get together, but don't be afraid to tell me when you need time to yourself. I know you came here to figure some things out. I'd love to be here to help you do that. As your friend, as a *we*, or whatever." Jack shot her a playful smile.

"I love spending time with you more than I can even say, Jack." She leaned in and placed a soft kiss against his cheek, then held her hand against it. "Just be patient. I'll get there."

"I've got nothing but time." He leaned into her hand, eyes closing.

I could love this man. The thought filled her mind as quickly as the *we* had escaped her mouth. It warmed her. With Sam, Livy would have been embarrassed over such a display of emotions. That wasn't the case with Jack. Instead, she had a renewed sense of hope for the future—whatever that held.

"Ready to go?" Jack asked. Livy nodded and Jack steered onto the road.

The Barnetts' home was just a few quiet streets off Main. Tall trees and pink budding bushes surrounding the backyard offered privacy and the illusion that they were farther out in the country. Livy sipped an iced tea on the deck and watched Jack with Owen and Jen's children—Beth, who was three, and Noah, who was almost five. Crouched with his hands reaching high, his shirtsleeves rolled up and tie thrown over his shoulder, Jack let out a fearsome, bear-like snarl. Shrieks sounded and children scattered in pretend panic. Livy's laugh matched Beth and Noah's as Jack sprung from his position and lunged at them. They ascended the deck and took cover behind Livy, Jack following close behind. Little hands pushed Livy toward Jack like a sacrifice. With hands still up, fingers curled like claws, Jack's eyes grew wide and flickered with a frisky playfulness.

"Jack." Amused, Livy drew out his name, warning him not to attack. Louder giggles sounded from behind, and the kids pushed her closer, until only inches from her predator.

"Y'all, don't wear out our new friend." The sharp clap of the screen door followed Jen's rescue. Beth and Noah scurried to their chairs at the patio table where their parents had placed lunch dishes. But Jack wasn't so easily distracted. He lunged the last step toward Livy, stopping just an inch from her face. His eyes were mischievous, forehead beaded with sweat. She almost kissed him, and probably would have had it not been for the audience. Instead, she tussled his hair and teased, "Aw, who's a big bad bear?"

"Grr." Then a quick peck on her cheek. Livy's hand touched the place his lips had briefly met her skin as they took seats at the table, side by side. What a turnaround from this morning. She started the day convinced her baggage was too heavy for her to carry. Too cumbersome and too scarring. Yet, opening up to Jack transformed her vulnerability into something that resembled hope. And it fueled a fire kindling deep inside her. Things were going to change. No longer did Sam have permission to sabotage her future.

"That was just great. It reminded me of the roasts my gram used to make every Sunday." Livy followed Jen into the kitchen with a few dirty dishes. The chain of the unbalanced fan overhead clicked in rhythm against the milk glass light cover. The kitchen had grown several degrees warmer than the sunny spring day thanks to the oven. Livy looked around and spotted a window air-conditioner unit, but the blue ribbon tied to the front grate wasn't blowing.

"It's the same for me." Jen rinsed dishes at the deep sink and placed them in the dishwasher. "But don't let today's meal fool you. We often have sandwiches or soup. We only invited you because we happened to have a presentable meal ready to go." Jen's honesty was refreshing where many southern women would have reveled in the appearance of perfect domesticity.

Jen dried her hands on a linen towel, and they retired to the porch overlooking the backyard where Owen and Jack played with the kids. From her

Adirondack chair, the cool spring breeze offered Livy a respite from the kitchen's heat.

"Jack is so relaxed." Jen turned to face Livy. "We've all been concerned about him these last several months. Don't get me wrong—he's a fairly positive guy. But those who know him as well as we do have seen the spark gone from his eyes. They used to almost twinkle—mischievously, like a little boy." Her gaze fixed again on the yard.

Livy chuckled. "Yeah, I know that look." Her eyes darted to Jen. Had she just given away some feelings for Jack? And was it really a bad thing if she did?

"That's just what I'm getting at." Jen smiled. "This past week since you've been in town, Jack's, well...back. Owen saw him when he stopped by the shop earlier in the week. When he came home, he told me that he'd just seen the old Jack. He said Jack had met a new girl and seemed pretty smitten."

A heat rushed Livy's face. "I think Jack is wonderful, too, Jen. It's so quick, though. I'm a little scared. But we've talked about that some, Jack and I. We're just enjoying the time."

Jen nodded silently, as if she understood Livy's reservations. Had Jack told his friends of her past?

"Timing is funny, isn't it?" Jen's voice was far off, her eyes fixed directly on Owen across the yard.

"Yes, it is." Livy wasn't even sure if Jen had heard her.

"Well," Jen said. "God has a way of surprising us around every corner. But I can vouch for Jack. He's the sweetest, sincerest guy you'll find. Besides Owen, of course."

For the next half hour or so, the women chatted and got to know each other more. Livy couldn't remember the last time she had a close girlfriend—probably not since high school.

Jack, Owen, and the kids joined the women on the wide, open porch. Jack sat next to Livy on the gliding swing, giving her a quick peck on the cheek and naturally sliding his arm around her shoulders. She soaked up the slow pace of the afternoon.

The kids asked Jen for water, and Noah rubbed his eyes, obviously sleepy to everyone but him.

"Naptime for you two." Jen scooped her littlest into her arms.

Livy joined Jack when he stood. "We'd better get going and let y'all enjoy a quiet afternoon." He turned to Owen. "Hey, any chance you're free one of the next few Saturdays? There are some big projects up at Livy's that I'd love some help with."

Livy fought the impulse to refuse the help. The last thing she wanted to do was take advantage of Jack's friends. But she trusted that Jack wouldn't ask if he knew his friends—her friends, too, really—weren't more than willing to help.

"Let me talk to Jen." Owen's eyes followed his wife and two chatty children. "We've got a birthday party for my brother next weekend in Johnson City, but I think we're free the next Saturday. I'll let you know."

Jack and Owen shook hands. "Sounds great. I'll mention it to Hank, Greg, and Jasper, too. If the girls want to come and help Livy with some of the lighter work that remains, I'm sure she'd appreciate it. Maybe we can do a barbeque afterwards."

"You guys are too nice," Livy chimed in. "I don't know what I was thinking, assuming I could do it all on my own."

Jack nudged her with his elbow. "Don't let her fool you, man. She knows her way with every tool I've seen her pick up."

"Yeah, right!" Livy chuckled. "I'm going to say goodbye to Jen and the kids." But as she followed the sounds of the children back into the house, she walked on air. Jack's compliments collected inside her likes shells in her pocket during a walk on the beach.

She and Jen agreed to meet up soon for coffee before the children were ushered back to their rooms for naps. On her way back to the deck Livy stopped short at the family room. It was clearly well lived in, with toys cluttered about, a half-done puzzle covering the square coffee table in front of an overstuffed couch. It was a true "family room." The sight pricked at a longing inside of her. A hope for what her future could one day look like?

"She seems just great." Livy overheard Owen from the kitchen table where she stood to collect her purse.

"But...?" Jack's chuckle trailed off with a questioning tone.

"No *but*. She's great. I'm just remembering when we talked after the divorce about the fear that kept you from dating for so long—of being able to trust again." She shouldn't be eavesdropping. But her feet were planted firm.

"I appreciate it, man." Jack paused long enough that Livy pulled her purse over her shoulder and took a step toward the screen door. She stopped with a hand on the door when Jack continued. "I've got to tell you, though, we've talked about taking things slow, mostly physically—because, well, we've already had to." Livy's cheeks warmed with the memory of the other night. "But, as I've said before, there's something about this woman. We'll see where things go. I'm in no big rush, but I can't imagine feeling more secure with anyone else."

Livy's mood soared, unencumbered by the weight of the doubt she'd harbored that morning. It dissolved into faint wisps like the sun-devoured fog over the Blue Ridge hills. His words were more than encouraging. More than comforting. They were confirming. Hearing Jack profess his confidence in them—in her—confirmed God's assurance that what seemed good and true might in fact be good and true. Livy stepped out on to the porch with a smile and a prayer. *Lord, let me cling to your assurance.*

CHAPTER
Thirteen

Jack's truck wove slowly through town matching the pace of the day—his favorite kind—church, lunch with friends, and a lazy drive. Livy had scooted next to him for the short drive back to the inn from Jen and Owen's, head resting on his chest. She smelled of lavender and sugar. Jack steered with one hand on the wheel and one around her shoulder, as if they were high school sweethearts without a care in the world.

If this morning had been any indication, Jack would not have guessed this is how the day would have turned out. Livy's eyes had given her away as soon as she'd met him and Jen in front of the church. They were cloudy, overcast with the burden of her worries. He was so grateful she'd shared her concerns. Now, her eyes sparkled again like the sun reflecting off a lake.

"Anything on your mind?" Livy pulled him back to the moment, those dancing eyes looking up into his.

"Just thinking about how much fun today was." Her eyes trapped him as the truck idled at the town's stoplight. A horn sounded behind them. He waved an apologetic hand to the driver and proceeded under the green traffic light, continuing up the hill toward the inn.

"Your friends are great. I think Jen's going to be a good friend for me here," said Livy.

"I can't tell you how glad it makes me to hear you say that." Jack adjusted his hands on the wheel, and Livy straightened as they arrived at the inn. "I adore her, and you know I adore you. My mom once told me that a woman's best asset is her best friend. So, she can be your best friend while I *keep you company*." He still couldn't believe they both had prayed the same prayer asking God for someone to keep them company. And though he delivered the phrase with a wink, he meant it with his whole being.

"Why, I believe you're flirting with me, Mr. Bowdon." Livy raised one eyebrow and looked at him sideways.

"Oh, man." In a dramatic fashion, he placed a hand over his heart, head falling against the seat.

Her laughter filled the truck's cab with a sweet melody. "What?"

He rolled his head against the headrest to look at her. "That's the second time you've called me Mr. Bowdon when you're flirting with me. No idea why, but let's just say coming from you, it's pretty darn effective."

"I'll keep that in mind...Mr. Bowdon."

"Oh, you are trouble." Their lips met softly, her cheek velvety against his hand. Jack's cell phone interrupted. He glanced at the number and every muscle in his body stiffened. Claire. He silenced the call without answering. The playfulness disappeared as if someone stabbed a pin to a balloon with no warning. What did she want? All this time and now she calls?

Keys jingled. *Livy.* "Oh, I'm sorry. It always catches me off guard to see her number." There was still so much Livy didn't know about Claire.

"Claire? Do you talk often? Does she live close by still?" All questions that she deserved to have answered—and questions he wished he didn't have to. If only Claire was truly and completely out of his life. "Oh my gosh, that's none of my business, Jack. I'm sorry." Livy waved her hands back and forth in front of her face as if trying to erase the question, an adorable gesture. The tension gripping and twisting his insides let go as he laughed loudly. He took both her hands, inhaling a deep breath.

"You're so sweet, Livy. Of course it's your business." He brushed a kiss against her hand. The brief contact with her skin threatened to distract him, as it always did. *Focus, Jack.* He leaned against the driver's side door to put a little distance between them. "Last I heard, she was living on the outskirts of town, but nearby. I haven't heard from her in quite some time, so it did surprise me to see her calling. But I'm sure it's nothing. Let me walk you up?" He wanted to believe it was nothing.

He left the phone in the console as they got out of the truck. Jack walked Livy around to the kitchen entrance at the back of the inn, which had a little more privacy than the public front porch. The building's siding was cool in the shade of the large magnolia as Jack leaned against it. Livy's dress blew in the gentle breeze, matching the hue of the clear afternoon sky. She took his outstretched hand and stepped forward to stand in between his legs. Her waist was small in his arms.

"You make me a little crazy, you know?" Her hair enveloped him like a curtain from the outside world as he whispered into her ear. Livy stood to increase the distance between them. Her lips turned up as she reached to straighten his tie, which had come loose during the afternoon.

"Do I?" She teased him, and he liked it.

"Kiss me, please." Jack's hands held tight to Livy's hips. She obliged, their lips locking in a deep kiss. The sound of a singing bird, motion of the breeze, and warmth of the afternoon sun swirled around them into a faded reality. Jack only heard his own heart beating, echoed by what might have been hers in perfect rhythm.

The back door flew open with a racket as Aunt Bea shooed an orange tabby cat out onto the steps.

"Oh, dear me!" The older woman let out a jovial shout. Livy buried her head in Jack's shoulder as he looked over to his aunt with a sheepish grin.

"Sure is a nice day for smoochin'." She shaded her eyes toward the sun as if surveying the weather. "Been years since that tree has hidden little lovebirds. Oh,

Jack, that running toilet upstairs seems to have fixed itself, so no worries about coming by tomorrow evening." Just as quickly as she had burst of the inn, she was back inside.

Jack and Livy shared a deep belly laugh.

"You have no idea how giddy that woman is to see me with someone good and sweet like you. No need to be embarrassed," Jack reassured her. He lifted her chin upward with a finger and looked into her emerald eyes. "Plus, even if she turned a hose on us, I doubt I'd care."

Their kisses lingered as sweet as the scent of new blooms hanging from the magnolia. When the breeze stilled and sun grew hotter, they retreated into the cooler kitchen.

"I may take a day off from working at the house tomorrow, sleep in and drive over to Asheville to do some exploring and shopping." Livy handed him a glass of ice water she'd poured from the pitcher on the small butcher-block island that sat between the stove and sink. They took seats next to each other at the small table.

Watching Livy move so comfortably in the inn made it seem as if she'd been here for years. "That sounds fun. I think it's supposed to rain, though. Be careful going down the mountain. Sometimes the runoff makes slick spots around the curves." Jack gave in to his protective instincts. He also wished he could go with her. "I'll be covering the store for two days. Jasper's got a meeting with one of our suppliers in Johnson City. Otherwise, I'd see about coming with you."

"I'd love that. But it'll be nice to do some exploring on my own, too." Livy's eyes danced with a sense of adventure, a subtle smile creeping to her face. Given what she'd told him about her ex-boyfriend, he knew it was good for her to be independent.

"How about we meet up for dinner at the café day after next? I'll have the store closed up by 6:00."

Livy paused for a wide yawn. "That sounds great."

"I should let you go relax," Jack said, though he wanted nothing more than to stay.

She nodded and stood, taking both their glasses to the sink. "Thanks for another wonderful day, Jack." Jack followed close behind her, waiting as she turned around.

"Oh, Jack, you startled me." Her hand went up by instinct, meeting his chest.

"It was a wonderful day, wasn't it?" Something came over Jack during these quiet moments with Livy. She had awakened the thing inside him that had gone dormant for so long after his ruined marriage. How could it be that just days before she'd come to town, he'd not even given dating a second thought? Now, he couldn't be alone with her without letting his emotions—and his attraction for her—take over all reasoning.

"I'll call you tomorrow evening when I'm back from Asheville, okay?" Livy said.

"Sounds great." Jack leaned and gave her one quick peck. She walked him to the back door, giving a quick wave, before he made his way to the front of the inn.

The truck had warmed considerably while it sat in direct sunlight. Reaching to turn on the air conditioner, Jack read the screen of his phone laying in the console.

Four missed calls. All from Claire.

CHAPTER
Fourteen

Jack woke the next morning with the call from Claire still on his mind. From not so far off in the distance, thunder rumbled. The stormy weather matched his mood. The message she'd left yesterday simply asked him to call her back. He hadn't yet, fearing what she wanted. It was just like Claire to inch her way in just when things were going so well for him. He drove into town under ominous clouds. Hopefully, work at the store would keep him occupied and distracted.

Almost two hours later, no such luck. Even with heavy rain pouring steady streams off the awning onto the sidewalk in front of the store, Jack's mind thundered with worry.

"Excuse me, Mr. Bowdon." A familiar voice interrupted Jack's thoughts.

"Oh, hey there, Harrison." Jack liked Harrison Clark, the eldest of the five Clark boys, who was polite every time he came in to grab something for his dad, Grayson.

Harrison held his weathered baseball hat in one hand and ran the other through his floppy hair. "Dad's looking for a new one-eighth-inch bit. Broke his off first thing today trying to get through a stubborn piece of wood. Didn't see any on the shelf."

Jack let a sack of feed drop from his shoulder with a resounding thud. "Sure thing. Let me check in the back." He pulled off his leather gloves and shoved them in the back pocket of his jeans, and retreated to the stockroom.

The easy task gave him a moment to breathe—and think. Not for the first time that day, his thoughts returned to how much easier it was with Livy, even with healing left to do. Compared to Claire, high-maintenance and in want of constant attention, Livy was comfortable. Telling Livy his feelings came as easy and natural as skipping rocks on a pond. How strange that, in the short time since he had reunited with Livy, he cared for and appreciated her more than he had maybe the entire time he'd been with Claire.

"Here you go, Harrison, last one I had. That'll be $4.78." Jack took the payment, gave change, and handed the teenager his bag with a receipt. "I heard you're headed to Western in the fall. Congratulations."

"Yes, sir. Thanks, Mr. Bowdon. Have a good day." Harrison replaced his hat, tipped the rounded bill, and waved on his way out.

Not five minutes later, Jasper barged through the front door with a strong wind at his back.

"What you are doing here?" Jack asked, following his steps with the mop from the storeroom he'd kept close all day.

"They're reporting a small rock slide north of Poplar on 197, so I turned around. Didn't think I should risk it with them callin' for rain through tomorrow. I'll have to reschedule with Mr. Renfro." Jasper jumped right in helping Jack finish hauling bags of feed to the front.

Jasper hated plans changing. "Sorry, man. I know you wanted to get that meeting out of the way." But with another person at the store, Jack could take time to return Claire's call before the day dragged on. "Now that you're here, do you mind if I step to the back and make a call?"

"Sure, why not?" Jasper stepped away to help an elderly woman studying their selection of birdseed.

In his office, Jack sat at the desk and gazed out the small window overlooking the store's rear parking lot. Uphill past the trees and roofs of small homes, the inn sat in the distance, blurry from the rainwater running down the pane.

Memories sprang forward of the first time Claire had called. Only a few weeks following their divorce, Jack had reached his lowest point, drinking more than he should and only coming in to work a few days a week. When he saw her number on his phone late one sleepless night, he had picked up right away.

"Hey, sweetheart." Her speech was a slur of country twang and booze.

"Claire?"

"Who else would be calling you this late?" Annoyance replaced her syrupy-sweet voice for a sharp, quick moment, then it softened again when she asked for a ride home. "I've got no one else to call, Jack."

Jack went to her, but the knots churning in his gut had warned him it was a bad idea. By the time he arrived at the bar, Claire was crying about how wrong she'd been.

"I love you, Jack. Everyone keeps telling me how crazy I am for letting you get away. Can't we put this behind us?" Jack knew better. But that night, he'd learned a cruel reality of infidelity. Even when a wife cheated on her husband, he didn't automatically stop loving her. Seeing Claire upset and drunk, needing to be saved, Jack offered help. He had taken his marriage vows seriously, even if she hadn't, and for a long time he had wanted to try to work through their differences. She hadn't been interested during the divorce proceedings, blaming him for sending her into the arms of another man by not being attentive enough to her needs.

With Claire stumbling to his truck under his support, showing regret for the first time, he lost his better judgment and let his guard down.

"Let's just get you out of here." He took her home to his house—what was supposed to be their house—and let her sleep in the guest room. He'd been foolish to think maybe there would be a fresh start between them. The next morning, however, things weren't as different as they seemed.

"I heard you'd finished the house," she'd mumbled as he handed her a cup of coffee, her eyes muddied by smudged mascara. "You must be doing pretty good for yourself. I'm almost bankrupt thanks to the divorce."

Jack hadn't said a word, sensing her mood had shifted since the night before.

"You know, if you're as nice as everyone says you are, you'd offer a little money to help out." She had looked him straight in the eye, as if convinced he owed her more than he'd already sacrificed for her. His chance at a happy marriage. His reputation in town. His heart.

Still grieving and feeling sorry for her, he had given her a few hundred dollars before taking her home. Ever since that day, Jack only heard from Claire when she was drunk and needed money. The silence these past several months had given Jack the chance to finally heal.

Then there was yesterday's call—out of the blue.

An impressive boom of thunder rattled the window, pulling Jack back to the present. He looked down at his fisted hands. There was nothing to gain by putting this off. He shook out his hands, picked up the phone and reluctantly dialed Claire's number. It took only one ring.

"Hi, Jack. Thanks for calling me back." She sounded calm. Maybe this was going to be easier than he thought.

"Hi, Claire. How are you?"

"I'm doing pretty good. I'd ask you the same thing, but I think I know the answer."

And there it was. Her voice might be calm and collected, but this was about him and Livy.

"Well, I am doing pretty good—" Jack started in before Claire interrupted.

"Imagine my surprise when Dorothy tells me she saw you in the coffee shop with some woman she'd never seen before." Her voice didn't sound as biting as the words themselves. Instead, she sounded artificially sweet, as if trying hard to hide her real feelings.

"Claire, listen…"

"Oh, I'm sure she's very nice. In fact, Dorothy said she was real cute, but a brunette? You surprise me, Jack. Then, Mary Sue said she saw you two together at the Blue Bird. Really getting around, huh?"

"Claire, listen." Jack's voice was firm. No more games. "You gave up the right to know my business or care who I am with a long time ago. Is there anything else you need today?"

A long moment of silence followed. Jack thought maybe she'd hung up, but she spoke again. Her voice was softer now, no longer artificial or sarcastic.

"I'm sorry. I guess hearing you might actually be with someone really threw me for a loop. How about we go to lunch sometime?"

"I don't think so." Jack sighed. At least she was calm.

"I understand. I'm sorry I bothered you." Jack strained to make out her last, soft words.

He offered his goodbye into a disconnected line. Something about the call left him unsettled. Maybe she regretted her actions that ended their marriage now that he seemed to be moving on. Despite their past, he hoped she could find peace—a calming peace like he had found with Livy.

Jack returned to the front of the store lighter because the call was over. The place bustled with the usual morning customers.

"Who'd you have to call? You were back there a while." Jasper whispered as Jack joined him to help bag items at the register.

Jack mouthed *Claire* to his brother, who returned wide eyes.

"Thanks, Mr. Moreland. Have a good day." Jasper handed the young man his bags and then looked around to make sure they were out of the earshot of any nosey townsfolk. "What in the world did you call her for?"

"She heard about Livy and wasn't happy. Called me four times yesterday and insisted we talk. But I think I made my point and doubt I'll hear from her again." Jack shrugged weary shoulders.

Jasper rolled his eyes and slapped Jack's back as he walked past him toward a cart full of coiled green hoses waiting to be shelved. Jack wanted to believe his own words. But things were never so easy with Claire.

Steady sheets of rain fell in a soothing pattern against the window of the dark room. Livy lay awake thinking of Jack. And Claire. She closed her eyes to a ticker tape of unanswered questions racing through her curious mind. Why did Claire call him yesterday? More curious, why did the call fluster Jack? Was Claire really just a long-gone part of Jack's past? How did Claire feel about their breakup?

But a peaceful calm enveloped Livy like the warm, soft blanket covering her old bed. Her confidence in Jack's feelings for her—and her only—matured every day.

Rolling to one side, Livy rubbed at sleepy eyes and pushed up on one elbow. The glowing numbers on the bedside clock were harsh against the darkness. *Eight fifty-four?* She reached for her wristwatch next to the clock. Sure enough, she'd slept until almost nine—the latest she could recall in recent memory. Pulling back at the window's curtain revealed fierce, dark storm clouds. Her arms stretched high toward the ceiling, toes pointed to the floor. A long, deep sigh shook off the remaining sleepiness.

She crossed the creaky wooden floor and headed for the bathroom. A mighty roar from the sky above made her jump. The thunder rolled on for several seconds, reverberating off the surrounding mountains.

Memories resurfaced of a storm that had come in the night the same summer she met Jack. Violent thunder and neon strikes of lightning had startled Livy awake at an early hour. She had bolted through the small house to Gram's bed, clinging to her side.

"There, there, my dear." Gram's whispers were faint, but they had washed Livy in comfort. Soon, Livy's heartbeat slowed and her eyes grew heavy again, finding sleep.

The morning light revealed a large tree had fallen across the length of Gram's front yard, crushing two precious flowerbeds and blocking the driveway. Even at ten years old, Livy had known how close the cottage had come to being struck.

"Oh, sweet mercy. Thank you, Jesus, for protecting us." Gram's voice was breathless, a trembling hand covering her chest.

"Audria! Hello? Can you hear me?" a man's voice bellowed beyond the fallen tree.

"We're here, Pete, and we're just fine." *Pete Wilson.*

Standing in the inn's bathroom, Livy paused with her toothbrush in her mouth, smiling at her reflection in the oval mirror above the pedestal sink. The elderly neighbor she'd met several days before—Mr. Wilson. He had come to check on them after that storm then called authorities to remove the tree. The realization filled her soul. Did he remember that storm? She'd have to ask him next time she saw him.

The floor vibrated again under Livy's bare feet as thunder roared across the mountains. The weather wasn't ideal for a casual shopping trip to Asheville, but she'd make the best of it. She took her time showering, sipped coffee from the single-cup brewer in the room, and left just after 10:00, decked out in a slick hooded coat, knee-high rain boots, and umbrella.

Getting to Asheville from Laurel Cove involved passing through several small towns before reaching a major highway. The two-lane drive down the mountain ridge was a gray blur as thick sheets of rain pelted the windshield, the wipers working full-speed as she gripped the steering wheel. The narrow lane offered no shoulder, so only a few feet from the line would be a deep ravine. So much for a pleasant scenic drive. Livy expelled a sigh as she steered the car onto the four-lane interstate.

The relentless rain kept her speed to a creeping 15 miles per hour. She couldn't see more than a few feet in front of her. Her white knuckles matched the tension in her gut. The car came to a large puddle and the back tires hydroplaned, veering into a sideways skid for a moment before regaining traction.

"Okay. Enough of this."

Next Exit Weaverville. Thank goodness. She steered off the interstate and followed the street into town where the rain was somewhat less aggressive. She could make out grand old homes with sprawling porches that appeared to house attorneys' offices, dental practices, and other businesses. As she waited at a stoplight, she spotted a quaint storefront lined with blue and white canvas awnings. *Blue Ridge Gallery.* In between passes of the wipers, she squinted to make out a smaller sign. *Fine Art Supplies Sold Here.*

Tingles surged through her fingertips. A sting pushed through her bottom lip as she bit down, the car now filled with a neon green glow. The car eased to a stop in one of the diagonal parking spots in front of the building. She couldn't remember the last time she'd set foot in an art store. It was time—no more avoiding. Tucking her purse inside her coat, Livy pulled the hood over her head and made a run for the door. A dainty ringing of a bell announced her entrance.

"Well, hey thay-er!" The deep, raspy drawl dripped over Livy like honey. The woman behind the counter, Livy guessed to be about fifty from the silver strands at her temples, peered over a magazine through red glasses. Her lipstick matched the bright rims.

Livy struggled to remove her coat without shaking water all over the carpeted floor. The hook she hung it on resembled a short tree branch made of bronze. "Hello."

"Didn't reckon I'd see anyone out in this mess, but am sure glad you're here. Anything you're looking for?"

My hibernating art career. "No, I actually just stumbled on you after pulling off the interstate until the rain let up a little. I'll just look around."

"Well, you just holler if you need somethin'." Her white teeth contrasted against dark caramel skin that suggested she frequented a tanning salon. "I'm Marge, by the way."

"Thanks very much." Livy couldn't recall the last time she'd been in an art store.

Stark white walls displayed more than two-dozen art pieces, some framed and some on bare canvases. Most were probably done by local artists, as the subject of the grouping was landscapes of nearby mountain sunsets, native flora and fauna, and recognizable landmarks. In a different area, colorful abstracts, pottery, and unique mixed-media pieces were also displayed, the last of which caught Livy's eye. Many of her own pieces used only paint, but her favorite projects involved layering paper elements over paint for a multidimensional effect.

She wandered past the gallery into a retail space that also included a few long, high tables, and several easels. *They must offer classes and demonstrations, too.*

Colorful paint splatters, uneven beneath her touch, covered the wooden tables, similar to the floor of her college art studio. Livy's pulse raced as she came to an impressive array of canvases and mountings. An entire wall held a rainbow of paints, charcoals, pencils, and clay. She hadn't sat in front of a blank canvas with her paints and papers in nearly eight months. The thought of that day, and why she'd stopped painting, quickened her pulse and knotted her stomach.

"*That* is what you've spent weeks working on?" Sam's words, laced with disapproval, had hit her with the force of a fist to her stomach. Her chin pointed upwards in protest, but acidic tears betrayed her.

"Oh come on, Liv. You're not crying again, are you? I'm just saying that surely you can do better than that. What is it supposed to be, anyways? At least I care enough to not let you embarrass yourself." He'd left her staring at her paint-covered hands before she had a chance to defend her work. She'd set the canvas aside and not looked at it again. In that moment, Sam had stolen her last bit of inspiration to create.

Standing in front of the store's selection of brushes, Sam's criticism faded. She was created to make art. Her body became lighter as her thoughts shifted to the new life she was beginning back in her home state. She'd stepped out in faith and moved to this place without any guarantees. Even if she had left New York to run away from loneliness and sadness, she'd also done it all on her own and despite her fears. *It's okay to be proud.*

"You're thinking some happy thoughts."

Livy jumped at Marge's gruff voice. The woman must have been a whole head shorter than Livy.

"Gracious, you scared me!" Livy's cheeks flushed with embarrassment over being so lost in thought. "Yes, ma'am, I am."

"Didn't mean to startle you. Just checking in. But I love a good story. What's got you so giddy?"

Livy chuckled at the twinkle in the woman's eyes. "I recently moved to Laurel Cove from New York City after a breakup." It wasn't in Livy's nature to open up to perfect strangers, but before she knew it, she took a seat on a stool opposite Marge at one of the art tables. "My boyfriend there wasn't supportive of my art at all—of anything I did, really."

Marge watched with the tip of her glasses between her teeth.

"Right after I arrived in town, I met up with an old childhood friend. He's been so nice since—"

"I knew it! There was love brewing in your pretty green eyes." Marge thumped her small hand on the table between them, punctuating her good guess.

"Ha! Yes, I believe there is. But it's been about two weeks. That's really fast, right?" Livy searched the woman's eyes for confirmation.

"Well, dear, my mama always told me that God's masterful plan is without flaw. There's a reason you're back here, a reason you've met your man again. No coincidences, only affirmations—little nudges from a heavenly Father who wants you to know you are loved and worthy of the grace he showers upon all of His people." Marge's hands rested over Livy's, cool as creek water in the heat of the summer. Refreshing and life-giving.

God knew Livy needed to revisit this life she'd once known, from which she'd found so much inspiration. Meeting Jack during her first hour in town. Discovering that she had the original key to Gram's house. Remembering old, sweet Mr. Wilson from her childhood. Now, finding this art store off the path from her planned route and Marge's kind words of encouragement. It all inspired her.

She needed to create.

"Marge, I can't thank you enough for your kindness." Livy smiled at the woman sitting across from her. "You've helped me more than you can ever know. Can you help me pick out some things?"

"Oh! I'd love to!" Marge squealed, throwing her hands in the air. The new friends strolled the aisles and picked out supplies.

"Don't be a stranger, love." Marge waved from the storefront, veiled in the afternoon sun, as Livy placed her bags in the back of her car.

"I'll be back really soon, Marge. Thanks again." Livy drove away from the gallery with a few canvases, brushes, and paints. Asheville could wait for another day. She'd grab her easel from her parents' house in a few weeks. Until then, she could surely find a makeshift one as she'd done plenty of times before.

Without the delay of rain, the drive back to Laurel Cove was smooth and quick. Back in her room at the inn, Livy scooted a square table against the window, narrow enough that she could prop the canvas up without having to reach too far with her paintbrushes. The spot provided abundant natural light from the now-sunny skies. She had cracked the window just an inch, welcoming a cool breeze and ambient sounds of life on the square. A coffee mug was filled with water for rinsing her brushes and dollops of paint waiting for her on the small palette she'd purchased.

She sat up tall in front of the blank canvas, stretching her neck from side to side.

Inhale. Exhale. Inhale.

Long exhale. She guided the brush to the waiting canvas.

Paintbrush still in hand, Livy placed the final stroke on the first painting she'd completed in almost a year. With each stroke emerged a prayer of gratitude. The blessings God had bestowed upon her life, a life she thought to be broken, were becoming clear.

"Not too shabby." A smile stretched her cheeks. It came from deep inside—as if coming up from her toes. The brush slid into the dirtied mug of water. She wiped her hands, loving the familiar pull of the dried paint on her skin. Her muscles cried as she plopped onto the edge of the bed, stiff from the position she'd kept all afternoon and evening. Glancing at the digital clock, the late hour urged her back to her feet.

Though sleep tempted her, she couldn't wait to tell Jack all about this unexpected day.

CHAPTER
Fifteen

H ello?" Livy answered her phone on the fourth ring, a towel barely secured around her. She was dripping wet, after bounding from the shower.

"Good morning, Livy. It's Jen. Hope I'm not calling at a bad time."

Her shoulders slumped, expecting to hear Jack's voice on the other end. Still, it was nice to hear Jen's sweet drawl.

"Oh no, not at all. It's so nice to hear from you." Livy adjusted her towel to fit tighter and stepped into her slippers.

"Well, I hope you don't mind, but I called Jack to get your number. Since it's supposed to rain most of the day again, Lane and I were going to head over to Meredith's place to watch girly movies and munch on snacks. Owen has the kids, so I'm escaping." Jen delivered the last sentence softly with a chuckle, as if someone would hear her, before continuing. "We'd love it if you'd join us."

Livy couldn't remember when she'd last hung out with other women. The friendship these women offered Livy, simply because she was Jack's friend, was such a blessing. Jack liked her, and that was good enough for them. "I'd love that, actually. With the weather still so wet, I don't see the point in working at the house today, anyway. Thanks so much for including me."

"Oh, don't mention it. I'll pick you up at the inn in about an hour. We can go by the store and pick up some goodies on the way. Lane is insisting we bring chocolate, and lots of it."

Livy caught Jen's contagious full-bodied laugh and giggled. "Sure. Sounds great. I'll be down in the lobby and will watch for you."

"Great. I'm in a white SUV. See you then. Bye, now, Livy."

Livy caught herself grinning in the dresser mirror as she pulled on comfortable jeans and a T-shirt. It was still new to have things to look forward to—things and people. Laurel Cove was proving full of such folks. *Folks.* The term was one of the southern colloquialisms she'd abandoned up in New York so she didn't stick out like a sore thumb. Yet slowly her roots were once again grounding her to this place, the people, the culture. A few minutes later, Livy bounded down the stairs to the lobby to meet Jen. What a fun day it was going to be. And with her resolution to put Sam behind her once and for all, nothing could ruin all she had to look forward to now.

Livy climbed in Jen's car just as fat drops of rain began falling from a dark gray sky.. As they made their way to the grocery store, Livy tapped her fingers on her knees to the contemporary rendition of "Come Thou Fount of Every Blessing" that was a mixture of a Top 40 hit with the acoustic-folk music she'd heard at summer festivals as a kid. Jen hummed along.

"We know Lane wants chocolate. What's your favorite snack?" Jen steered into a parking spot near the store entrance.

"I'm not picky, but I never turn down popcorn."

"A girl after my own heart. Ready?" Jen had one hand on the car door and one on her umbrella. Livy nodded and they made a run for the store's automatic sliding doors.

They leisurely browsed the store's candy aisle, selecting a bag of chocolate squares and a package of gummy bears. They made their way down to the next aisle full of chips, pretzels, and other salty snacks. Jen stopped and put her hand on the end of the grocery cart that Livy pushed.

"See something you want?" Livy asked, stopping in front of the canned nuts.

"Um, well..." Jen turned to Livy with wide eyes. "Maybe we should head over to the soda and come back for popcorn in a bit."

Curiosity pulled Livy's eyes down to the end of aisle. A woman standing at the other end stared at them. Her blond hair fell past her shoulders in long, salon-fresh ringlets. Despite the weather, she wore a short sundress and high heels. A grocery hand basket hung from the crook of her elbow, carrying what looked like a bottle of wine and bag of chips. But the look on her face told Livy the most. The woman's eyebrows rose into high arches, her pink lips pulled into a tight purse.

"Let's go, sweetie." Jen swiveled the cart around to face the way they'd come. Livy followed Jen's lead, pushing the cart past the frozen section and to the drink aisle. Staccato clip-clops on the linoleum floor followed.

"Hi, Jen." The woman rounded the same corner and stopped just shy of their cart.

"Hello." Jen's voice carried an edge that made Livy take notice. It wasn't like Jen to be unfriendly. Who was this woman? What did she want? And why in the world did Jen want to avoid her?

"Who's your new friend?" The woman's intense gaze was unsettling.

Livy refrained from introducing herself. Jen could handle this awkward encounter.

A sigh escaped from Jen, and her shoulders dropped, as if she were waving a white flag in the woman's direction.

"This is Livy Johnson. Livy, this is Claire." Jen looked apologetic when her eyes met Livy's.

The Claire? Livy gripped the grocery cart bar to steady herself. Why couldn't Jack be here? She tasted acid at the back of her throat as her stomach twisted. Was it possible to break a sweat in a matter of seconds? *Act cool, Livy.*

"Well, now. What are the chances? I've sure heard a lot about you around town." Claire set her basket at her feet and folded her arms across her petite frame, layers of gold bracelets clinking together. "You're the one dating Jack. Isn't that right?" Claire's painted eyes looked Livy up and down.

"I wouldn't exactly say we're dating, but..." Her voice actually trembled.

Claire threw up a meticulously manicured hand. "Well, it sure seems that way from what I've heard. Dancing. Out for breakfast. You have no way of knowing this, seeing as you're from up north," Claire's tone snapped with sarcasm. "But I'm Jack's wife. As a matter of fact, we just spoke earlier today."

They did?

Jen put a hand up in protest. "Now, wait a minute, Claire. You are *not* his wife any longer."

"We may not be married at the moment, but you mark my words..." Claire took a wide step closer to Livy, pointing a long painted fingernail at her face. "We will be."

Silence filled the space between the three women for what felt like an eternity. Livy stared down at her hands, knuckles white around the cart's bar. First Sam, now Claire. One blow after another from exes who just wouldn't go away.

"Y'all have a nice day, now," Claire finally continued, her southern drawl shifted from biting to thick and sweet as molasses. She grabbed her basket and clicked down the aisle toward the front of the store.

Jen and Livy stood in her wake. "The nerve of that woman." Jen grabbed Livy by both shoulders. Could she see the tears threatening? "You listen to me. Do not pay one tiny bit of attention to her. Jack has eyes for you and you only. Trust me. She's a bitter woman still learning to live with her mistakes."

Livy inhaled deeply, trying to find comfort in her friend's words and will the tears to stay put. "Okay" was all she could manage. Livy numbly followed Jen through the store for the last of their snacks. Her gut told her Jack was indeed done with his ex-wife. But would they ever completely escape their pasts?

"I cannot believe the nerve of that woman." Lane lounged on an overstuffed sofa, hands resting on her round belly and her swollen feet extended on an ottoman. Next to her, Meredith sat staring with mouth gaping at Livy, with Jen sitting opposite them on the matching loveseat.

Livy's hands were still damp and her throat still dry from the encounter. Even though she had heard from Jack himself how terribly things had ended with Claire, her confidence was shaken. Did Claire really want him back? Had she called him the other day because she'd seen Livy and him together?

At this moment, the anonymity of New York's bustling environment would have offered a welcomed hiding place. Tiny Laurel Cove left her too exposed.

"You know," Meredith spoke up. "Dorothy asked me the other day if I knew who the woman with Jack was. I assumed she meant you, so I casually told her it was an old friend back in town. I sure hope I didn't stir a pot. Dorothy and Claire are friends, but I never dreamed she'd run and tell her."

Jen's cool hand rested on top of Livy's. "Are you okay?"

"Yes, I think so. It was just so unexpected. She talked at me as if I've done something wrong. Don't get me wrong, I like Jack—very much." Her cheeks warmed. "But, we've only just started connecting. There's nothing all that interesting happening, you know." Did they believe her? Deep down, Livy knew that wasn't the whole truth. Things with Jack were very interesting to her. Very interesting and very exciting.

"Well, leaving Claire out of it for a second, you must know that Jack does adore you," Meredith offered a throw pillow to Lane, who was rubbing her hip. "I haven't seen him look at a woman the way he looks at you since even before Claire."

Livy squirmed a bit. "Jack has been very sweet, and we get along great. That's all I know for now, I suppose."

She wanted desperately to believe that Jack could adore her. But things with Claire seemed unresolved. What if she let herself give in to her budding feelings for Jack, just to be left broken when he returned to Claire? She wanted to believe he wouldn't do that. But once a man was married to a woman, even past transgressions could be overlooked. So many times, she'd looked past Sam's unkindness, judgment, and cruel remarks. And they weren't even married. Who was to say Jack wouldn't do the same thing if Claire begged him to take her back? She put her fingertips to her tight temple.

"This is such heavy talk for a movie day!" Jen swatted at Livy's leg playfully. A nervous laugh caught in Livy's throat at her friend's attempt to rescue her from the conversation.

"Well, all I know is Claire had better watch herself." Lane's eyes narrowed. "No one messes with us."

"And what are you going to do, mama? Throw your pillow at her?" Meredith teased. The group erupted in laughter. Lane's head fell against the back of the couch in defeat.

But as they started the movie, the run-in with Claire dominated Livy's thoughts. She and Jack had a lot to discuss over dinner tomorrow. She looked around at the women in the room, who were focused on the movie. Not agonizing over bitter ex-wives. For now, she'd have to draw strength from them. Her friends.

CHAPTER
Sixteen

The late afternoon sun cast long shadows on the floor of Bowdon's Supplies. The storm that lingered over Laurel Cove for two days had finally cleared. It was Jack's favorite time of day at the store, when the old fixtures gleamed in the golden late-day sun and all was quiet. Few customers came in as dinnertime approached.

The familiar squeaky turn and click of the old door handle pulled Jack's eyes to the front door. Claire walked through, closing the door gently behind her. Jasper let out a cough and walked to a nearby merchandise rack, leaving Jack at the front counter alone.

As usual, she dressed much fancier than the casual pace of Laurel Cove. Long, blond hair cascaded over her shoulders in soft curls, set as if she'd come straight from the hairdresser. Her jarring red lipstick, designer jeans, and high suede boots had the look of a former pageant queen aiming for the perfect mix of wholesome and sexy. Livy achieved that look without even trying.

"Hi, guys." Claire's tone was as casual as it had been at the beginning of yesterday's call.

The woman had some nerve. "What are you doing here, Claire?" Jack didn't hide his frustration. First, she had called out of the blue. Now, here she stood.

"Well, lunch yesterday didn't seem to work for you, so I thought I'd see if you were free for an early dinner. I hear Greg has your favorite chicken salad today. How 'bout it?" The artificial sweet voice returned, putting Jack on alert.

"We've got some more work to do here," Jasper chimed in. Jack could hug his brother.

Claire didn't even look his way. Her eyes were fixed on Jack. He looked to Jasper, then back at Claire, clenching his jaw. *Stay calm.*

"Why don't you head back to the office, and we can talk there." It wasn't worth risking a customer coming in during what could be an unpredictable conversation. She obliged, eyeing him with a flirty smile and squeezing his arm as she walked to the office.

Once she was out of sight, Jasper closed the gap between him and Jack. "What in the world was that all about?" His whisper was gruff and incredulous.

Jack closed his eyes, rubbing a hand across the back of his stiff neck. "I don't know, man. I think she's really struggling with me seeing Livy. But I didn't think she'd show up."

"The people in this town never cease to amaze me!" Jasper shook his head, resting a hand on Jack's shoulder. Rumors spread like wildfire. And the likes of Dorothy and Mary Sue were usually behind most of the juicier rumors.

"I'm going to have to handle this. Can you look after things for a few minutes?"

"Sure. But I'll check on you if she's not out of there in ten minutes." The brothers shared wary smiles. Hopefully she'd be good and gone in half that time.

Jack's steps were slow and deliberate toward his small office. The cold knob chilled his clammy hand. *Lord, help me keep my cool.* Inside, Claire looked through the same small window Jack had stared out just hours before. There was something childlike about her posture, arms wrapped around her narrow shoulders. Did she wipe a tear from her eye? He couldn't be sure from where he stood. Memories flashed through his mind—happy ones and others he wished to forget. Then, like storm clouds parting to reveal blue skies, Livy's beautiful face filled his mind. That cute messy braid. Her unforgettable emerald eyes. The sweet way her lips curled when she spoke of her grandmother.

Jack sucked in a deep breath and stepped toward Claire. This had to end.

"Do you have any idea how badly you hurt me?" Why was his throat tightening? She didn't deserve his emotions.

Claire closed the remaining distance between them and placed a hand on Jack's chest. "Oh, that was so long…"

"Enough. That is enough." Jack grabbed her wrist and extended his other arm to encourage her to step back. "I was prepared to build a life for you. *Our* life. And you casually threw it away. For what? Some cheap thrills? You broke my trust in the very worst way. You did that, Claire. All by yourself. You were selfish and careless with our marriage and my feelings, with no regard for consequences. There is no world in which you and I have any future together. Do you understand me?"

Fury shooting at him through her narrowed eyes quickly faded to a tempered blank stare. But the floorboards creaking under Jack's shifting weight was the only sound in the office. His chest tightened, and he clenched his fists. "Do you understand, Claire?" His shout sent chills racing up his arms.

"Yes." Barely a whisper and she was gone.

Jack let the weight of his body sink into the old chair in front of his desk. The encounter had lasted only a few minutes, but he might as well have run a marathon. He ached physically and mentally. Saying those things to Claire after all this time should have been therapeutic and brought him relief. And it would have, if he believed this would be the last he heard from her.

As if on cue, his cell phone vibrated in his pocket. Reaching for it, he found an unfamiliar local number on the screen. "Hello?"

The familiar sound of a car door slamming sounded in the background. "You sure know how to put me in my place, Jack Bowdon." For crying out loud. In the time it took Claire to cross through the store and make it to her car, her temper had swung back and she sounded ready to fight.

Jack rested his head on a hand propped up on the side of the chair. A headache began throbbing behind his eyes. "Claire, enough. Can't we just be done with this? Please."

"Let's just get one thing straight, Mr. Perfect. I wouldn't have gone looking for those cheap thrills if you hadn't always been so busy with your stupid building projects." Jack could picture her pointing her finger at him, manicured nail and all.

He shook his head—never mind that the biggest project was the cabin that was supposed to be their home. There was no arguing with her when she was like this. "Ok, Claire. Whatever."

Her rage-fueled huffs silenced. She exaggerated an inhale and exhale. "Jack, dear. I don't mean to get so angry. My therapist wants me to practice breathing through these situations, but it's hard. You know I don't really blame you." And just like that, the calm Claire was back. This was really something. Jack didn't know whether to be annoyed or concerned. She continued, "Speaking of my therapist, why don't you come with me sometime? Maybe it would be a good start to working all of this out and getting back to the good old days."

Jack couldn't stifle an incredulous laugh. "I'm sorry you're struggling, Claire. I really am. But more than a year has passed. I've moved on and it's about time you did, too. So, no, I won't go. You're on your own."

Jack listened for a reply but only heard a click disconnecting them. *Lord, please let that be it. I don't know how much more of that I can take.* He believed God was in the business of miracles, but not hearing from Claire again surely would be a big one.

"Well, here we are." Jen rolled the car to a stop at the top of the hill.

The sight of the inn pulled a sigh from Livy. She needed at least a few minutes to herself before meeting Jack for dinner at the cafe. Her body was a weight anchoring her, tired from wrestling the thoughts that kept creeping into her mind about Claire.

Jen must have sensed the tension in her. "I'll be praying for you, Liv. It's not an easy position you're in. Just trust God—and trust Jack."

"Thank you, Jen. And thank you for today. I'll give you a call soon." Livy's cheeks tingled in the cool spring air as she made her way into the inn. Prayers from her friend did bring comfort, but they wouldn't still the churning in her stomach, like riding violent waves on a stormy sea.

Her room invited her in with a happy amber glow from the westward sun beginning its descent behind the mountains. Livy was due to meet Jack in about fifteen minutes. The anxiety of relaying to him what happened with Claire tamed the excitement of seeing him again after two days apart. How would he react? Had he heard from her?

Livy swapped her T-shirt for a green knit sweater and worked her fingers through her braid so her hair fell down around her shoulders. With purse and key in hand, she stepped into the hall and pulled the door shut, but not before a final look at the painting leaning near the window.

Jack had ignited the spark in her to paint again, made her feel alive and special and adored. She couldn't wait another moment to see him. She made quick work of the short walk to the café.

A crowd larger than she'd ever seen at Brewed filled the space with the hum of friends and family chatting over their meals. Another couple occupied their usual table near the window. Livy panned the restaurant twice before spotting Jack at a table in the very back. His head was down looking at his phone. She sat down and removed her lightweight coat before Jack looked up.

He gave a halfhearted smile, eyes brooding over a furrowed brow. "Oh, hey there." Something was up. She stiffened as the doubts resurged.

"Hi." She played up the enthusiasm to hide her concern. "How was your day?"

"I'm not quite ready to talk about my day." His short reply left her deflated. He took in a deep breath and managed a genuine smile. "But I sure am happy to be here with you now. It was strange being apart two whole days. I didn't like it at all." He reached for her hands across the table and gave them a squeeze. "What sounds good to you tonight? I think their special is chicken salad sandwiches and corn chowder."

"That sounds great." She nodded and asked for an iced tea, too, before watching him cross the sea of people to place their order at the counter. She needed to be on guard and give him the chance to talk—if he would—before she told him about her run-in with Claire. Hopefully, he would confide in her, but she shouldn't push.

Livy's chair faced the back wall of the café, which was decorated with various mismatched and multicolored framed mirrors. Livy found Jack's reflection in a yellow-framed oval mirror. Meredith wrote their order on a ticket as Jack spoke. Jack said something more. Even through his reflection across the room, Livy noticed Jack's jaw tense. He had the same look after Claire had called the day before. Meredith looked over to Livy.

Livy's seat creaked as she shifted her weight. She couldn't take her eyes off the mirror—and Jack. What was going on? Meredith shook her head then reached for Jack's hand. Jack paid and maneuvered his way back to their table.

No. Livy wouldn't let her worry get the best of her this time. *Just trust Jack. Talk to him.*

"Are you sure you're okay, Jack?"

Jack's eyes closed as he leaned on his elbows and rubbed at his temples. "Thank you for caring. I've never been good at pretending everything is okay when it's not. The last thing I wanted to do tonight is drag you down by complaining about my day—but it has been monumentally awful." The breath left her. She squirmed at the urge to go to his side and wrap her arms around him. Seeing Jack anything less than happy awakened an instinct in her to mobilize—find a way to both remedy and defend. Make it all better.

"I'm sorry. What happened?" Livy offered him her hands again. It never occurred to her that his day could be as hard as hers. But her story could wait.

"Remember yesterday when I received a call from Claire? After I got home, I listened to the message. She simply asked that I call her back as soon as I could. Usually the calls are made from some bar when she's drunk. She's sorry for her mistakes and wants to see me. But it was different this time." Claire surely had been busy today. Livy's grip on Jack's hand tightened. "She showed up at the shop today. I didn't want her to make a scene, so we talked in the office. Thinking of you gave me courage to say some things I've really needed to say." He paused, and Livy's breath caught again.

Sam almost never said what he meant, littering their conversations with subtle suggestions, opinions, and jabs for Livy to decipher, but Jack wasn't playing any games.

"Livy, you make me feel stronger than I have in a long time. I finally feel like I deserve to move on past the heartache I've held on to so tightly." A sincere determination resonated in his voice.

Confidence rose up in Livy as his words sank in. They were healing one another's heartache.

Meredith called out their order number, and Jack retrieved their meals. Livy would need to fill him in on her ordeal, too. He returned with two plates and sat with arms crossed on the edge of the table. "Is this too much for you?"

"No, it's not too much, Jack. This is your life, so I'm interested." Sure, it was unnerving to know Claire didn't like her, but maybe it wasn't too abnormal after a divorce.

"It dawned on me standing there in the office with Claire, that I never told her face to face what her actions did to me. Throughout the divorce I was just so numb. So, I told her. It was hard and I let my anger get the best of me, but it had to be said. Now there's no way she doesn't know that it's over." His eyes darted back and forth across Livy's face. Then his shoulders slumped, as if deflating in front of her, and his gaze fell to the table.

"What did she say?" Livy gritted her teeth. What she'd give to have another shot at telling Claire what she thought now.

He offered her a timid smile that bore deep into her—but it didn't reveal hope, really. "Well, she walked out. But the relief only lasted a moment, because just a few moments later she called from her car. At first she was very defensive and gave me a few of the same excuses as before—that I was too busy and never available for her. She was angry and put the blame back on me. Then, like she has been doing off and on since she called last night, she changed her tune again on a dime. She admitted that she's been seeing a therapist. She actually asked me to come with her to talk this out together." His laugh reminded Livy of someone who was being swindled and knew it. He fixed his eyes on Livy for a long moment, as if searching her for something. The confident, charming Jack had faded.

Anger toward Claire swirled with worry for Jack in the pit of Livy's stomach. "Well, is that something you're interested in?" Jack didn't owe Claire anything.

Livy tried to remain as impartial as possible, but her care for him made her completely biased.

"No. I tried to be kind, but I was firm. Too much time has passed for this to be an *us* thing anymore. She's on her own." A warm and intense smile came over his face as his eyes locked on Livy's, but it didn't last longer than a second. He sipped his tea.

From the little bit she'd seen during her own encounter with Claire, Livy could only imagine Claire's reaction to not getting her way with Jack.

"I was expecting her to blow up. Protest. Maybe even give me more of that fake sweet talk." He shook his head. "But she just hung up without another word. I'll tell you, Livy, the whole thing has left me pretty unsettled."

"I know what you mean." Livy muttered the words as she took a bite of her sandwich.

Jack froze and stared at her.

"How would you know what I mean?" A deep wrinkle formed between his brows.

"Well, I thought Meredith might have said something to you about it, but Jen and I ran into Claire today at the grocery store." Livy searched Jack's face for a reaction.

He sat up straight, rubbing the side of his face hard with one hand, visibly irritated. "What did she say to you, Livy?"

"Well, she made it pretty clear that she'd heard about you and I seeing each other. Apparently people around town have told her. And she said that even though you weren't married now, you would be." Livy wrinkled her nose, bracing herself for Jack's response.

He let out a belly laugh that drew looks from the other patrons. Livy startled, almost knocking over her glass.

"That's really rich," he finally managed. "It's so far-fetched that it's actually funny. I guess that's why she showed up today at the store. After hearing about you, then actually seeing you, she must have been jealous. Desperate." He shook his head, still chuckling under his breath.

"Well, she can be pretty intimidating."

"Oh, believe me, I know. There was something about her today that left me with chills up my spine." Jack rubbed a thumb over the back of Livy's hand, and his blue eyes softened.

"Do you think she's upset enough to do something...crazy?" Livy leaned in across the table, the words barely above a whisper.

"I don't think so. She obviously has no problem dragging you into it, though, which is truly the last thing I wanted. And just when we were having such a good time, you and me." Jack returned a boyish grin. Livy couldn't help returning a flirty look.

"So, where do we go from here? What if Claire doesn't back off?"

"I honestly don't know. Tell me you don't scare easy?" They both laughed.

But Livy's stomach still flipped. Was she replacing one complicated relationship with another, just different sorts of complicated? She took in a deep breath. One thing was certain—Jack was a man worth standing her ground for.

"I can't promise I'll always know the right thing to say or do. I'm pretty bad with confrontations, but I'm in this with you, Jack. I'm not going anywhere."

Jack's eyes twinkled above a wide smile, looking for the first time that evening like the Jack she'd known the past several days. The old Jack. They finished their meals, both sitting taller and laughing more. Livy told Jack about her failed trip to Asheville in the rain, Marge and the gallery, and how she'd spent so much time painting.

"What did you paint?" Jack asked as they were finishing their coffee.

"Would you like me to show you?" Livy bit her bottom lip.

His eyes widened. "Oh yeah. I'd love it."

Hand in hand, Jack and Livy walked to the inn as the last bright orange sliver of sun sank beneath the horizon. The spring sky, clear and clean after the rain passed, swept with strokes of brilliant pinks and purples. The town's buildings and trees were silhouetted, intricate cutouts in a masterful creation.

"This is my favorite time of day." She tucked her arm under his, their steps falling into rhythm. Jack just sighed long and slow—sounding much more content than at the beginning of the evening.

Together they climbed the slight hill toward the town square. Though thankful that dinner ended on a high note, Livy's stomach fluttered waiting to show Jack the painting. Slowly she was peeling away layers of herself before him—each time bringing with it the hope of acceptance and fear of rejection.

Staccato creaks sounded through the quiet inn as Jack followed Livy to her door. He'd seen each guest room countless times, of course. But there was something exciting about being inside the space where Livy lived. Jack stood close behind Livy as she unlocked the door. The braid falling over her shoulder exposed the soft skin of her neck. Together they stepped into the cozy room lit only by a small table lamp. The same sweet scent of lavender he'd often admired on her cloaked the small quarters.

"Well, this is it. Home sweet home—for now, anyways." She hung her keys just inside the door.

She was a neat tenant, with things stored where they would be had this been her actual home. There was no sign of living out of a suitcase. She attempted to discreetly stuff a black bra into a dresser drawer. Jack politely turned to focus on an old framed photo of the inn, his pressed lips reflecting back at him in the glass. Why did it have to be black? He had a thing for black lingerie.

The room illuminated as Livy flipped a few switches. A makeshift painting station came into Jack's view at the window, her coveralls draped over a wooden chair. A canvas, maybe two feet by three feet, leaned against the windowsill. He knew that view. It was the mountain range from the tall windows of his house, the same view he and Livy had admired together on their first date.

"This is amazing." He joined her at the window, his words just above a whisper. He didn't know a lot about art, but he knew good art when he saw it. And this was *good*. He'd never seen such a unique style before. The strokes were long and smooth in some places, short and thick in others. There was no denying the subject, but the abstractness invited imagination. The freehand lines of the cabin melted into fluid forests, eventually becoming vivid sky. He could imagine Livy's hand moving with grace over the canvas. Maybe one day he'd see for himself.

"It's for you." Livy rubbed a hand across his back. "I won't soon forget that night, and I didn't want you to either."

"That's not possible, honey." Her thoughtfulness and talent amazed him. Her cheeks were cool in his hands, her mouth hot on his lips. Jack lowered himself into the chair in front of the desk, closing their difference in height. Livy nestled close to him with her arms wrapped around his shoulders.

"Your aunt doesn't make me swoon quite like you do when *she* calls me honey," Livy said between soft pecks.

"I sure hope not." His eyes closed. The softness of her lips and occasional tease of her tongue stole his breath. Kissing Livy intoxicated him. He guided her to sit on one of his knees and studied her features. The slight upturn of her nose. The dark freckle next to her left eyebrow. The intense black of her lashes against bright, jewel eyes. He smoothed wisps of hair with the back of his hand and took a deep, full breath.

"This short time we've spent together has been so unexpected and wonderful," he said, placing kisses on the palm of her hand. "I know this might sound insane, but I believe I'm falling for you, Olivia Johnson."

"It does sound insane." Her breathy sigh and loving eyes told him what he wanted to know. "I wouldn't believe you for a minute if I didn't feel the same way."

Their bodies came together in a long embrace, Jack's heart pounding hard against his chest. "You make me happier than I thought I could ever be again. It's unexplainable, but when I bumped into you in the hallway out there"—he gestured to her door—"I just knew you were going to be a very important part of my life. You were going to mean something to me. Turns out, you mean everything."

"Jack…"

She kissed him with such passion that the room began to spin, and he nearly forgot where he was.

Dizzy, Jack inhaled deeply to collect himself. "If I want to remain a gentleman, I should go."

She gave him a playful wink. "Are you going for sainthood or something?" She teased him with nibbles behind his ear between compliments.

He let out a moan signaling her efforts were having their desired effect. But his hands made their way from her waist to her arms and held her wrists. He eased her away from him and looked straight into her brilliant green eyes. "I'll tell you on the night I make you my wife."

Silence. Her eyes darted around every point of his face. Then, a whisper as thin as a cloud. "I like the sound of that very much." As if it came from within her very soul.

"I love you, Olivia Johnson."

"And I love you, Jack Bowdon."

His mouth once again drew to hers like a magnet. It took all the strength he could muster to pull away from her embrace and say goodnight—he'd kiss her all night if he could.

The occasional chirp of crickets was the only noise on Jack's quiet drive home that evening. If ever a day had turned around, this was it. What a monumental swing from the awkward encounter with Claire to telling Livy he loved her. And she loved him.

For now, that was all he needed to know.

"Yes, Mama, I know it sounds crazy." Livy's toe pushed against the wooden slats of the inn's front porch, keeping the rocking chair moving at a slow, easy pace. She'd mentioned Jack once or twice during quick calls to her mom, but it was time to fill her in on how serious things had gotten since last night when Jack had professed his love. She stopped short of mentioning his intentions of marriage. There would be time for that.

"You know how quickly your father and I fell in love—married three months after meeting—so I can't exactly tell you it's not possible."

"I used to believe in love at first sight," Livy said. "But all those years of disappointment and discouragement with Sam left me really jaded. In these few short weeks, Mama, Jack has changed all that. We just can't help it."

"You know, Olivia, I had a hard time with Sam. I didn't understand you two together. But you sound so relaxed now, so content. This Jack might be an answer to my prayers." The tenderness in her mother's voice warmed her.

A sturdy breeze blew through the porch. Livy bent to pick up the bloom of a rose that tumbled in front of her. Aunt Bea must've been cutting flowers earlier. Even with half its silky petals missing, the deep red flower was beautiful. "Mine, too, Mama."

"Well, I'll need to meet this swooner who's knocked my daughter off her feet."

Livy grinned and let her head rest against the back of the rocker, the rose cradled in the palm of her hand. "I'm thinking of coming to pick up some of the bigger things I've got stored at your place. Maybe I can bring Jack along." Jack would surely want to come. Hopefully he could take time off from the store for a few days.

"Well, then. Guess I'll have to tidy up the place and iron my good dress."

"Okay, Mom. I get it. You're excited." Livy laughed as a childlike giggle came through the receiver. Any time her mother sounded this happy, it gave Livy a sense of peace and calm. "I'll let you know when." Livy drew in a breath, the fragrant aroma of the rose filling her nose, and paused. "There's something else to tell you. Actually, I could use your guidance."

"Of course," she replied softly. Her mom must have sensed Livy's change in tone.

"Jack's ex-wife, Claire, is not happy about us dating." Livy stopped the rocker's motion. She lost grip of the rose, and it rolled to the ground.

"Really?" The emphasis her mother placed on the question surprised Livy a bit. "How do you know?"

Livy's mind flashed with memories of their encounters with Claire. How easier life would be without all that mess. But nothing worth having was usually easy, as Gram would say. "To make a long story short, she has approached Jack with mention of them getting back together. And she basically told me to stay away from him when I ran into her in the grocery store." Livy swallowed hard.

A long pause from her mother. "I'm not sure you'll like what I have to say about that."

"What is it, Mom? Say what's on your mind." Livy and her mother usually saw eye to eye on most things. However, their track record for agreeing on ways to handle relationship problems wasn't great.

"It's just that divorced couples are complicated. Though I trust your instinct about Jack, there's always more to the story when another person is involved. Broken hearts lead people to do unfortunate things. If things seem uncertain and strained with Jack and Claire, you have to let them work it out first. Make sure he's closed that chapter completely before opening yourself up to him."

Livy closed her eyes and rested her head against the hard back of the rocker.

"Mom, I have no doubts about Jack and his intentions. He's not interested in getting back with her." It was Claire she doubted.

As if reading her mind, Livy's mother replied. "Something tells me Jack won't be the problem, honey.

Haven't you heard the quote about a scorned woman?"

"I'm the first woman Jack has been with since they split. And it's a small town, Mom. Claire is bound to run into us. I bet she'll settle when she sees I'm not going anywhere." Livy tried to believe her own words. "Plus"—she forced an upbeat tone—"who doesn't like me?"

"Well, no one in their right mind." Another giggle. "Just promise me you'll be careful, honey. Guard your heart. It's been through so much."

"I know, and I can't tell you how much I appreciate you being protective, but even Claire deserves a chance to make the right decision." Livy hadn't really considered that until she said it out loud. But she did believe it. Livy herself had experienced a second chance. God led her to this place, to the memories of her happy past, to Jack. Everyone deserved that chance.

"I love you, my darling daughter." Her mother's words echoed what she'd said to Livy as a child.

"And I love you, darling mother."

Livy ended the call and set the chair in motion again, accidentally crushing the rose bloom under one of the rockers. *Oops.* She sat back, eyes skyward, and traced a line of birds flying north. The distant mountain peaks had a light green hue as spring buds turned to tender leaves. Jack and Livy's relationship was just as new and fragile as those leaves. They both had also awakened from a bleak winter of heartache.

God, if it's part of your will for Jack and me, let us continue to grow stronger and survive whatever is in store. Her prayer floated away on the breeze as the line of birds disappeared over the ridge.

CHAPTER
Seventeen

The smell of sweet and salty kettle corn filled the Laurel Cove athletic field. The Laurel Cove Bluegrass Festival was the perfect way to relax for an evening with Livy and put the drama of Claire behind him. He nodded to the twangy beats floating from across the field and scanned the crowd for Livy. A group of teenage girls in matching frilly skirts pushed passed him—he hoped they hadn't missed the last clogging dance.

"Jack." He turned toward the sound of his name and found Livy waving, stepping away from a tented craft booth. The sight of her struck him like the final chord of a bluegrass song, lingering a satisfying melody in the air. She was stunning in a white cotton dress, jean jacket, and brown cowboy boots. Instead of her signature braid, her hair fell in soft waves well past her shoulders, a daisy tucked behind one ear. But it was the way the twinkling strung-up festival lights danced in her green eyes that really struck him—well, speechless. How did he get so lucky?

She smelled sweet, like fresh apples, when he bent to greet her with a kiss. "Hi. You, uh, look spectacular."

"Well, thanks, honey." She poked at him, impersonating Aunt Bea by drawing out the syllables, and laughed. Her joy was infectious. "This is so fun. I just met so many nice folks. Have you seen Georgia's handmade soaps? And Patti—with an I and not a Y, she made sure to tell me—has these peanut butter balls that are so delicious. I think I talked her into giving me the recipe one day."

"That's pretty impressive. Patti doesn't give that out to just anyone. You must've made a good impression."

She laughed, grabbed his hand, and pulled him in the direction of the music on the far side of the field.

Out of the crowd of craft shoppers, Livy threaded her arm through Jack's, and their steps slowed to a gentle stroll. It was darker across the grassy field, away from the tents and food trucks.

"I really like it here, Jack."

It was the first time Jack noticed she was beginning to slip back into her native drawl. He smiled at the realization and knowing she was happy. "I'm glad."

"Laurel Cove has always been a little bit of home, with Gram being here and all. But I'm starting to really picture a life here. The people are so nice—well, save a few." She squeezed his arm tightly, a laugh as sweet as a songbird drifting into the night. It was good she could now joke a little about Claire. "And Gram's house looks so great after the work the last week or two. It's hard to believe how we found it, isn't it?"

"It really is. I'm proud of you. Evening, Gentry." Jack waved at the man passing them several yards away, wearing the same worn overalls he had for years. He leaned in close to Livy. "The poor guy lost his wife of over fifty years back at Christmas. I'll never forget what he told me the first time I saw him at the store after the funeral." Jack looked back over his shoulder and watched the old farmer disappear into crowd.

"What's that?"

They reached the edge of the red clay field. Folks sat on lawn chairs and blankets tapping their toes to the plucking of banjos and fiddles. "He said that the love they shared flooded into the deep cracks of his grief like grains of sand. That it didn't stitch the cracks closed, just filled in the wounds so that they were bearable."

Livy led them to two blue camp chairs she'd saved by tossing a quilt over. "Wow. That's actually beautiful." Livy squeezed Jack's hand as they took the seats.

He couldn't take his eyes off of her. When she turned to the band, the profile of her face under the starlit sky matched the soft features of the mountains he'd called home his whole life. "You know," he whispered so only she could hear. "That's how I feel about you." She turned tender eyes in his direction, ruining any chance he had at paying attention to the music. "I know it might sound cheesy, but when you got to town, I still had some cracks in my heart. You've filled them in just being the wonderful person you are."

"Thank you, Jack. I love you."

He was about to tell her the same when Patti came bounding up to them carrying a domed plate covered with aluminum foil. "Hey, there Livy. We're breakin' down the booth for the night and I thought you might like to take home these last few balls. And I might've written the recipe on the bottom of the paper plate. But if anyone asks I'll deny it and said you made up the whole thing. Y'all take care now."

Livy took the plate and Patti was gone as quick as she came. Jack shook his head, laughing. There was no shortage of quirky characters here. Peeling back the foil, Livy handed him a chocolate covered candy before taking one for herself. Her eyes closed as she savored the homemade treat. This had truly been the best evening he could ask for. Life with Livy was really taking shape, despite their rocky start.

"I love you, too, by the way." He settled back in the chair, licking his fingers and tapping his toes.

"Lane looked miserable when I saw her leaving the library last night." Livy squeezed some local honey into her hot tea as she spoke over her shoulder to Meredith. The steam warmed her knuckles, still chilled from the early walk to the café.

"No kidding." Meredith arranged fresh sticky buns in the pastry case. "I'll be surprised if she goes until her due date."

Livy turned toward the window and spotted Jack

coming out of the storefront several doors down. He wore dark jeans and a red T-shirt, sleeves tight on his muscular arms. She knew first hand just how strong and tender he could be with those arms. And when he smiled at a neighbor passing on the sidewalk, her breath caught—those dimples were going to be the death of her one of these days. "Hmm ..."

A chuckle sounded from behind her. "Earth to Livy."

Livy looked down at her mug. *Tea.* Deep breath. *Meredith.* Good gracious. She'd completely spaced out. But who could blame her? "Um, what was that, Mer? Yeah, Lane's huge."

A full-on belly laugh ensued between the women just as Jack came through the door. "What's all this ruckus about?" He gave Livy a lingering peck on the cheek that produced an audible whimper from her.

Meredith leaned on the counter in a fit of giggles. Livy was hopeless. Hopelessly in love with the most handsome man in Laurel Cove. And she didn't care to admit it. "Meredith caught me ogling you coming down the street, okay? It's not my fault you look so good even in a T-shirt." She waved a hand at him, hitting him in the chest, which she stared at long enough that when she tilted her head to meet his eyes she found arched eyebrows and a crooked grin. They all joined in a chorus of laughter.

"Hey Casanova, take your princess and sit on down, will you? I've got work to do and you've distracted me long enough." Meredith sighed and waved them toward their usual table by the window.

Jack pulled out Livy's chair for her then took the seat across from her. "You sure know how to make a guy feel good. So, no coffee today?"

How was she supposed to think about her drink moments after that whole scene? "Uh, tea sounded good."

"Don't look now, but you're being watched," Meredith nodded toward the window as she approached with coffee for Jack.

Jack and Livy both turned toward the street. Claire stood looking at them from the curb on the far side of Main Street. She carried an oversized bright red purse in one hand and wore an expensive-looking denim wrap dress.

"Oh, boy." He muttered the words, but didn't sound particularly alarmed. Funny, because Livy's palms instantly became clammy, her heart in her throat. He raised a hand to give Claire a wave, keeping the other on top of Livy's. Claire's eyes stayed fixed on Livy but were not unkind. Maybe she'd finally admitted defeat. Jack squeezed Livy's hand, and she looked for a brief moment back to him before returning to the window.

A Yancey County school bus made its way down Main Street. Once it passed, Claire wasn't there. Livy followed her blond hair down the street until she turned the corner and disappeared out of their sight. Fear or anger would have made more sense, but instead, there were subtle shadows of regret and pain in Claire's face. Livy knew those feelings well, but applying them to Jack would be crushing. The encounter had been so brief and uneventful that Jack and Livy didn't even talk much about it and went about their day as usual.

Yet, when Livy's head hit the pillow late that evening, the imprint of Claire watching them would not fade. She pulled the blanket up tight under her chin and stared at the ceiling until sleep came and relieved her.

CHAPTER
Eighteen

May in the mountains was a fickle thing. The long-sleeved coveralls Livy wore comfortably that morning lay in a heap next to empty buckets of paint. The cool morning had turned into a downright hot and muggy day at the cottage. Storm clouds off to the west caught her attention as she took a breather from rolling fresh paint along the siding.

Jack walked by and swatted at her, the tip of his towel stinging her thigh. "No slacking on the job."

"Hey, now. Isn't it bad enough I'm sweaty and aching all over?" Her back popped as she arched, stretching muscles she hadn't used in a while. In work mode, Jack just laughed and kept walking back to his section of the siding with a fresh can of paint.

Livy was surrounded by activity. Jasper, Hank, and Greg raked the last of fresh gravel into place down the driveway from a pile delivered that morning. Owen changed out the porch light fixtures with vintage copper lanterns Livy had found a few days ago at the antique store near the Blue Bird. She'd bought them on a whim to remedy her disappointment that the easel she was saving up for had recently been sold—but they actually were perfect for the cheery porch. And from an open kitchen window, Livy could hear the chatter between Jen and Meredith as they repainted the cabinets. The only friend missing was Lane, who used the excuse of grading papers while everyone knew she and her growing belly required air conditioning and proximity to a good napping spot.

A loud rumbling sounded in the distance, echoing between the valleys. "Storm's comin' in quick." Hank set down a rake in the pile of tools next to the porch and pulled off worn leather gloves.

"Yeah, bet it will be pouring in about an hour. Let's go ahead and call it a day," Jack called out to the others. Like ants, they all scurried to store tools in the shed, tap paint lids into place, and roll up tarps before the stormy weather arrived.

With her friends gathered around their vehicles starting on goodbyes, Livy choked with emotion. "Guys, I can't tell you how much your help means to me. I can't believe you've given up three Saturdays in a row just to be here." Jack's arm draped over her shoulder and squeezed.

"My bowling game's probably suffered." Greg's jeer was defended by a swift elbow jab from Meredith and arguments from everyone else. What a crew they all were. Sarcastic, funny, and so incredibly genuine and caring. Livy had never known such true friends.

An angry crack from the sky sent everyone scattering to their cars. One by one, they pulled off the grassy side yard and onto the driveway, christening the new gravel, and drove off toward the darkest of the looming clouds.

"Let's close up the house and go get some dinner. I've got some leftover chili at my house." Jack wrapped both arms around her and pulled her close. "You can ride out the storm at my place, if you want."

Those blue eyes of his danced with mischief. "Don't flirt—I can't take that look." Livy lifted to her tiptoes and waited for her lips to find his. "But I can't. I promised Aunt Bea I'd play cards with her tonight. Mr. Smith went to a family wedding over in Johnson City today so she's on until 8:30." Fat raindrops tore them apart and sent them running for shelter in Jack's truck. Thankfully, she wouldn't have to navigate the slippery winding roads to the cabin.

"How sweet you are with my aunt only makes me like you more." Jack reached for her hand over the center console. "Care for a third player? Maybe I can talk Aunt Bea into rustling us up some goodies from the kitchen, too. It can be like an old-fashioned storm party."

Livy shook her head at his persistence. "How can I say no to you?" No matter that she didn't want to. The storm dumped a deluge of rain on them, and Jack concentrated on delivering them safely to the inn. One day she'd know these roads like the back of her hand like Jack did. It was getting easier and easier to imagine life in Laurel Cove turning into a lifetime. She'd stopped holding her breath waiting for the other shoe to drop, but the drama really had subsided.

White hot lightning struck to Livy's right with a deafening crack. Jack steered the truck hard to the left, missing a fallen tree by inches. Her body jerked back to the right, smashing against the truck door as Jack veered to regain placement in the lane. He let out a long whistle. "That was close."

Maybe someone was trying to tell her not to count her chickens quite yet.

The next evening, the sweet scent of blooming jasmine blew across Jack's back porch and cascaded over Livy through a warm breeze. This porch had become her favorite spot to enjoy dinner. Perfect view over the mountains, now carpeted fully in lush greenery as spring neared completion. Jack stepped from the house and set down a basket of garlic bread. The company wasn't bad either.

His lips were soft on her cheek before he took a seat. "You might have beaten me at cards last night, but no one can rival my pasta skills."

"No argument here." As Livy cut her spaghetti, she continued with a planned announcement. "So, I think I'm about ready to move into the cottage."

"Finally! I was getting pretty tired of driving all the way to the inn to pick you up all the time." He winked playfully, as if he knew nothing of the socked foot rubbing her leg under the table. He'd been extra flirty all evening. But she had no complaints.

His reward was a sarcastic smirk. "That means I'll need to head home soon to Raleigh to grab the furniture and dishes and other things my mom is storing for me. Would you like to tag along?"

His fork of twirled pasta paused halfway from his plate to his mouth. "That sounds amazing. I'd love to meet your mom and see the farm. I've also got a supplier in Raleigh I've been meaning to go see, so maybe I can work that in while I'm there." He set his full fork back on the plate and drummed his fingers on the patio table. "Jasper owes me some favors, so I bet I can manage a Friday off if you'd like to make it a long weekend. How about next week?"

The sooner the better. "Perfect! I've got some other news, too." Livy took a slow sip of her wine.

"Well? Let's have it, Miss Chatty." Jack sat back in the chair, hands behind his head, and laughed. He was so distractingly handsome when such a playful mood mixed with those rugged good looks. His skin was tanned to a caramel hue from a lot of time in the warmer weather. And the five o'clock shadow he was sporting today added to the rugged arm muscles visible under his rolled sleeves. *Whew.* Sure was warm this evening.

One more sip allowed her to refocus. "I drove up to Weaverville today to get a few smocks. The coveralls bit the dust last week when I snagged the back pocket on part of the fence out back."

"Very *I Love Lucy* of you."

"Oh, hush." She tossed her napkin at him. "Anyway, out of the blue, Marge asked if I'd be interested in hanging up some of my pieces in the gallery!" Livy had painted a few times a week since finishing that piece for Jack. Marge had asked to see some and was always complimentary, but her offer to feature Livy's canvases in the gallery came as a welcomed surprise.

Jack's hands flew out from behind his head with excitement. "Honey, that's fantastic!" He leaned across the table, standing enough to reach her lips for a congratulatory kiss. He'd encouraged her painting so many times already, but it never lost its impact on her. She let her hand rest on his cheek and whispered, "Thank you," before he returned to his seat.

Jack motioned with his hands as if outlining a sign. "I can see it now, *One of a Kind Paintings by Local Renowned Artist Olivia Johnson.* And I've got a custom one. I feel so special." He nodded toward the painting hanging near the fireplace inside.

"Jack, you're crazy." Her body shook with laughter. "Let's not get carried away. But I am excited, and thank you for thinking it's a big deal. Marge and I also talked about me maybe coming to do a class once a week. Which is great, because I could use a little extra money."

Jack scooted his chair around the table until their knees touched. "Well, you're on a roll." He nuzzled her neck, his hot breath sending chills down her arm. "I bet you could teach *me* a thing or two."

"What's gotten in to you, Jack Bowdon?" Livy squirmed as his large hand rubbed the small of her back. "Greg and Mer are going to wonder where we are if we don't get moving." They were scheduled to meet their friends for drinks in a bit.

His soft lips explored the tender spot behind her ear. His whispers stole her breath. "Well, you show up here in this black silky shirt that you know I love, telling me you're taking me home to meet your mother, being the brilliant artist you are, and flashing those irresistible eyes at me. It's all your fault, really." It was her turn to take on the role of intimacy police. They were a good team, and she knew when their wedding night came, it would be worth the wait.

"Okay, Casanova, I'll take the blame. You go change that shirt that you've spilled spaghetti sauce on and I'll rinse these dishes." She pushed away Jack's hands and carried their plates over to the sink as he seemed to notice the spot of sauce for the first time.

Jack's steps followed and Livy started to rinse the dishes and place them in the dishwasher. "I guess you're right, Livy. We'd hate to be late." When she turned around, Jack had indeed taken his shirt off—and stood right in front of her. She gasped, tingling as she took in her first look at his bare chest, fit and muscular. Her hands had wandered up his shirt a time or two when they'd made out over the last few months, but this was a first. *Is this man trying to kill me?* Her restraint might not be enough for the both of them tonight if he kept this up.

He had that telltale twinkle in his eyes as he took another step closer. She leaned against the edge of the sink, nowhere else to go. "Am I making you uncomfortable?"

"Uh, no." *Play it cool.* But her heart raced, and knees went weak. Just when she thought Jack couldn't surprise her anymore, he did something like this and sent her reeling. "I don't know how you expect me to keep us on time when you're throwing yourself at me."

He inched closer still, eyes fixed on hers. "I texted Greg a minute ago and told him we'd have to reschedule, that something had come up."

Livy put a hand up to block him, but his bare skin only sent shivers running down her spine. "Any other excuses?" She had none. Her fingers explored tight muscles. Suddenly weightless in his arms, he lifted her to the counter. His chest met the smooth fabric of her shirt, and he kissed her, romantic and passionate and unexpected.

Lightheaded, Livy pulled away from his mouth and let him kiss her neck so she could catch her breath. Her stomach rolled, the ceiling spinning above her. Jack found her collarbone, wrapping both arms around her waist.

Something was wrong. "Jack…"

"Jack…" Livy's voice trembled.

Hearing her whisper his name only encouraged Jack as his mouth explored the curve of her neck. But the third time she delivered his name, something made him pause and look up at her face.

She'd gone pale. Beads of perspiration formed along her forehead. Before he could ask her what was wrong, she bent over the sink next to her and vomited.

Instinctively, Jack pulled her hair to one side so it stayed out of the way, and steadied her with an arm around her waist. When the first wave passed and she sat up, he wiped her face and helped her to his bathroom, the closest one to the kitchen.

"I'm so sorry." Livy moaned through obvious pain, doubled over. The nausea had come on so strong and quick. "Oh, my shirt." It hadn't survived the incident unscathed.

Bless her heart. Seeing her like this, unable to make it better, was torture. "Don't worry about it. It's okay." He stroked her damp hair a moment before going to his dresser for a clean T-shirt. He handed it to her and she began unbuttoning her shirt, seemingly unaware that she had an audience. He turned to give her a moment of privacy.

Moments later, another wave of nausea hit her, and she leaned over the toilet. Jack held her hair back again, his own stomach sinking with regret that there was nothing else he could do.

When it seemed to have subsided for a while, Jack offered her mouthwash and helped her into his bed. She was asleep almost immediately. What if she needed him again? He changed into some comfortable sweats, grabbed a quilt from the living room, and camped out in the reading chair in his room by the window—feet propped up on the small side table that held a few magazines and his Bible. Jack picked it up.

He often turned to a random page and read whatever passage his eyes fell upon, finding that the scripture would have something to say to him about his life at the time. Tonight, by the blue light of the full moon shining in through the window, he turned to the book of 1 Peter, chapter five. When he got to verse ten, he stopped and reread it several times.

And after you have suffered a little while, the God of all grace, who has called you to His eternal glory in Christ, will Himself restore, confirm, strengthen, and establish you.

Jack glanced at Livy again, peaceful and still now, then out the window to the glorious view of the mountains silver-tipped from the bright moon. He'd indeed suffered during and after his divorce. He'd doubted that he was strong enough to love another woman. But here he sat, just a few months after meeting Livy—restored as a man who needed and wanted to love a woman the way God intended. Although having a companion was the biggest answer to his prayer and the most noticeable change in his life, his painstaking hardships with Claire had strengthened him, like iron forged in the fire.

Now here he sat in the home he'd built for a wife but had so far lived in alone. With Livy in his bed for the first time, though under unexpected circumstances, it was clear their relationship was much deeper than he and Claire ever managed. Just in this one evening, he had enjoyed Livy's casual company, been attracted to her beyond belief, and had been called into duty to tend to her needs. He had no doubt that if the situation were reversed, Livy would do the same for him in a heartbeat.

One minute, Jack was in the middle of a prayer, and the next, the sound of running water woke him. The shower. Rubbing his neck, stiff from sleeping in the chair all night, Jack opened his eyes. The covers were pushed back on his bed. Livy had made it through the night without getting sick again.

To give her time to finish up, he went to the kitchen to boil water for tea. A few minutes later, Livy came out in her jeans and his T-shirt, hair wet and framing her face. She had no makeup on and, though still a little pale, she had never looked more beautiful.

He welcomed her into his arms. "How are you feeling?"

"A little weak, but pretty normal otherwise. I'm so sorry about all of this. I guess I ate something earlier in the day that was bad." She accepted the mug he offered her.

He'd trade places with her if he could. "Don't worry about me. I felt terrible for you. At least we'll have a funny story to tell one day," he said, trying to make her feel better.

"One day." She managed a sideways smile as she walked toward the windows. She seemed smaller next to him when he joined her. "And thanks for the shirt. I bet that wasn't what you pictured undressing me would be like." She gave him a little joking jab with her elbow. "Seriously, though, thank you for taking care of me, Jack. You're wonderful."

Good to see her sense of humor was back. He returned to the kitchen and made her a piece of dry toast to be safe. "I know we were planning to go kayaking today, but would you like to spend a lazy Saturday here instead?"

"I don't think I can refuse that. And, by the way, you are too adorable in those plaid pajama pants." Though her eyes revealed how worn-out she was, her gentle squeeze around his waist was playful. "I sure love you."

"I love you too, honey." He kissed her forehead. Having her close was just *right*. There was no other word for it.

They finished the morning on the porch, watching the mist over the mountain peaks evaporate as the sun rose in the sky. Later, they went for a stroll on a trail through the woods surrounding the house—one of Livy's favorite things for them to do together, she often said—and then spent the rest of the day on the couch watching old movies.

Where the night before had been one of the most passionate nights they'd *almost* had, the time since had been the most intimate. If this was what their future together might be like, it would be nothing short of wonderful.

CHAPTER

Nineteen

hen, out of the trees, came the big bear with a furious roar and scared away the fire breathing dragon!" Jack's wild hands cast long shadows across the wall, captivating even Livy.

"No, Jack! A brave knight saves the princess, not a bear!" Beth, Jen and Owen's youngest, fell onto the floor in a fit of giggles.

Jack and Livy were watching Beth and Noah that evening while Jen had parent meetings at the school and Owen was on his way back from a conference.

Livy sat on the couch with Noah tucked under her arm, his hand covering his mouth to hide laughter. "It's getting late, you two. Your mom will be home soon. Time for bed."

"Aw, man," Beth protested.

Noah wriggled down from the couch and reached for his sister's hand. "It's okay, Sissy. I'll help you get your teeth brushed."

Jack flopped down next to Livy. "Wow. I've never seen Noah be so agreeable about bedtime. I think he's showing off for you."

"Well, maybe so, but both those kids are pretty great." Livy let her head fall against Jack's shoulder.

"Jack!" Beth's cry rang from down the hall. "Noah pushed me!"

Jack rolled his eyes and shook his fists in the air dramatically. "Proven wrong again!" Livy laughed for the countless time that night. He slowly pushed himself up from the couch and started for the hallway. "I'm coming back there and expect to see pajamas on."

A contented sigh escaped Livy. Jack was so natural with the kids. Sure, he'd known them since they were born, but not every man had such instincts. He'd make a wonderful father someday. How easy to imagine a life with Jack and kids and a home—a life. Her heart skipped at the thought. Believing in such happiness wasn't without its risks, but a night like tonight sure encouraged it. She busied herself by moving to clean the kitchen from supper.

"Victory!" Jack whispered when he came into the kitchen a few minutes later.

Man, he *was* good. "Already asleep?"

He bounced around the kitchen on light feet in a victory dance, ending by swooping her up in his arms. "Almost. And it only took one book." Following his lead, they moved through the kitchen, past the dining table, and into the living room. Jack had turned out most of the lights during his story about bears and dragons. The dim light that remained from a table lamp cast a warm glow across his already handsome face. Their pace slowed, he pulled her in, and they swayed to music that didn't play.

"You're beautiful." Jack stared into her eyes. His chest was warm against her hand. "And you're going to make a great mother someday."

He thinks about it, too. Heat rose in her cheeks. All the words she wanted to say caught in her throat. If she told him that she thought about such a full future with him, would it scare him? Would it tempt the riskiness of hoping? She offered him a sheepish shrug of her shoulders. The thought of being a mother thrilled her, especially if he was the father.

Jack leaned down, a finger lifting her chin. He grazed his lips over hers.

They jumped at a jingling behind them. Jen stood in the doorway of the kitchen holding up her car keys, her purse still hanging on her shoulder.

"Caught you," she said through an amused grin.

Livy buried her head in Jack's chest as they all laughed.

"Mommy, Jack messed up the fairytale again," Beth stood at the end of the hallway rubbing tired eyes, a teddy bear hanging from the other hand.

"Oh, did he, sweetheart? Well, I'll have to talk to him about that. Let's get you back in bed."

Jack smiled, picked up some throw pillows and set them on the couch. "We'll see ourselves out, Jen. The kids were great."

"Thanks, I really appreciate the help. You two go straight home, now. No stopping to smooch." Jen's eyes sparkled.

Jack grabbed Livy's hand as they headed for the front door. "Can't promise that."

"That was fun," Livy said when she was settled in the truck next to Jack. She hadn't really given much thought to having kids before now. So many years with Sam, and the topic had never come up—though he'd never talked about marriage, either. Why had she stayed with him for so long? In just over a month with Jack, she'd imagined marriage and children.

"I'm glad you came. Two-against-two is better odds." Jack lifted a hand for a high-five, which she returned. His cell phone glowed on the dash from a call coming in. "Oh, it's Owen." He answered with the push of a button. "Hey, man. We just left your house. I've got you on speaker. Liv's here with me."

"Hi, Jack. Hi, Livy." Owen's monotone voice was serious. "Jack, listen, I just received a voice message from Claire."

Their eyes met across the middle of the dark truck. This couldn't be good.

"What did she say?" Jack stopped the truck in an empty parking lot.

Jack wasn't the only one interested in hearing this. Livy stared at the glowing screen.

"You sure you want to talk about this now? Wouldn't you rather finish your evening?" Owen's slow delivery was suggesting, not really asking. Whatever Owen had to say, it must be best for Jack's ears only.

"Nah, that's okay." Jack's shoulders met his ears in a shrug, as if trying to dismiss the oncoming conversation.

"Well, ok." Owen paused a long second. "She asked if I'd talk to you, Jack, and try to convince you to go to counseling with her."

Jack stared into the phone, both hands resting in his lap. What ran through his mind?

"How did she sound, Owen?" Livy bought Jack a moment.

"Well, she sounded normal, I guess. She wasn't crying or anything like that, if that's what you mean. I haven't called her back yet, Jack. I wanted to talk to you first."

"I told her I won't go, and that's all there is to it." All joking faded from Jack's demeanor. Even in the darkness of the truck, Livy could see his hands loosening and tightening around the steering wheel. Just as she reached to place a hand on his shoulder, his hands flew up.

"Who does she think she is?" Livy pulled back sharply at the anger in his voice. "Hasn't she done enough? She doesn't deserve a chance to explain things!"

"Now, Jack—" Owen tried interjecting reason, but failed.

"She cheated not once, not twice, but four times! She not only broke our vows, she destroyed them. It's a wonder I trust anyone, thanks to her. And now she wants me to go to counseling with her? Why? To hear some sob story about why she deserves a second chance?" Jack let out an incredulous laugh.

"Jack." Livy rested a trembling hand on his arm. Did he forget she was there? Surely when he calmed down he'd regret doing this in front of her. But Livy was no stranger to outbursts when such rotten pasts were involved.

"I'm the one who deserves to be happy." Jack's voice dropped to a near whisper. His face fell.

"Jack, I need you to listen to me." Owen's voice carried from the phone, even and calm.

A long silence lingered. Jack rubbed a hand over his face and leaned an elbow against the window ledge of the truck. *Look at me, Jack.* But his gaze settled on something—nothing—beyond the glass. Livy started to scoot closer to him, but deep husky words stopped her. "Yeah, Owen. I'm here."

"I know you've had this sitting on your heart for a long time. It's a really tough situation, but forgiving Claire is more important for you than it is for her. Why don't you and I meet tomorrow and talk. Maybe for coffee?"

Livy looked up at Jack and waited.

"Yeah, okay." Jack sat up a little straighter, picked up the phone, took it off speaker and put it to his ear. "Can you come out to the house around eight?" He listened and nodded his head. "Sounds good. And thanks, Owen."

The call ended and Livy watched his chest rise with a deep breath. The air in the truck hung stagnant like a thick fog. What if that phone call changed everything? What if Jack decided it was easier to be with no one right now? *Not possible.* Livy shook her head as Jack put the truck back into drive and started for the main road.

She couldn't let her weakening insecurities gain strength.

He stared straight ahead. "Olivia, I'm so sorry." His voice broke under his words.

The change in him was like storm clouds smudging out a noonday sun. Livy ached for him. "It's okay. I don't blame you for being upset."

"I'm not upset." He finally looked at her. "I'm angry. I didn't realize just how angry until now." They arrived at the inn. Livy looked up at the window where she'd first seen Jack, before she knew they'd fall for each other. Before she knew what torment he'd endured.

"I bet talking to Owen will help." Did Livy dare ask the other question on her mind? When Jack didn't speak, she couldn't help but ask. "Will you meet her for counseling?"

Jack held her gaze for several moments. His silence told her he considered it. If he went, what would this mean for them? Would Claire take it as a sign that he'd give her another chance? In his fallen face, Livy saw uncertainty. Doubt. Hurt. She knew those feelings too well. Yet, in that moment, seeing the burden of anger and resentment on Jack's shoulders made her realize that she'd forgiven Sam. She wasn't sure when or how, but she had. Jack needed to find his way there, too.

When Livy was about to leave him to his thoughts and say goodnight, Jack spoke.

"I don't know. But please promise me that you know this has nothing to do with you. You make me so happy. And you don't need to worry." His fingers wrapped around hers with a tight, determined squeeze.

She placed her hand on his cheek, and he leaned against it. "I won't. Call me tomorrow if you want."

"Goodnight," he said with a nod.

"Goodnight, Jack."

The walk to her room was arduous. Livy's entire body seemed to buckle under the stress of what had just happened, their sweet evening with the children ground to a halt with Jack's outburst.

"Will we ever be done with Claire?" The soft words filled Livy's room. The floor was cool under her feet as she removed her sandals. Her prayer continued in her heart as she readied for bed.

Father, please be with Jack. Show him the way to forgiveness. And if meeting with Claire is in your plan to help him get there, please help me to be patient. Calm my fears and guard my hopes. You tell us your grace is sufficient. Help Jack to see that. Thank you for your faithfulness, Lord, to see me through to the life you want for me. It's not easy, but it's worth it.

The words faded in her mind as sleep came.

CHAPTER
Twenty

Aunt Bea set a vase of bright pink gladiolas on the coffee table in the middle of the lobby. Their scent was as sweet as their color. "You feeling all right, honey?"

Livy stretched her neck, aching muscles screaming at her. "Fine, thanks." Her eyes returned to the newspaper in her hands, but she hadn't read a single word.

The older woman stopped in front of Livy, hand on hip. "You've been sitting here for an hour. It's almost ten o'clock. You waiting for Jack or something?"

"No, ma'am. Just taking it easy." But Livy was waiting for Jack. To call, or show up, or somehow tell her about his morning with Owen. She'd woken up that morning with last night's prayer fresh on her mind.

And a troubling new awareness of her place in between two people once connected by marriage. Despite Claire's terrible infidelities, what if Jack decided to forgive her and give her another chance? That didn't seem likely, but anything was possible when love—old love or new—was involved. She picked up her phone from the table and pushed the button to illuminate its screen. Only five minutes from the last time she'd checked.

"Well, whatever it is, you're making me more nervous than a hen in a fox den." Aunt Bea snickered, waving at a fly buzzing near her face. "It's sure pretty outside. Why don't you go for a walk? I do my best thinking on my feet."

If only her feelings didn't camp out on her sleeve. She wasn't fooling Aunt Bea or herself.

"Sorry, Aunt Bea. I'm just letting something worry me a bit. A walk does sound good." The newspaper folded into its natural shape as she set it on the table. Livy patted Aunt Bea's shoulder and headed for the front door. What would she do without these wonderful women in her life?

Sunlight drenched the porch. Livy shielded her eyes from the glare and stepped down to the small garden in the front yard. Her fingertips explored velvety petals adorning the tips of tall rosebushes. The squawk of a blue jay in a nearby tree pulled her eyes upwards. Her gaze landed on the mountain behind the row of shops on the western side of the square. Meredith had told her about an easy trailhead that began just behind the antique store. She slid her phone in her back pocket and made her way westward.

By the time Livy's phone came back into service range, the clock showed her short walk had turned into a two-hour hike. Except for a bug bite screaming on her wrist, it was just what she needed to clear her head. But still no call from Jack.

She crossed through the square's center toward the inn. She'd come to a conclusion on the trail. It did no good to fret over anyone's decisions but her own. Her actions, after all, were all she could control.

Lord, let me seek your guidance and will, no matter what the future holds. Be with Jack as he makes important decisions for his life, too. Help him to find forgiveness in his heart born from the grace you give us all. I know you love us, Lord. Amen.

She approached the inn's gate and noticed a car parked next to hers. One she hadn't seen before. Maybe she'd finally have a floor mate. The possibility of new faces ignited a lighter pep in Livy's tired legs as she closed the distance from the gate to the front door.

"Oh, there you are." Aunt Bea's cheery voice greeted her. "You won't believe what happened while you were out."

Livy poured herself a cup of complimentary ice water from the pitcher at the check-in desk. "What's that?"

"A new guest checked in. Totally unexpected. No reservation."

Livy smiled at her confirmed assumption. "How wonderful. I know you're happy with a fuller house."

"He's definitely not from around here. Wasn't much of a talker when I took him upstairs. But nice enough for a Yankee, I suppose." Aunt Bea's nose wrinkled before she stifled a giggle.

"You're too funny, Aunt Bea. I need a shower after that walk you suggested." Livy turned for the stairs. "You haven't by any chance seen Jack, have you?"

The woman shuffled papers behind the desk then reached to answer a call. "No, honey. Sure haven't."

Livy retreated to her room and enjoyed a hot shower. She dressed, slipped on some new flats she'd bought shopping with Jen recently, and took out her cell phone. In a new message, she typed to Jack: *Hi there. Hope you are feeling better about things. Text me later. I think I might go antiquing. Love you.* Send.

The early afternoon sun blanketed Livy's freshly washed skin as she made her way to her car. A wall of gray clouds was forming over the western ridge she'd hiked earlier. If rain was on its way, the gardening would have to wait.

"Livy …"

The familiar toneless voice stopped Livy in her tracks. *It can't be.* Her heart revved to a dizzying speed. After a deep breath, she willed her torso to turn around. There, on the top porch step, dressed in blue jeans and a NY Yankees T-shirt was Sam. Tall, lanky, and more strikingly handsome than she cared to admit.

No, no, no. The sight of him drew a sharp breath, though Livy was without air. She took a step backward as he left the porch and approached her. Like in a bad dream, she wanted to run, but her legs seemed as heavy as concrete. She'd put so much distance between them—and worked so hard to distance herself from being vulnerable his discouraging habits. She'd started to grow. How could he be here now?

"What … what are you … why …" Livy's shaky voice gave away her shock. Was he the new guest who'd just checked in? How did he know where she was staying? She bristled as he grasped her upper arms and his lips brushed a soft kiss against her cheek.

"I know. Crazy, right?" Sam placed his hands on his hips and studied his surroundings, a satisfied smile pulling his thin lips up. He actually looked pleased with himself.

The smug expression helped Livy find her nerve. He had nothing to be smug about. "Sam, what are you doing here? How did you find me?"

"Well, it's not like you were hiding. Just poked around a bit before I figured it out. Can we sit?" He motioned toward a bench at one end of the yard.

Arms crossed, she held her ground. "I'd rather not." She refused to fall into whatever trap he had set for her.

His eyes shifted to the ground. "Well, I suppose I do owe you an explanation." There it was again, the same softer tone she'd detected on the phone the night she'd arrived in Laurel Cove. The almost undetectable hint of regret.

"Yes, you do. You have no right to show up here unannounced, to the place I now call home, and disrupt everything I'm trying to build for myself." Tears threatened. She pinched the inside of her arm. *He doesn't deserve your tears.* Plus, she refused to show him any weakness in her armor.

"Okay. Maybe I should have called, but I thought surprising you would make more of an impact."

More impact than this? You've got to be kidding. Livy raised her eyebrows in protest.

"Listen, I said some things I didn't mean that night I called. Hearing you'd moved away really floored me. I guess I didn't think you'd really move on without giving me another chance." He swatted at a swarm of gnats that migrated through the yard, a momentary scowl replacing the tenderness that had formed in his eyes. "I've done a lot of soul searching and can see now how terribly I treated you back in New York. Can you blame a spoiled single child of rich parents?" He forced a laugh and shrugged his lanky shoulders.

It was hard to ignore the obvious change to his usual defensive and arrogant attitude. Livy chewed on her bottom lip. "I can't believe you came all this way to tell me that. Thank you, but you could have just called, Sam. And you shouldn't have just shown up here unannounced."

"Don't you miss me? Miss us? Even a little bit?" His eyes searched hers the way a misbehaved dog looked to his owner for reassurance that he was still loved.

She had no words for him. Livy turned away, searching the sky for—what? In all the years she'd known him, Sam had never once looked even remotely lost. Strange how the tables were now turned. He was here, on her turf, putting the fate of his happiness in her hands. Livy could not ignore the timing of his arrival, after she prayed for God's guidance—*no matter what the future holds*. She never would have guessed her future might still involve Sam in any capacity. And what about Jack? Where did things stand with him and Claire? Had she become too attached too soon to a relationship that carried no promises? One thing was for sure. Sam deserved kindness. He'd come all this way for her. But kindness did not have to come at the expense of her heart's safety.

"Listen, why don't we talk over some food. Any good places around here?" A hand landed on Livy's shoulder, pulling her eyes shut. Compassion and fear wrestled inside her, oddly matched opponents. As if unable to bear her silence, he continued. "I'm starved. I haven't eaten since I left the city this morning. That's two crowded plane rides and a drive from the airport in a rental car that's way too small for me. Come on, Liv. Surely a meal with me won't hurt anything."

"I don't know, Sam." Livy caught movement from the curtains of one of the lobby windows.

She'd bet anything Aunt Bea was keeping an eye on the developing situation, which both comforted her and made her anxious. The notion of mixing her two worlds—her past and her present—was dreadfully heavy. But Livy was hungry, Sam was here, and Jack was busy dealing with his own ghost of relationships past.

With a long inhale, she allowed her eyes to connect with Sam's again. "Okay. There's a diner a few miles out of town." More aware now than ever just how small Laurel Cove was, she knew Brewed held too much possibility of running into someone. She wasn't exactly hiding Sam, but being seen with him would take more explanation than she cared to give right now.

His smile was victorious. "That sounds fine. I can drive us."

"No. I think it's best we drive separately." He didn't need to think he'd won her over or anything.

His keys jingled as he pulled them from his pocket, his posture suddenly looser. "Livy, we're staying at the same hotel. It only makes sense."

"I'd prefer to keep my options open, if you don't mind." The last thing Livy wanted was to be stuck relying on Sam to transport her if the old Sam showed up.

"Whatever you say." His hands went up in surrender. "But thanks for not refusing to talk to me. I'm not stupid. I know this could have gone a lot different."

Before she could keep the distance between them, Sam stepped forward and hugged her. She stiffened from head to toe with fists clenched at her sides. She'd give anything to be leaning in to Jack's comfortable embrace. Still, there was an acquaintance with Sam's form that her body remembered. Funny how odd comforts could be found in the places that caused the most pain.

Distant thunder matched the dull pounding in Jack's head. Owen had called earlier that morning on his way to the home of a church member whose husband had died, asking if he could come over later in the afternoon instead. Since he hadn't slept at all the night before, Jack had agreed and went back to bed. More than the exhaustion, his emotions needed rest from the turmoil of indecision. What was he going to do about Claire?

He pressed his temples between his middle finger and thumb to ease the throbbing pressure and rolled over. Black digital numbers read 3:39 p.m. *Livy.* He'd let the whole day go by without calling her. What must she think, under the impression that he'd already talked to Owen?

Turning on his phone, there were no missed calls, but two new text messages appeared. One was from Owen, sent only fifteen minutes ago. *Be there around four.* There was just enough time for a shower. Throwing back the covers, Jack swung his legs to the side of the bed and rested his head in his hands a moment before standing. Wait—the second text. Hope surged through him as he navigated to the message. The short but sweet message from Livy gifted him with just what he needed. She seemed ok. He texted back a quick *Hi. I'm ok. Text you more soon. Love you.*

Yet, the thought that had kept running through his mind overnight still plagued him. *This isn't just about you, Jack. It's about Claire. The woman you once loved. And now, it's about Livy. The woman you do love.* Jack gritted his teeth. He didn't even want to engage with Claire anymore. That part of his life was over. Yet his faith had taught him that forgiveness was important despite his reasonable fear that talking to Claire would only bring more suffering.

He turned on the hottest water he could bear in an effort to clear his head. Minutes after he dressed and put some fresh food and water down for Rex, the doorbell chimed.

"Hey, man. Sorry you had to wait on me all day." Owen extended a hand, which Jack took and pulled in for a hug. How many times had his friend come over following the divorce? And here they were again, still talking about Claire.

Jack led them into the living room. "It's no problem. I slept most of the day. Want anything? I could put some coffee on."

"No, thanks. So, how are you?" Owen took a seat on the couch, crossing his legs and placing his hands behind his head. Straight to the point.

There wasn't any use wasting time on pleasantries with Owen. Jack stepped over Rex who lay between the coffee table and loveseat and sat across from his friend. His hair was still a bit damp as he ran his hands through it. "I'll be honest, man. I'm struggling."

"With what exactly?"

Could he articulate what had been plaguing him— the flood of emotions he'd worked hard to bury, but never *really* worked out. "Mostly, figuring out why all of this bothers me so much. It's been over a year. And now there's Livy, who is wonderful and great for me. Sure, it's annoying that Claire won't leave us alone, but it shouldn't have caused such an explosion in me." Jack looked to his friend. What he'd give for some magic nugget of wisdom that would help make sense of it all.

For a long moment, Owen just stared at him. Just as Jack was about to interject some more rambling, Owen cleared his throat. "Can I tell you something?"

Jack managed a half-smile. Owen's classic tell. "Of course. That's why you're here."

"I think I know why your reaction is so severe. You haven't really forgiven Claire for all the cheating."

A heavy silence fell between the men. Jack sat back, a hand to his chin. Hadn't he though? Hadn't he forgiven Claire after all this time?

Owen broke the silence first. "Often during outbursts of emotion, people say what they have really been feeling but trying to hide. From others as well as themselves. Do you remember the things you said last night on the phone?"

"I know I'd had it, that she'd gone too far trying to get to me through you." But was there more? Jack closed his eyes, thinking back to the scene in his truck.

"You said she doesn't deserve a chance to explain her actions. You called any explanation she has a 'sob story.' Do you remember that?"

Jack approached the fireplace, resting a hand on the brick mantle, and stared at the cold, gray ash of burnt logs. Shame pricked at him—or was it residual anger? Probably both. Why had he been so harsh? That wasn't like him, but this wasn't just any simple annoyance. "That was pretty rough, I know. But she had her chance at counseling before the divorce and refused. How will hearing her side of things now change what happened?"

Jack turned back to face Owen, his heart starting to pound with a dizzying effect.

Frustration took the lead, and Jack couldn't hold back. "I'll tell you. It won't erase any of the turmoil I went through. Being rejected, lied to, talked about around town. And for something I could do nothing about. What good would it do to rehash that nightmare? No. I've moved on. She's only reacting to seeing me with Livy. She's jealous. Well, that's just tough." A heat rose up Jack's neck and flushed his cheeks.

Owen's caring eyes offered compassion. "I get what you're saying. And I agree that getting counseling with her is probably not a good idea. For some reason, she's just now beginning to deal with her own guilt. Maybe seeing you with Livy did spark that. And that's her burden to carry. Her guilt to work through. You aren't responsible anymore for her happiness."

Jack nodded and sat down again. Of course, his friend was right. The words gave Jack permission to breathe deep for what might have been the first time all day.

"As your pastor and your friend, I'm more concerned with *your* heart," Owen continued. "Unresolved anger and resentment can eat away at your spirit without you even knowing it. Then it becomes a big problem."

A lump formed in Jack's throat, an unyielding mix of emotional and physical exhaustion. "Sure, but offering her forgiveness now feels like more of a gift to her. She's already taken enough, Owen. I don't know if I can give her any more." Jack looked down at the floor and took a few long, deep breaths. "I've waited so long for a woman like Livy to fill the place in my heart I figured Claire had left dead. Why does Claire have to do this now? It just doesn't seem fair."

Owen let out a loud belly laugh and stood, taking the seat next to Jack. "At the risk of sounding like your mama, what's right isn't always fair, Jack."

He couldn't argue with that, but he wasn't ready to return more than a half grin and a simple nod. Jack had no business talking about fairness. Owen was right about that. Fairness assumed something deserved. He didn't really deserve Livy. He wasn't perfect—never would be. But if what was *right* included continuing to accept Claire as a presence in his life, he didn't know how to handle that.

As another chuckle faded, Owen sighed. "Man, I tell you, if fairness led the way, God would never forgive any of us for anything. And grace is really what we're talking about here. Claire might not deserve your forgiveness, but for each of you to heal, you need to forgive her and she needs to forgive herself. Plus, until you resolve this in your heart, you won't be really ready to give Livy everything."

Jack's shoulders slumped like a child who knew his ill-schemed plans had been thwarted. "Yes, I know you're right." Forgiving Claire once and for all meant exposing parts of himself he'd rather leave in the dark.

Rex slowly wandered toward the men, as if sensing the tension. Owen reached in front of him and stroked Rex's shiny ebony head. Satisfied, the dog walked a step closer to Jack and pushed his wet nose into his hands. Rex's copper-colored eyes searched him with an unconditional adoration.

"Maybe I need more healing than I care to admit. I suppose a healed person wouldn't snap when provoked in such a nasty way like I did last night." It was exhausting carrying around this weight. If opening himself up to deep, true healing would allow him to set aside this burden, he'd at least try.

"Give yourself some time, Jack. Complete healing from something like this is tricky. Even though it's been over a year, starting your first relationship since Claire is bound to bring a lot of things to the surface. It's understandable." Owen stood and walked to the kitchen, helping himself to a glass of water. "What do you think your next move is?"

Jack stood to join him, sending Rex's tail into a frenzy. "I don't want to see Claire. And she's got to stop going through other folks to get to me. I'll text her in a bit and tell her that—and that she's just going to have to be patient with the rest of it." Jack approached the kitchen and leaned on the back of one of the stools lining the island. "But I've got some hard praying to do about finding true forgiveness before I can engage in any sort of conversation with her again."

"I think that's smart." Owen placed a hand on Jack's shoulder and gave it a squeeze. "I wish I could stay longer, buddy. But Jen's got lasagna in the oven, and they're waiting on me to eat. Hang in there and call whenever you need to. I'll check in with you tomorrow."

Dinner. Maybe he'd luck out and Livy would be free, and he'd get to talk to her about what had happened last night and apologize for pulling her into the middle of his rollercoaster.

Jack saw Owen out the door. With a wave as Owen pulled down the drive, Jack found his phone and dialed Livy. No answer. He checked for new messages but found none. Maybe she needed a little space. Or she could have run into the other women while out shopping. There wasn't really a scenario to alleviate the disappointment of not connecting with her.

The sound of Rex's leash dropping at his feet brought Jack back to the moment.

"Sure, boy, let's go for a walk. It's just you and me tonight."

"This is it?" Sam hands rested on his hips, and he stared at the unassuming building. *Cook's Diner* was hand-painted in black on a long sign affixed to the ledge of the sloped roof.

"This is it." Livy didn't even pause as she passed him on her way to the front door.

A rooster roaming the side yard ruffled his feathers before pecking the ground. The aroma of fried cooking mingled with the earthy sweetness of a fireplace burning nearby. If he followed her to the country, a true country experience was what he was going to get.

Inside, Livy followed the directions scrawled on a small dry erase board and sat herself on one side of a corner booth. Sam sat opposite her and reached for the small plastic menu she handed him.

"It's, uh, sure different from the city." Sam's eyes roamed the place as if he expected aliens to come out from behind the swinging doors to the kitchen.

Livy pressed her lips together and rolled her eyes. "For goodness' sake, Sam. We're not on Mars."

He reached and pulled down an old worn blind, craning to look outside. "Where are we exactly? Is this still Laurel Cove?"

Livy admired the scene framed by the window. The clouds were beginning to clear, revealing a cotton candy pink early evening sky. "No, we're north of Laurel Cove, not too far—maybe ten miles—from Finnegan's Hollow."

"Finnegan's Hollow? Geez, I thought names like that are just made up in movies." His scoff was a bit arrogant, but Livy couldn't really argue with him. Names of towns, roads, and even people were quite unique in these parts, even compared to Raleigh.

"Many towns are named after generations-old families or natural landmarks. Jack told me the Finnegan family founded the biggest limestone quarry up there that brought a lot of people to the area. It's still in operation, I think. Apparently, it's so high up that there are only a few roads that'll take you there." Livy looked up from her menu to find Sam staring at her, his lips pressed thin. "What?"

"Who's Jack?"

Livy's mouth went dry at the weight and suspicion in his words. How should she answer him? How would Sam react to hearing she'd met someone? Where was their waitress? She'd give anything for some water.

As if she'd spoken the need aloud, a silver-haired angel wearing an apron approached the table. Norma, according to her nametag. "What can I get you fine folks to drink this evenin'?" She held her pen at the ready over a ticket pad. When Livy didn't answer right away, the woman turned to Sam. "What about you, honey? Coffee? Some sweet tea?"

"Sweet tea, I guess. When in Rome, right?" He laughed, but Norma looked confused.

"What about you, sweetie?" she asked Livy.

"Water's fine. Thanks."

"Be right back with those. The special's country-fried steak, taters, and fried okra." She turned to leave, calling over her shoulder, "We still got some of Cook's banana puddin' for dessert."

Livy dared to look at Sam again. He grinned as he unwrapped his silverware and placed the napkin in his lap.

"The guys won't believe this place." The grin faded, but what replaced it wasn't exactly threatening. What was it? She didn't like not being able to read him. After a moment, he asked again, "So, who is he?"

"Funny story—"

Saved by Norma again. Livy reached for the water the waitress approached with and thanked her. They each ordered the special, Sam with corn instead of okra, and Norma was gone.

"Jack and I played together when we were kids at my grandma's house when I visited for the summers. Now he owns the supply store in town with his brother."

"Well, that's convenient." Sam took a sip of his tea, squinting a bit, probably not expecting the cloying sweetness. New York didn't serve the common southern beverage.

"What's that supposed to mean?" There it was. The first underhanded comment of the evening. Livy straightened in her seat, arms crossed.

"It doesn't mean anything. Aren't you repairing that house? Knowing a supply store owner will be beneficial." His tone was matter-of-fact.

Livy studied him. Should she believe him? She'd been burned too many times giving him the benefit of the doubt. It would be careless to let down her guard after one grand gesture of showing up here or a few genuine moments. And what investment did he have in the repairs going well?

"Sam, this is nuts." Livy rubbed her collarbone, fixated on an old leak stain on the ceiling, and drew in a deep breath. "What exactly do you want? Why are you here—really?"

He matched her long exhale, leaning his elbows on the table. "I don't exactly know."

After a long silence, Norma appeared with two large dinner plates full of steaming food and a plastic basket of rolls. "Let me know if you need extra gravy, ya' hear? Butter for yer bread is in that cup next to the salt and pepper. Y'all enjoy, now."

Surreal. The perfect word for being here in the mountains with Sam. Eating at this diner with him instead of Jack. She suddenly appreciated, better understood Jack's outburst the night before. Ultimately, Sam had intruded on her life. He'd come uninvited, with no warning.

The steely scratch of Sam's knife across his plate startled Livy's focus back to the table.

"Listen, Liv. When you said you wanted to split, I was angry. I didn't get it. I mean, I know we weren't some *Leave It to Beaver* couple, but I thought we were doing okay. No one likes to feel rejected. My pride got the best of me and I mouthed off like I always do. Told everyone it was fine." He paused to take a bite of the steak. His eyes grew wide. "Wow, this is actually really good."

His eyes were the color of rich chocolate cake. She'd told him that on one of their first dates. Eyes the color of cake and black hair that waved on top like the tail of a manicured show stallion, only much softer. They had laughed so hard that night. Back when things were good. But it hadn't stayed that way, and she couldn't remember the last time they'd laughed like that.

"One day I ran into that friend of yours at the coffee shop off Eighth Avenue where you worked, and she told me about your move. Later that night, I asked my brother if he could believe you left the way you did. He said he didn't blame you. Then I started asking our friends. Apparently nobody blames you. Seems I'm the only one who didn't realize what a jerk I'd been."

What was she supposed to do with this revelation of his? She didn't owe him anything. She shook her head. "But, Sam, what about the night you called me several weeks ago? You insulted me and hung up. If you've had some kind of epiphany, you sure have a funny way of showing it."

"You're right. I've got a lot of things to figure out. When I called that night, your voice sounded stronger, more sure of yourself. I didn't like thinking that you'd moved on. I guess a part of me figured you'd be back and hoped that we weren't really over. My impulse was to be angry, and ..."

"Because you weren't getting *your* way." Livy flung a hand up to stop him. "That's what you always do, Sam. Any time I say, think, or do something you disagree with—even in the slightest—you lash out in anger, spitefulness, hatefulness. No one's perfect, but I don't deserve it." She placed her arms protectively across her body.

"You're right."

She waited for the *but*—the excuse to explain away his behavior. Her stare softened as the silence between them grew. He offered no excuse. His face fell and his shoulders slumped as he searched her eyes. Sam looked like a different person sitting across from her at Cook's Diner. People changed every day after encountering a turning point, their rock bottom. Was Livy's leaving Sam's rock bottom? Had he really changed?

Norma came to clear their plates. "I'm assuming you two are together, but is one check all right?"

"We're not..." Livy shook her head at the waitress.

Sam cut in. "One check will be fine."

After Sam paid, they made their way to the gravel parking lot. The last of the rainclouds had moved through without leaving one drop. Livy reminded Sam which turn to take on the highway.

"You're not going back? I figured we could go for coffee or something. Plus, we're sleeping under the same roof." He took a step toward her and reached for her hand—she retreated a step back. Like some crazy two-step of the exes. Was he flirting?

Livy chuckled and shook her head, turning towards her car. His confidence was slightly nauseating. It would be awkward enough sleeping a few doors down from him. And she certainly didn't care to say goodnight to him right outside her room. "I've got some errands to run, Sam. You're on your own."

She turned to say goodnight but was cut off by the closing of his car door. He didn't even look back at her as he revved the engine and steered the car across the gravel lot. He always was sore when he didn't get his way. Nothing had changed really, just passing time blurring reality.

Livy took her time driving back into town, her only errand avoiding Sam the rest of the evening. And thinking of Jack, of course. She longed to tell him about her unexpected day and yearned for the comfort of his arms. How would Jack react to knowing Sam was here in Laurel Cove? How did he feel about Claire? Maybe he'd spoken with or seen her today.

She held down the center button of her phone and gave instructions, "Call Jack." The automated voice accepted the command and Livy listened, waiting for Jack's voice to greet her.

On the third ring he answered. "Hey, you."

She sighed into the receiver. "Hi. You won't believe the day I've had. How are you?"

"It's been an interesting day, really. Owen came over and we talked a while, but I got a lot of things off my chest. What happened today for you?" His low voice sounded exhausted, his drawl even more pronounced.

If it wasn't so late into the evening and she wasn't almost back at the inn, she might have turned the car around and headed up to the cabin. Now probably wasn't the time to drop the news of Sam on him. "Um, it's probably best to tell you in person. Are you up for breakfast tomorrow?"

"Yes, please." If a smile had a sound, Jack's voice delivered it. How wonderfully skilled Jack was in making Livy feel special in the subtlest ways.

They set a time and said goodnight. The brief call centered her. She'd sleep well tonight after all, with the promise of seeing Jack in the morning.

Jack set his phone on the wide, flat arm of his Adirondack chair. The short call from Livy was just what he'd needed. His gaze returned upwards, where stars blanketed the dark sky over the Blue Ridge. The gray clouds that hovered on top of Laurel Cove earlier had been swept away on a strong spring wind. From where Jack sat on his back porch, the sight was brilliant.

And the world was quiet.

He hadn't received a response from Claire since sending the brief text after Owen left. Set against the drama brewing with Claire, Livy was a bright beacon of hope, fun, and—yes—love. The dreamy image of her emerald green eyes and affectionate smile filled his mind. Closing his eyes, he could almost smell her sweet scent.

But as much as he tried, Claire once again invaded his mind, like a mean girl pushing her way to the front of a line. Even when Claire had resurfaced shortly after the divorce, Jack never considered getting back together with her. And at the moment, forgiving her seemed no more likely. *Lord, please intervene. I know my anger isn't pleasing to you. Help me find the forgiveness I need to give Claire so that I might fully live into your plan for my life. And, Lord, if it is part of that plan, please continue blessing my relationship with Livy. I love you, Lord. Amen.*

A familiar ding sounded from his phone. *Loved hearing your voice. Can't wait to see you.*

Jack's mood lifted, accompanying the smile that broke across his face. Their breakfast date couldn't come soon enough. He also couldn't imagine what it was she had to tell him. He'd detected a hint of nervousness in her voice, but compared to his predicament with Claire, nothing could be too big of a deal. Right?

CHAPTER
Twenty-One

Even from a distance, Jack's rugged good looks warmed Livy's cheeks when she spotted him waiting outside Brewed. It was hard to tell if the knots in her stomach were from the excitement of seeing him or anxiety about telling him that Sam was in Laurel Cove. Instead of running to him, she returned his wave and strolled as casually as she could.

"Well, hey there." Livy raised a hand to block a harsh glare. Before she could focus on his face, Jack's tall shadow moved in front of the sun. His large, smooth hands embraced her face as he pulled her close for a sweet, tender kiss. Rising to her tiptoes, Livy threw her arms around Jack's neck and gave in fully to him. Everything else faded—the sun warming her skin, the noise of town around them, and her worry over

Claire and Sam. Being in Jack's arms was where she belonged.

"Oh, darling." Jack's whisper raised the hairs on the back of her neck. "I'm so sorry."

Their embrace was tight and lingered long enough that Livy's stretched calves began to burn. "There's nothing to be sorry for." She followed Jack's lead toward the bench in front of the coffee shop.

"Yes, there is. I put you in a very tough situation the other night. I was selfish and didn't think of how you'd feel. I let my anger get the best of me." Jack's hold on Livy's hands was almost crushing. She freed them and touched his cheek.

"Jack, I'm no stranger to being hurt. Do you feel better after talking to Owen?" She searched his eyes for a clear answer but found none.

"Yes..." He closed his eyes, leaning into her hand. "And no."

The rumbling engine of a passing truck offered them both a moment to pause. Livy watched it disappear. The turmoil she heard in Jack's voice was all too familiar. But she was invested in him, in them as a couple. If they were going to have a chance at a healthy and thriving relationship, she had to let him work through this. Her head knew that, but the thumping in her chest told her that her heart wasn't so sure.

"I didn't realize until I talked to Owen last night how much I was still holding on to. Even before you came to town, I hadn't heard from Claire in quite some time. I'd moved on, or at least I thought I had." He leaned forward, elbows on his knees, and looked at the ground.

Livy's hand traced across his wide back. She knew all too well the complications that lay in the wake of being jilted. Especially with Sam in Laurel Cove. Her heart did an entirely different sort of flip than when she'd set her eyes on Jack just moments before. More of a sinking into the pit of her stomach. How would Jack react to hearing Sam was in town?

Jack straightened. "Owen helped me see how stuck I've been. I haven't dated in over a year. I haven't returned to fixing up houses. I haven't fully enjoyed the things in life I used to." He took Livy's hand and searched her face. "Until you."

There was no mistaking the adoration in his eyes.

"Since you came back into my life I've dated, obviously. I've put time and energy into fixing up Gram's house with you. And anyone in their right mind can see I'm enjoying a lot that life has to offer me now."

Livy savored his words. "Me, too, Jack." But she had to ask, "So, that's the 'yes' you meant to feeling better. What's the 'no' part?"

Jack released Livy's hand and rubbed the back of his neck. "Well, I have to find a way to truly forgive Claire for me—for us—to have a healthy, full future. And I'm not quite sure how to do that."

She didn't have any advice. Though she'd forgiven Sam, how could she articulate how she did it? "I wish I knew a way to help you figure that out. Forgiveness is so hard. Do you plan to go talk to Claire?"

Jack stood and paced the length of the sidewalk in front of the shop. "I've come too far to rehash everything, and I can't risk giving her any false hopes. I think it's best that she figures the rest of her issues out on her own. At this point, forgiveness has to take place in my heart, on my own."

"I know what you mean..."

Jack cut Livy off before she had the chance to mention Sam's unexpected arrival. "Well, that's enough of that. How about that coffee?" He reached for her hand. His charming smile took the words right out of her mouth. They made their way into Brewed and took seats at their usual table. What would it hurt to wait until after breakfast?

"Thanks, Mer," Jack said as Meredith placed a plate of blueberry scones on the table, but his eyes were busy taking in the sight of Livy sitting across from him. Her delicate hands wrapped around her steaming mug. A slightly curled strand of chestnut hair cascading down the soft curve of her neck. The round line of her full lips. They'd only been apart one full day, but he'd experienced a newfound appreciation for her. When her green eyes traveled from her coffee up to his face, his breath caught for an instant.

"Jack, there's something I need to..."

"You are so beautiful."

Her mouth turned up at the corners. He reached for her hand, stroking his thumb across its soft skin.

"Thank you. You're sweet."

"You know, I was thinking...it's supposed to get pretty warm this weekend. Maybe we could dust off my canoe and head for the lake."

From behind him, the bell rung above the door to the shop. Livy looked past his shoulder in the direction of the noise. Her eyes widened before darting back to Jack. She hunched her shoulders and turned toward the window as if trying to hide.

"Liv, what is it?"

She gave her head a short shake and whispered, "Jack, I'm sorry. I was trying to…"

"Well, *hey there*. Isn't that what *y'all* say down here?"

Jack turned toward the unfamiliar voice. A tall man with jet-black hair stood at their table with a hand extended to Jack, but his dark eyes were focused on Livy. She offered no introductions, her eyes begging Jack for something, though he wasn't sure what exactly. Jack's chair made a severe scraping sound against the linoleum floor as he stood. The man's cold hand returned a shake firmer than Jack expected.

"Morning. I'm Jack Bowden. And you are…?"

"Sam." Both men turned at the sound of Livy's timid voice. "This is Sam Battaglia."

Livy's Sam? Jack jerked his hand back. The man let out a casual chuckle, igniting something inside Jack. What in the world was he doing here all the way from New York? Had they been in touch? How long had he been here? Why hadn't she told him Sam was here in Laurel Cove? All of the questions swarmed in his head, a tornado of confusion. He looked to Livy and found in her eyes something akin to a child being caught doing something she shouldn't. A look all too familiar stole his breath. *She's not Claire.* But the room became a swirling sea of confusion.

"I—uh—I just realized it's about time to open the store up." He reached for his wallet and took a ten-dollar bill from its folds. It fluttered to the table, landing on top of the untouched scones.

"Jack ..." Livy reached for his hand, but he stepped away before her fingers could grasp his.

On his way to the door, he made brief eye contact with Meredith, standing a few tables away holding a full coffee pot. He couldn't take the pity he saw. He had to get out of here.

In a few long strides, Jack stood on the sidewalk, the cool air hitting his flushed face. He looked down the street both ways before turning toward the Bowdon's Supplies sign. *She's not Claire.* But his chest thundered and beads of sweat formed along his forehead. Was this a panic attack? He unlocked the door, stepped past Rex, and retreated to his office. He'd just sunk into his desk chair when he heard Livy's voice and the creak of the front door.

"Jack? No, Rex, not now."

Jack pushed off on one foot, rolling his chair to face the window behind his desk. His eyes shut and he swallowed past the lump in his throat. He wasn't ready to hear her explanation. He couldn't lose her. Quick footsteps approached, stopping at the office door.

"Jack, please. I'm sorry I didn't tell you first thing this morning. Will you please look at me?"

Jack slowly turned back around in the chair, elbows resting on the edge of his desk. Her green eyes glistened with threatening tears. *She's not Claire.*

She took another few steps into the office and took the seat opposite him. "Sam showed up completely unexpected yesterday. Except for that call from him my first day in Laurel Cove, I hadn't heard from him. Then, there he was at the inn and ..."

Jack sat up straighter. "Wait. He's at the *inn*? Well, that's convenient." Jack heard the cutting tone of his own words. That wasn't fair.

"Believe me, I was just as surprised as you are, but you and I both know there's no other hotel in town." Her head shook. She sat back in the chair and sighed, hands folded in her lap. She looked past him toward the window. The morning light streaming in illuminated gold flecks in her eyes. Was this their first fight? Even if it wasn't truly a fight, he hated it. She leaned over and reached for his hand across the desk. "Jack, can you hear me out and let me tell you the rest?"

There was more? He took a deep breath and braced himself. "Sure."

She sat back in the chair and looked down at her hands. "We went for dinner last night. I guess I felt like after our history, and him making the trip, it was the nice thing to do."

The dizziness returned. "You went out with him?" Jack dropped his head into his hands. If there was any question whether he harbored anxiety and trust issues post-Claire, this confirmed it.

"Please, just let me explain."

Jack's nerves exploded and he shot a look up into her pleading eyes. "Explain what, Livy? How I'll have to compete for your affections with a man who didn't know what he had when he had it? How everyone deserves a second chance, and you owe it to him to hear him out after he's come all this way?" Jack swallowed hard past the lump screaming in his throat. He slammed his eyes shut, turned back toward the window, and ran his fingers through his hair. Images of Claire in bed with another man flashed in his mind. Sam's arrogant laugh, the soundtrack to this nightmare.

"I'm not Claire, Jack."

She's not Claire. How did he convince himself he could trust Livy? "Maybe I just need some time to think. I'll call you later, okay?"

"Please, Jack ..."

The pounding in Jack's ears was almost deafening. It took several deep breaths for it to quiet. When he turned around, the room was empty.

A few moments later, the click of the front door sounded and Jack perked.

"Hey, man. You here?" Jasper's voice echoed.

Jack's heart sank. Had he just let the woman he loved walk right out the door—and possibly right into the arms of another man?

CHAPTER
Twenty-Two

Hot tears flowed down Livy's cheeks as she climbed the hill toward the inn. Things had gotten so turned around. Jack didn't even let her explain everything. Of course, she hated the way Jack and Sam met, but Jack hadn't given her any chance to tell him that she had no intentions of rekindling anything with Sam. If only he'd listened.

She paused and bent at the waist, leaning on her knees as a wave of sobs threatened.

"Liv. Wait up." Sam's voice sounded behind her.

The last thing she wanted was to deal with him. Not here. Not now. She resumed her climb toward the inn and the sanctuary of her room.

"Man, you're fast." Sam caught up with her as she crested the hill and followed the white picket fence along the inn's yard.

"Not now ..." Livy bit her bottom lip to stifle the cries that begged to release. As she reached for the latch on the gate, her hand grazed against something sharp. "Ouch! For goodness' sake, what else can happen?" The thorny stem of a rose bush growing around the gate's post must have been the culprit. Her eyes searched the sapphire sky as if God would send an answer on the mild mountain breeze.

Sam took her hand and inspected the scratch. His tender eyes searched her face as he bent to graze his lips across the back of her hand. Livy pulled back, shaking her head.

"Oh, come on." His dark-brown eyes twinkled with the seductive charm she knew too well. He closed the short distance between them with one step. "You know I can't stand to see you cry," he whispered.

Since when?

"You always were the emotional type." The subtle double-edge in his voice was all too reminiscent of the Sam she knew. "I'm not surprised Farmer Jack wasn't up for fighting for you."

As his words hit her, Sam pulled Livy to him and kissed her hard. She wriggled her hands between their bodies and pushed hard against his chest, releasing from his grip.

A deep breath gave life to her confidence that had begun to take root here in Laurel Cove. She wasn't some injured prey, easy to take down, already weakened by another fight. No, it wasn't that easy. Not anymore.

Livy turned, her steps wide and determined up the walkway to the porch. "Go home, Sam."

"Don't walk away from me, Olivia."

How dare he think he could boss her around any more. "Watch me."

His steps sounded behind her. "I'm not leaving this hillbilly town without you. You don't belong here." His curt, annoyed voice bellowed through the lobby as he followed her through the front door.

"She most certainly does, young man." Aunt Bea stepped from behind the desk, positioning herself between Livy and Sam. She held her arms wide as if ready to protect Livy from whatever might come next.

Sam scoffed and kept walking toward them. "You stay out of this, old lady."

"Well, I never! Didn't your mama teach you any manners?" Aunt Bea stepped toward Sam, shaking a finger in his face. "Too bad for you I'm the owner of this establishment, and we reserve the right to refuse service to anyone who can't mind their manners. I'm afraid I'm going to have to ask you to leave— immediately. I'm also born and raised here in these parts. I'd reckon the whole town wouldn't mind one bit if I spoke for them all and asked you to leave Laurel Cove altogether."

God love the old woman's spunk.

"You're crazy. Both of you." Sam pushed past Aunt Bea and Livy and bolted for the stairs, taking two at a time.

"Well, that shut him up. Good riddance." Aunt Bea brushed her hands together, as if getting rid of pesky crumbs. "Being nosy finally paid off. When I saw you two out front, something told me to pay attention. I didn't much like the way he moved in on you, and apparently neither did you from the way you marched your pretty little self up here."

Livy lunged into the old woman's embrace and whispered, "Thank you, Aunt Bea—so much."

"Oh, honey. We mountain folk look out for our own."

Livy's eyes swelled with tears of gratitude. Laurel Cove was more than a familiar place of her childhood summers. It was home. It was, indeed, where she belonged. And she wasn't going to let her past—or Jack's, for that matter—keep her from fighting for the man she truly loved.

Several minutes later, Livy was sitting with Aunt Bea on the antique loveseat in the lobby's center, when Sam descended the stairs with fervor. Still fuming, he awkwardly struggled to keep his suitcase and duffle bag from banging in to each other. Livy just shook her head. The difference between the New Yorker who arrived the day before and the New Yorker leaving today. Then again, she had changed a lot too since arriving in town. Things were becoming clearer. With Sam on his way out, things would be okay. God was revealing his path for her. It wasn't without hills to climb, and there was still debris to clear away. But she belonged here. She was sure of it.

Talking things over with Jack would be difficult. But as Gram used to say, "Seldom do the most worthwhile things in life come easy." They'd get there. They had to.

Jack sipped the coffee Jasper had brought him, compliments of Meredith.

"She would've come herself to check on you, but couldn't get away for a while. Livy's ex showed up, huh? She said it looked pretty tense. And apparently Livy left the guy high and dry to go after you. You okay?"

Maybe he had overreacted. A deep pang twisted in his gut, a gnawing concoction of remorse, confusion, and grief. "I will be. But I wasn't fair to Livy. I didn't even let her tell me everything." As soon as she'd left, Jack was just as alarmed by his jealousy as Livy had been. No matter what had happened with Claire, he had no right to jump to any conclusions without hearing Livy out. In fact, he knew nothing about why or how Livy's ex was here. He didn't give her the chance to say.

"You know, she's not Claire." Jasper stood in the doorway of Jack's office.

Jack couldn't stifle a laugh. "I've been trying to tell myself that all morning." With that, Jasper nodded and headed for the front of the store.

A few minutes later, the familiar click-clack of Rex's nails against the hardwood sounded from the stock room but stopped before continuing into Jack's office. Jack looked up from the spreadsheet he'd pulled out and twisted in his chair. Rex stood in the office doorway, tail wagging furiously. A slender hand patted the dog's head. Livy. Jack hadn't heard the back door open. She stepped forward, illuminated by the soft light streaming from his office window, and Jack straightened.

"Hi." Her eyes were puffy, the tip of her nose pink— likely from crying. But she offered a timid smile.

"Hi."

"I'd like to talk, if you're ready." She stopped in front of his desk. Just a couple of hours earlier they'd enjoyed a tender embrace and kiss. Now, the room was thick with tension.

"I'd like that. Have a seat." Jack stood and cleared a stack of inventory papers from a spare chair. She deserved to be listened to before he showered her with a deluge of apologies. He owed her that, so he'd take her lead.

Settled in the chair opposite him, Livy looked at him and cocked her head to one side. He leaned forward, elbows on the table, and rested his chin on his folded hands.

"Jack, I'm really sorry."

He didn't expect an apology. "What? No, you don't have to …"

Her hand went up. "Please hear me out. I should have tried harder to tell you about Sam showing up. I didn't mean to catch you so off guard. I do wish you'd given me the chance to explain earlier, but I can understand how it may have triggered the trauma of past experiences." She leaned up to the edge of the desk so that their faces were only about a foot apart. "But,

Jack, please hear me. Nothing happened between Sam and I. He showed up yesterday out of the blue. Yes, we went to dinner. It seemed innocent enough, especially since I hadn't heard from you all day. But I was naïve to think he was a changed man. He made that very clear this morning. As a matter of a fact, he's just left town—thanks to your spunky aunt—and I don't intend on seeing him ever again."

Jack closed his eyes as her hands rested over his. He didn't deserve such graciousness—such forgiveness—after his behavior. "Livy, I'm the one who owes you an apology." He stood and made his way around the desk, kneeling in front of her, taking her hands in his. Her vibrant green eyes darted across his face, from his eyes to his lips, to his hair as she reached up to brush her fingers through it. "I'm so sorry." He leaned into her hand, her palm warm against his cheek. "You've never given me any reason not to trust you. I had no idea how much I'm still struggling to overcome—the insecurity, the need to forgive. But I promise you now, I will never again talk to you the way I did earlier. You deserve better. I want to be better…for you."

"I forgive you." Her soft lips gently pressed against his, her words refreshing whispers to his soul.

Relationships were such funny things. Some broke your heart and some healed it. The past few days made it painfully clear that his relationship with Claire left parts of his heart still broken. But it was time to believe in the new relationship with Livy. Time to let the healing really begin.

CHAPTER
Twenty-Three

ou sure you're not just making him up?"

Livy snickered. "Oh, come on, Mama. I told you before. He and the guys are in Johnson City for some fishing since they had to go up to meet with a few vendors." Livy rose to her knees and wiped her brow with the cuff of her gardening glove. "Gosh, it's got to be near 80 degrees today."

"Well, I guess it's better than the storms they predicted earlier in the week. Though the farm could use the rain. Things are already looking pretty dry in the fields. But it sure is pretty here. Real green and lush." Livy's mom reached for another seedling.

Contentment rushed over Livy like a welcomed breeze. Her mom bent over the flowerbed and placed the young plant in the shallow hole. With her gray hair pulled back in a loose braid, her mother resembled Gram, even though the two weren't blood related. Memories of gardening together those summers long ago sharpened into focus. The run-down cottage took on more of its original charm right before Livy's eyes, and yet it was simultaneously new and hers. The old and new formed a future Livy had never imagined.

"There. That's the last of it." Livy's mother patted the dark soil and straightened.

A rainbow of pansies peppered the newly tilled bed in front of the kitchen window.

Livy pulled off her gloves and rested her sweaty hands on her lap. "I wonder what they'll have to say to me."

The rough fabric of her mother's still-gloved hand rubbed against Livy's. "Whatever you need to hear, dear." They exchanged soulful smiles and stood to admire their handiwork.

"I wish Gram was here. She was so gifted at gardening. I hope I can do her garden justice."

Livy stood, then helped her mom up so they were shoulder to shoulder. Her mother held on to her hand, giving it a tight squeeze.

"She is, sweetie. Her hands have been in this same earth, turning it over to prepare a way for new things. Just like you're doing." Heat lightning illuminated distant storm clouds high above the mountain ridge. "And I don't just mean the flowers."

She searched her mother's eyes. "How do you mean, Mama?"

"God gives us all the same nutrients—the same gifts of grace and love to nurture us—just like this soil.

Chances are, this dirt isn't much different from the soil your grandmother worked with. You have everything you need right here to build the life you want—the life God wants for you. It's up to you what you do with the opportunities you're given, and I think you're really on your way here. I'm proud of you."

Livy rested in her mother's embrace. They spoke on the phone a lot and her mother often gave good advice, but it never lost its soothing effect on Livy's tender heart. *Thank you, God, for this woman. Thank you for using her to remind me so often of your goodness and faithful provisions.*

Thunder echoed along the peaks and valleys in the distance.

"We should get going. The girls will be expecting us soon."

"I'm a cow." Exaggerated moans bellowed from the end of the couch. Lane's head rested against the back cushion, her feet propped on the ottoman. Her spoon clinked against the ice cream bowl sitting on top of her round belly.

"You are so much cuter than I was at eight and a half months pregnant." Jen positioned a standing fan so it pointed right at Lane's face.

Livy's leg warmed under her mother's touch from next to her on the loveseat. "This one was born in August. I really wasn't sure I was going to make it, and neither was Livy's father. Imagine going through the summer while pregnant and without air conditioning."

The room enlivened with gasps and uproars of laughter.

"That sounds excruciating. I guess I shouldn't complain, Mrs. Johnson. Hank is happy to run ours all day and night even though he had to fish out his long johns to sleep in."

"Oh, Lane, please call me Katherine. Same goes for the rest of you."

"Katherine, we're just so tickled that you're here. Livy has fit in perfectly with our little group." Jen turned off the kitchen light, dimming the living room to a golden coziness, and took the seat on the couch between Meredith and Lane.

"So, Katherine, has Livy told you about Jack's crazy ex-wife?"

"Lane!" Meredith flew forward, leaning past Jen to gawk at Lane.

Lane's candor was a bit surprising. But all heads turned toward Katherine's amused giggle. How did she deserve such an easygoing, kind mother? Fact was, she didn't.

"Yes, she's brought me up to speed about Jack and Claire."

"Well, we want you to know from someone other than Livy how wonderful Jack really is." Jen's voice was characteristically tender and genuine. "We've all grown up together. I am confident I can speak for us all when I say he's the most genuine, caring, and thoughtful man out there."

"Except for our own husbands, of course." Meredith snickered. "Just had to get that out there in case we're being recorded." Snickers sounded all around the room.

Ice cream pooled in Livy's bowl, her spoon swirling bits of chocolate around the bottom. She and her mother had spoken about Jack and Claire, but the conversations had, so far, been pretty brief. Would her mother share more about her opinion with her friends? What if Livy didn't like what she had to say? Her mother's approval of Jack and her relationship was so important.

The room fell quiet again.

"Listen, we all grow up wanting perfect, hoping for perfect, and unfortunately, expecting perfect. In life, and certainly in love, perfect simply does not exist." Her mother's hand, cold from holding her bowl, brushed a wisp of hair from Livy's face. "So what if Jack has a past? We all have pasts that scar us. And I, for one, don't want to be judged for my past mistakes, misjudgments, and failed relationships. But we can hope for better. Better than we had, better than we think we deserve. If we find that, it's as pretty close to perfect as we can get this side of heaven."

"Thank you, Mama." Livy's head found the gentle curve of her mother's shoulder.

"That's very well said. I might just have to quote you to Owen and make sure that ends up in a sermon." Jen winked at Livy.

The chirping of her cell phone righted Livy on the couch. She stood and dug in her back pocket for the buzzing device.

"Oh, I know that look. Tell Jack we said hey." Lane waved at her as Livy stepped out of sight and through the foyer.

From the Barnetts' front porch, the warm evening breeze delivered a sweet, pungent odor of distant rains. Livy eased the door closed behind her and stepped out far enough to watch the passing clouds.

"How's the trip going?" She and Jack had not talked all day.

"Well, that sweet voice sure does make everything better." His words dripped like honey into the phone.

She swooned, leaning against the porch railing. "Did you call just to flirt with me?" She wouldn't have minded if he did.

His laugh was hearty. "That and to see how the visit with your mom is going."

"It's been wonderful. We just finished dinner at Jen's and are enjoying some ice cream. I sure miss you, though." Livy closed her eyes and conjured up his face in her mind. Those blue eyes, strong jaw, and scruffy five-o-clock shadow he likely had going.

His sigh on the other end only made her miss him more. "Oh, I miss you, too, honey. The guys wanted me to ask you to say hello to all of the girls, and tell them we'll be back around 4:00 tomorrow afternoon. Just in time for a home cooked meal." Those last words hinted at a not-so-subtle request. "I'll miss your mom, won't I?"

"Yes, she'll be on the road again, but I actually wanted to talk to you about that." Her heart raced with anticipation. "Since I'm so close to finishing up at the house and should be ready to move in soon, I'm going to need to go get my things. And you've got your big truck. And ..."

He paused. "And you'd like to borrow the truck to go back to your mom's all alone?" His voice teetered on the edge of a laugh. Oh, how he teased her.

"You're so very clever. No, my mom has invited you to come with me." She looked down at her free hand shaking. "It would, of course, help to have your truck to haul my things back here, but it would also give the two of you the chance to meet." Why was she so nervous about whether he'd agree to the trip? She acted like a teenager asking a boy to the prom.

"That sounds amazing." Not a second went by before he answered. "I'd also love to see where you grew up. See my sweetheart's roots." Again, the dripping sweet tone.

"Oh, Jack, you've got to put that husky voice away. You know what it does to me."

"Yes. Yes, I do."

Hearty laughter from the women she loved most rumbled from inside the glowing house, pulling at the corners of Livy's lips. What a wonderful day. And now soon—but in a much better way—her past and her future would meet.

CHAPTER
Twenty-Four

*J*ust here. To the left."

Jack pulled the truck through a tall ranch-style iron gate that framed a long dirt drive. The four-hour drive east on Interstate 40 had passed quickly, though Livy's stiff legs told another story. She rolled down her window and inhaled the familiar earthy, red-clay dirt. Rows of mature summer corn, as tall as the top of Jack's truck, ushered them toward her childhood home about a quarter-mile down the drive. It was a relief to see her family's land still producing crops, now managed by the neighboring farmers.

Jack parked the truck in front of the long porch where Livy's mother stood, hands on hips and an elated smile dancing across her face. Though it had been several years since her father passed, Livy still expected to see him standing next to Mama. He would always be waiting to welcome her with one hand waving and the other holding the snap of an overall suspender. Even without her father here today, her heart thumped with excitement. Jack was about to see this part of her life.

"Hi, Mama." Livy climbed two squeaky steps into open arms. The fresh scent of baby powder enveloped her as her mother's slender fingers pulled Livy's face close enough to rub their noses together. It had been their signature greeting since Livy was young.

"And who is this handsome fella?"

Livy pressed her lips to keep a laugh from escaping. "Oh, you're so coy, Mama. Really." Her mother grinned at Jack, who was standing just off the porch.

Jack's boots were loud as he stepped up with one hand outstretched, removing his ball cap with the other. He towered over them both. "Hello, Mrs. Johnson. I'm Jack Bowdon. It's so nice to meet you."

"Well, what nice manners." Her mother's cheeks flushed pink. "But I must insist you call me Katherine. It's nice to have you here, Jack." Oh, how Livy could relate.

Jack excused himself to retrieve their bags, and Livy turned to her mom. "Well?"

"He sure is a cutie pie—and a tall one!"

Livy couldn't agree with her mother more. Her eyes settled on Jack as he brought the bags into the house. She showed him to the guest room where he'd be sleeping while Katherine put the finishing touches on lunch.

Jack dropped his bag then followed Livy to her room next door. "So, there's only one wall separating us." His raised eyebrows and thin smile made him look impish. "Then again, I've already had you in my bed."

"Jack Bowdon, you're so bad." She swatted at him, but he grabbed her wrist and pulled her in for a quick kiss. He followed close behind as they made their way through the open living room into the kitchen.

Over a lunch of egg salad sandwiches, Katherine shared stories about what Livy was like as a child— headstrong, creative, and kind to everyone she met. They both answered Jack's questions about farm life and reminisced about Livy's father. He would have loved Jack, she was sure. After lunch, Livy helped her mother clean up while Jack looked at the family photos hanging on the living room walls.

"This man loves you, Olivia. I see it all over his face. And you love him, don't you?" Katherine held her daughter's hands and spoke in a whisper.

A tightness formed in her throat. "Yes, I do."

Her mother fixed her gaze out of the window above the sink. "He reminds me of your father in some ways. Strong and capable. Tender and open." What was it like being a parent, wishing the very best for your child but understanding how vulnerable life was, with no guarantees and no real power to stop sadness? Glancing at Jack again, it was impossible not to wonder exactly what their future held.

Livy patted her mama's arm then joined Jack, linking a hand through his elbow. "Want to see the farm?"

"I'd love to. Nice hair." He nodded toward a framed photo of Livy's eighth grade picture, her frizzy, teased hair just as awkward as the silver braces that peeked through an unfortunately timed smile.

She covered her eyes, head falling to her chest. An embarrassed moan escaped. "Yeah, time to go outside." She pulled him toward the door, which he tried to resist, craning to look at the wall of family photos.

"No, wait. I want to take that one home with me."

"Oh, there'll be time for more pictures," Katherine chimed in, patting Jack on the back. "Y'all enjoy looking around. Livy, watch for Buster. He's not getting around too good these days and sometimes plops down in the middle of the road if he's tired. The old hound wasn't good for much even when he was in his prime, but he's still good company and barks at any approaching vehicles. So I guess I'll keep him a while longer."

"Yes, ma'am," Jack said. "We had one a lot like him before I went to college. The old ones are worth keeping, for sure." He walked through the screen door to meet Livy on the porch.

Livy led Jack around the homestead, pointing out the pink birdhouse she and her father had painted for a Girl Scout project, the antique rosebush growing near the back steps of the house from clippings of Gram's bush back in Laurel Cove, and her favorite tree behind the garage. Jack's fingers ran over the bumpy edges of her name carved in the tall pine.

He rested against its slender trunk and arched his eyebrows. "Who carved this? A boyfriend?"

"No, Daddy did." She stepped closer to inspect the worn lettering and the jagged heart scratched around it. "He said he did it the day they brought me home from the hospital because he loved me so much, right from the get-go."

Jack reached under her chin and tilted her face to his. "That's really sweet."

Livy took in his eyes, ran her hands over the bristles of his two-day-old scruff, and pushed up on her toes to meet his lips. Having him here, at her tree, was like a dream. The pine didn't provide much shade, though, and in the afternoon sun, it was pretty warm. "Let's go for a drive."

Livy drove Jack's truck through town and showed him the highlights—her high school, the restaurant where she had her first job, the town hall where one of her paintings still hung after she won a county award. That evening, Jack insisted on treating Livy and Katherine to dinner at a local steakhouse.

Jack and Livy sat on the porch late that evening after her mother went to bed. The swing rowed in lazy rhythm, back and forth under Jack's outstretched foot. Shrill chirps of distant crickets and the swaying of the tall corn serenaded them from the darkness beyond the porch steps. A clear night displayed a blanket of silver stars.

"My mom sure likes you. She called you a cutie pie twice today." Livy spoke without lifting her head from Jack's shoulder.

"What can I say? The moms love me. I wasn't worried." He rubbed her arm.

"Oh, is that right?" Though he couldn't see her eyes roll, she was sure her sarcasm came through.

"Yep. Every mom of every girl I've ever dated has loved me. It's a gift, really."

Livy sat up so he could see her rolling her eyes this time.

He laughed. "But I have to admit, your mom is the sweetest of them all."

At that, Livy let out a loud laugh. "Exactly how many moms of girlfriends have there been?"

"You know what I mean! I just really like your mom. You look a lot like her, you know?" His eyes softened in the dim yellow porch light next to the front door.

"I've been told that my whole life. You should have seen us back before her hair turned gray. People used to think we were sisters."

Jack pulled Livy in close. "I can't wait to grow old and gray with you."

She breathed a dreamy sigh and rewarded Jack with a lingering kiss, her arm draped around his middle. Their eyes settled back on the expanse of land. Heat lightning danced across the sky in the distance. A delightfully surprising possibility struck her. What if he proposed here at the farm?

"I used to sit on this swing with my father." Livy tucked a flyaway strand of hair behind her ear. "We'd talk about everything, what was planted and how the weather had been, some boy at school who had broken my heart, the dreams my dad had for my life. One time he told me to not settle for a guy who didn't make me feel special. I wasted a lot of time ignoring his advice. And now, sitting here with you, I realize how wise his words were. You make me feel special, Jack, like no one else ever has. Thank you for that."

Jack pushed against the porch floor, keeping the swing in motion. "You *are* special. And I feel honored to have the chance to try and live up to the hopes your father had for you. To be treasured. I hate that I didn't get to meet him."

It had crept into her mind several times the last few months. "Me too. He would have loved you—maybe as much as my mom does."

Livy rested her head against Jack's shoulder again. The warm spot had become her place of comfort, respite, home. *He feels like home.* The thought covered her like a cool bed sheet on a hot summer night—satisfying and comfortable. She closed her eyes and secured the moment with him in her memory.

A warm hand rubbed up and down her arm. "Honey, time for bed." Jack's voice was as smooth as velvet against the sounds of the night. How much time had passed? From the crick in her neck, she must have dozed off for a while. She sat up straight on the swing, and rubbed at it.

"What time is it?" She stretched through a yawn.

Jack followed her yawn with his own and rubbed his shoulder she'd been leaning against. "After midnight."

Memories of her dad poking his head out about curfew earned a chuckle. "Wow. Why didn't you wake me sooner?" She pressed her palms to her eyes to clear them. "I'm so sorry you sat there so long. Your arm must be killing you."

"And miss the chance to watch you sleep? You know, your nose twitches sometimes. It's adorable." He winked at her, though his heavy eyes revealed how tired he was, too.

Livy rewarded his compliment with a hug as they stood, both stretching one last time before heading inside, saying goodnight, and retreating to their rooms. This time, in pajamas and snuggled under an actual cool bed sheet, Livy returned with ease to sleep and her thoughts of Jack...and home.

CHAPTER
Twenty-Five

With less than thirty minutes left of their trip back from Raleigh, Jack steered the truck and trailer through hairpin turns up the mountain that led into town. Moss-covered rock faces towered to their right, a dramatic drop-off and magnificent views of the valley to their left. Trees soon closed in on both sides, swallowing them into the lush late-spring shadows of Laurel Cove.

"It's good to be home." Livy waved at someone on Main Street a few minutes later.

"Yes, it is. I'm glad to hear you call it home." His words didn't adequately describe how wonderful that sounded. Livy considering Laurel Cove, there with him, home was just about the best feeling in the world.

She turned to him and raised the back of his hand to her lips. "You've made it feel that way, honey."

"I'm so glad." He reached over and took her hand in his. "So, I know you've got some art classes in Weaverville and want to get some things done at the house, but think you can spare some time on Saturday?"

Livy nodded while she dug her feet around the floorboard to slide on the sandals she'd kicked off. "Sure, what's up?"

"Well, we could use all the help we can get finishing up inventory that morning at the store. Then I thought I'd finally take you up on the Parkway to some of my favorite spots." She'd mentioned wanting to explore the Blue Ridge Parkway a few times recently. And the forecast was perfect for this weekend.

Livy clapped her hands and squealed. "I'd love to, Jack. Jen said the flowers are perfect this time of year. Oh, and I'll help with inventory, too, I guess." She leaned over the armrest between them and pressed an exaggerated kiss on Jack's cheek as he turned past the tall flowering hedges and trees that bordered her driveway. He couldn't wait to give her a proper kiss.

"What in the world?" Jack's stomach dropped, the truck rolling to a stop at the top of the drive.

Livy turned and gasped, hand flying to cover her mouth. "No."

White flowers Livy had planted in front of the porch were torn up. A kitchen window was shattered, and a woman sat on the porch steps, long blond hair hiding her face, which she held in her hands.

"Claire." Jack reached for his seatbelt, hands shaking. Something inside him warned to proceed with caution. "I think you should let me go talk to her. Stay here, okay?" He squeezed Livy's hand, insides twisting at the concern he saw in the lines on her face, and slowly exited the truck.

"Claire?" The gravel crunched loudly under Jack's boots. She didn't look up, but he could hear her whimpers. Hadn't she noticed them drive up? "Claire, look at me!"

She startled, shoulders shaking and eyes flying up to his. Streaks of mascara and tears covered Claire's cheeks. Trembling hands patted at her wet face, as she attempted a smile.

Jack stopped several feet from the porch, hands on his hips. "What in the world are you doing, Claire?"

"Hi, darling." She wiped her hands on the front of her jeans and stood, uneasy on her feet, clinging to the rail for support.

He gestured to the flowers, the window. "Claire. What the—?" His jaw flexed, teeth clenched.

"I went up to your house on Friday, but you weren't home. Then I drove over to the store and Jasper told me you were out of town and wouldn't be back until Sunday." Claire's voice sounded strange, as if she were desperate to sound normal. But something was unstable about her, her voice and body strained.

"You can't be here. You need to leave," he insisted firmly, working to control himself.

She didn't even look at him as she stepped off the porch, eyes glued to the grass. "So I came back to your house this morning, hoping to surprise you when you got home." Instinct told him to back up, keep the distance between them wide. "I sat on the back porch admiring the view. You really did a bang-up job on the house, Jack."

They were in the middle of the front yard now. "That is *enough*, Claire."

"I couldn't resist peeking in those huge windows." Her voice sharpened, an eerie shift from the almost childlike whimpers. "Imagine my surprise when I noticed a pair of women's shoes by the door and a picture of you with her on the end table." Her eyes met his, the forced smile pressing into a thin line. "How could you be seeing another woman behind my back? Did you think I wouldn't find out about the two of you?"

"What?" Jack's jaw relaxed, but his breath caught as if someone sucked the air out of his lungs. He was having trouble putting all the pieces together. She'd been irrational before, but this worried him. He chose his next words carefully. "Why don't you head home, calm down, and we can meet up later to talk more about this. Okay?" Jack just wanted to get rid of her. He'd deal with the damage she'd caused to the house later.

Just as quickly as the anger had surfaced, it was gone. "Come with me, please, darling." As if on cue, tears flowed again in glistening streams, dripping from Claire's nose and chin. She stepped forward with arms opened, close enough that he could hear her muffled whispers. "We belong together, no matter what. Even though you screwed up, I still love you and forgive you for what you've done. I just want us to be together." She reached for his hands, but he pulled away.

"Jack, stop it! You have to forgive me!" Her sudden shout made him jump. With eyes squeezed shut, she began pounding hard at his chest with her fists. He backed away and grabbed for her wrists. She swung her arms wildly, sobbing. Behind him, the truck door slammed. *Livy.* He turned to look for her as Claire's fist landed hard on the side of his face. His ear rang, his jaw instantly stinging down to the bone.

"Jack!" Adrenaline coursed through Livy's veins as she ran in long strides toward Jack and Claire now stumbling in a tangle around the yard.

Claire's crying stalled at the sound of Livy's voice. "Of course she's here!" she yelled at Jack, pointing in Livy's direction.

Livy stopped several feet short from where they stood, threatened by the intense hatred in Claire's voice.

"She isn't any of your concern." Jack rubbed at his jaw.

Livy collected her nerves with a deep breath. "Claire, it's okay. We can talk this through. I know it's hard."

"You don't know anything about me," Claire insisted through clenched teeth, though Livy saw fear and exhaustion in her dark eyes.

"I know you're sad and can't understand how your life turned out so different than you imagined." Livy gave Jack a slight, reassuring wave when he took a few steps closer to her, trying to keep distance between the two women.

Claire blinked hard, sending several tears down her worn face. It must have been so hard for Claire to see her ex-husband love another woman.

Silence fell over the yard. Claire's frame softened, her slumped shoulders swallowing her. Then Claire spoke, so low that both Jack and Livy took a step closer and leaned in to hear. "Last week, I overheard Lane and Hank talking at the market. Lane wondered how your trip to meet Livy's mom was going." Claire's gaze lifted in Jack's direction. "Hank said he thought she was perfect for you. At that moment, something inside me snapped."

"Claire, now hang on, I…" Jack's protest died in the breeze that teased the trees above them.

Livy looked to Jack and back at Claire. This had nothing—and everything—to do with Livy.

"I know we've been apart a long time, but it just seems wrong." Claire's arms extended with palms out, one in Livy's direction, one in Jack's—as if instructing them to keep their distance. "I screwed up. Now you've screwed up. I just want us to be even."

"*Even*?" Jack yelled, stepping dangerously close to Claire. "I've done nothing wrong, Claire. We aren't married. You can't be cheated on by someone who isn't with you!"

Oh, Jack, stay calm. His anger wasn't going to help matters at all.

Livy dared a step closer. "Claire. Claire, can you look at me?" The woman was consumed by guilt.

Claire met her eyes. "I think you need to forgive yourself for the past. It's okay to move on."

For a fleeting moment, Claire's face relaxed, anger melting to exhaustion again. Livy drew in a hopeful breath.

A strong wind blew through the yard, rustling the tall trees behind the house. What was that smell? Jack and Livy's eyes connected in shared awareness—panic replacing all hope.

Gasoline.

CHAPTER
Twenty-Six

*L*ivy's stomach retched. She'd give anything to wake up from this nightmare.

"Claire." Jack's voice was firm, resolute. "Is there gas here?" Claire suddenly crumpled to the ground, sobbing. Livy and Jack sprinted up the porch steps, the pungent smell almost knocking her over. Two spouted, plastic containers sat off to the side of the front door. One was turned on its side.

"Jack, what do we do?" Livy blinked against the sting of tears. Was all the work and love she'd put into Gram's house, and all the memories, about to be taken away forever?

"Do you see matches or a lighter? Something she'd use to start a fire?" Jack turned wildly in circles. Nothing.

Livy stepped into the yard to keep looking and froze, as if she'd hit a wall. Claire stood just feet from the porch pointing a small gun at her. Livy's eyes moved from Claire to Jack, pleading for him to do something.

"We can figure this out, Claire. Please put the gun down." With his hands out in front of him, Jack inched toward the two women.

What was happening? She'd heard people say that during life-threatening situations, their whole life flashed before their eyes. For Livy, it wasn't the life she'd already lived that ran through her mind, but rather the life with Jack she may never have the chance to live. She'd been so sure God had brought her back to Laurel Cove and to Jack for a reason. It wasn't supposed to end this way. *Please God, protect us and enter Claire's heart.*

"I'll always care for you, Claire." Jack was just a yard or two from them. Livy's chin quivered, tears threatening to fall.

Claire turned to Jack but kept the gun aimed at Livy. "Do you mean that?"

"You were my wife. That means a part of me will always care for you." He reached for the gun.

Claire took a step backward, though her arm went limp, gun pointing at the ground. "I can't believe what I did to you, Jack. You were so good to me." Hysteria filled her voice.

Livy felt the hot trail of a tear along her cheek. She locked eyes with Jack. His calmness willed her to keep her composure. She wiped the tear away with the back of her hand and took a deep breath.

"It's not too late to do the right thing." Jack addressed Claire again. "I can help you find someone to talk to and work all of this out."

Claire's arm straightened lazily toward Livy. "But what about her?"

Livy winced and stiffened. The barrel was even with her face.

"What on God's green earth?" A new voice sounded from the direction of the truck.

Claire spun and the gun released a shot in the direction of the voice.

Livy fell to the ground, covering her head with her arms. There was a scream. Feet running. Muffled cries. And then Jack tackled Claire, knocking the gun several feet away under a bush as they fell to the ground.

Mr. Wilson. Over her shoulder, Livy saw him lying on the ground against the truck. After a quick glance to Jack, who seemed to have control of Claire, she jumped up and ran to her elderly neighbor. His eyes were closed tight. "Mr. Wilson! Are you hurt?" She ran her hands over his chest and arms, searching for a wound.

He grimaced. "That crazy woman shot at me!" His voice was gruff but clear.

"Did she hit you?"

"No, she didn't hit me! She had that gun dancing all over the place like she was aiming at rotating ducks at a carnival."

Livy let out a relieved sigh.

"That bullet is probably still flying through the air somewhere in Tennessee. But it about scared the Holy Ghost out of me. I fell right down. Guess my survival instincts aren't quite as old as my body."

Livy chuckled. "But you look like you're in pain. Do you think you hurt something when you fell?" A broken hip or knee, maybe?

"Yes, dear. I fell on top of my cane, and it's poking me right in the kidney. Help me up, would you?"

Livy heaved Mr. Wilson to his feet, handing him his cane, and helped him to the back fender of Jack's truck. Across the yard, Jack knelt in front of Claire as she sat cross-legged on the grass, still crying. He had one hand on her shoulder, speaking softly.

Mr. Wilson spoke up. "I was out for my walk and heard some commotion when I neared your driveway. I made it about halfway up before I overheard some of what y'all were discussing and decided you might need some help. My daughter insisted I start carrying this stupid cell phone"—he pulled one out of his pocket— "so I called the police and told them they'd better get out here. But I never dreamed she'd have a gun." He shook his head. The gravity of what had just happened was likely sinking in for the old man. For Livy, too. Someone could have died—any of them, all of them. And the cottage, the memories of Gram, her hope for the new beginning she'd sought in Laurel Cove—it could have all gone up in flames. She collapsed against the side of the truck, and began sobbing into her still-trembling hands. Mr. Wilson shuffled closer and wrapped an arm around her shoulders.

They both looked up at the sound of sirens in the distance. Moments later, two police cars pulled up the driveway. Livy gave one officer an account of the incident while another approached Jack and Claire, taking Claire into custody. It struck Livy how civil it all was now—though nothing about this seemed real. As Claire was put into the back of a squad car, Jack joined Livy and Mr. Wilson near the truck.

Jack embraced Livy in a hug that enveloped her, his head bending to rest in the curve of her neck. He trembled. "I'm so sorry."

"Okay, you lovebirds. That's enough cuddling." Mr. Wilson rapped his cane against the bumper of Jack's truck.

Livy chuckled as she tightened her arms around Jack's shoulders. "It's okay, Jack. We're okay. It's over."

It took about an hour for the police to collect statements from Livy, Jack, and Mr. Wilson after they'd taken Claire away. Livy watched Jack shake the officer's hand before he left. Jack had the weight of the world on his shoulders as he approached her and Mr. Wilson where they sat on the porch steps. It would take some time for them all to recover from the day's events. Jack probably most of all.

"Let's get you home, Mr. Wilson." Jack reached to help the old man stand.

Even with such a personal trauma, Jack was still focused on others. Livy's heart swelled with pride and gratefulness.

While Jack drove Mr. Wilson back to his house, Livy began cleaning up. She stared at the house from the yard—the destroyed flowers, the broken windows, and the porch doused in gasoline. Livy climbed the porch steps, set the empty gas container upright, and unlocked the front door to assess any damage from the broken windows. As the screen door creaked open, something light yellow in her peripheral vision caught her attention. Crumpled by the edge of the porch was a lightweight jacket. It had to be Claire's. Livy picked it up. Underneath was an ink pen and a box of long fireplace matches. A chill crawled along her arm and up her neck. Things could have turned out so much worse. *Thank you, God, for protecting us all.* She folded the jacket over her arm. Something stiff inside a pocket caught her attention. Reaching in, she pulled out a folded piece of paper. One side was an advertisement from the Blue Bird Café Livy had gotten in the mail on Thursday. On the other side was a handwritten note. *Dear Olivia,* it read at the top. Livy drew in a short breath, following the elegant curl of the lettering. Why not a letter to Jack? Was she ready to read anything Claire had to say to her? But with Claire on her way to jail, it was difficult to maintain anger. Not for someone so taken over by guilt and heartbreak.

Instead of heading inside, Livy left the porch with the letter in hand and walked along the edge of the front yard where she could fill her lungs with fresh air.

> *Dear Olivia,*
>
> *I am Jack's first wife, Claire. I had my chance to be happy with Jack, and for a while, I was, but I was not able to hold true to the vows I made to him on our wedding day. For better or worse. But in my mind, I was expecting perfect. Selfishly, I went looking for perfect somewhere else, not realizing*

until it was too late that life with Jack—even the hard days—was as near perfect as life could get.

But I'm so confused. So tired of feeling guilty. I didn't know how to love Jack like he deserved. Now I can't get thoughts about the two of you together out of my head. It should be me and Jack. But I never gave us a chance to work, never wanted to admit my mistakes. It was so easy to blame him for my unhappiness.

I recently overheard a good friend of Jack's say that he loved you and is planning to ask you to marry him. I loved him, even when I made my mistakes. But the truth is, I don't deserve him. I never deserved him. Any woman who can heal Jack's wounded heart after what I did to him deserves the nearly perfect life he can give.

I'm sorry for what I've done to your house. I can't bring myself to light the matches. But I know I can't live watching Jack love another woman the way he could have been loving me, had I let him. Let him love you the way only he can.

Claire

A tear rolled down the curve of Livy's cheek and over her quivering lips. Claire had intended the gun for herself. She had written the note on whatever she could find after breaking the windows and destroying the flowerbeds. Sadness overwhelmed Livy, clutching at her chest. This woman, so broken and riddled with guilt, did not see any chance at being truly forgiven.

Livy gazed at the gentle cascades of the mountains in the distance. Her own sins may not have been as severe as Claire's choices today, but how miserable would life have been if she didn't believe in a loving Father God whose endless grace poured over her and washed away her bad choices, disappointing behavior, shortcomings, and failures? Indeed, that grace was what she'd found in Laurel Cove after her own sorrow. What she'd found through a fresh start.

"I forgive you." Her words, heard only by the lush nature around her, floated away on the breeze. Maybe one day she'd get to tell Claire in person. *Lord, be with Claire. She's hurting and needs to know your saving grace. You've already rebuilt my life. Rebuild hers, too.*

She read the letter again, this time her eyes catching on Jack's intended proposal. The familiar sound of Jack's truck made its way up the driveway. Even given the day's awful circumstances, Livy could not help but smile. She folded the note and tucked it in her back pocket. They had quite a bit of cleaning up to do, and she knew Jack would get around to his plans in his own time.

CHAPTER
Twenty-Seven

Jack could have predicted it. Two weeks had passed since the incident with Claire at Livy's house, and Laurel Cove residents were still in a tizzy about it. And Jack found himself at the center of town gossip once again.

"Another afternoon like this and I quit." Hoisting himself onto the counter behind the store's register, Jasper thumbed through a stack of receipts before tossing them aside.

Jack's shoulders hunched over the register as he struggled with a new roll of receipt tape. The store had finally resumed a manageable pace after a busy morning and afternoon. "I hear you."

"Claire goes nuts and everyone wants to come get a look at the poor ex-husband turned victim. It's not even died down. Don't get me wrong, the extra business is great, but no one's fooling me." A thump sounded behind Jack. "I'm going for a cold soda while I can. Want one?"

The register hood clicked into place. "Got it. And yeah, sure. Thanks."

Jasper was right. Ever since news had spread around town about what happened at Livy's house, he and Claire were once again the talk of the town. Folks he'd never seen step one foot into the store suddenly needed odds and ends. Many purchases amounted to less than ten dollars, which Jasper called the entrance fee to the circus. Several folks came right out and asked how he was. Most were nice about it and wished him and Livy well. Others were bold with their inquiries, proving just how fast facts could get stretched. Was Claire in jail? Was it true she'd punched Livy? One little old church lady even slipped him a card for her lawyer, who she said was ruthless about justice.

He had no intention of dragging Claire's name through the mud any more than the rumor mill would. Yes, she was incarcerated, but only from charges brought on by the police. And he was angry. Claire had put everyone in danger—including herself, but, thankfully, no one was hurt and the drama with Claire was over.

The front door creaked open, its bottom scraping the floor. Jack had been meaning to fix that.

"About time. Meredith and Greg busy today?" Jack brushed the eraser shavings off the sales ledger and set the book aside, his mouth watering at the thought of the cold drink Jasper was bringing him.

"Hi, Jack."

His eyes jerked up at the small but terse voice. Mary Sue and her mass of bright auburn curls approached the counter. He straightened. What did she want?

"Hi, there. Something I can help you find?"

"Jack, listen, you know I don't mince words."

He nodded. The *Closed* sign on the door begged to be turned outward. Another half-hour and he'd be free, off to dinner with Livy.

"I came to say I'm sorry." Every hardened feature of her freckled face softened. "I was just awful to you and Livy when you came into the restaurant a while back. That is her name, right? Livy?"

Of all the things Jack expected from Mary Sue, this beat all. "Uh, yes, that's right."

"As you can imagine, Claire had her own side to y'all's story. She was pretty convincing about your fault in what happened between you two. I know you and I were never friends, but I see now that I had no right to throw gas on the fire."

Jack couldn't help but chuckle at her choice of words.

"I honestly had no idea how troubled Claire was about everything. I'm sorry I was so nasty. Okay?"

"Okay. Thank you for saying so. That's really big of you." Jack extended a hand across the counter, which she shook quickly before turning to go.

Mary Sue paused with a hand on the door and turned to Jack. "She asks about you. She hopes you'll forgive her one day."

Jack hoped so, too. The doorknob pulled from Mary Sue's hand as Jasper walked in with two longneck sodas. She slipped past him and was gone.

"Geez, I can't leave you for five minutes, brother. Everything all right?"

Perspiration dripped down Jack's wrist from the bottle. He pulled the cap off under the edge of the counter and clinked the glass against Jasper's bottle. Cold, refreshing fizz filled his mouth.

"Yeah. Everything's going to be fine."

"Oh, dear, I'm sure going to miss having you here. The place will feel so empty." Aunt Bea stood with Livy and Jack in the parking lot of the inn. She shifted her weight back and forth and wrung her hands around the end of a pink handkerchief.

"I'm going to miss seeing you every day, too. You've been so gracious and welcoming." The Laurel Cove Inn had been the perfect place to spend these last few months. The two women embraced for a long, tender moment.

"I sure enjoy seeing my two girls lovin' on each other." Jack put his arms around Livy and his aunt, and they laughed.

Livy helped Jack load her car with the last of her things. "I'd love to have you over for Sunday lunch after church one day."

"I'd love that, honey. And come by any time!" The pink handkerchief waved in the air with more pomp and circumstance than the moment called for, but it was endearing.

Livy looked up into Jack's blue eyes and her contentment wrapped her like a blanket. "Thanks for helping me with these things. I'll see you in the morning around eight for breakfast, right?" Her love for him, with her whole heart, hit her most during simple times like this.

"Yes ma'am. And I like my bacon crispy." He winked before kissing her and closing the door. She headed out of town, no longer a resident of the old, charming inn.

The drive to the house felt different this time, both an ending and a new beginning. She'd anticipated this day ever since arriving the few short months ago. But the inn had become her home and Aunt Bea her family. Still, she was finally on her way to her home—where old memories waited to welcome new ones.

When she saw Gram's house that first full day in Laurel Cove, it looked sad, tired, and neglected—reflecting her own disappointed and disheartened state coming from New York. Now, the gravel under her tires sounded about the same as the car climbed to the end of the drive. But the view that greeted Livy today was everything she hoped it would become.

Standing outside the car, she took in the bright white siding, tin awnings gleaming under the sun, and the rainbow of blooms outlining the windows. The yard was free from rusty debris and patches of dirt, replaced by a fresh carpet of grass the color of limes. The house's signature pink concrete steps had a fresh coat of paint. It was cheery, inviting, and reminded her again of the beloved home she had visited as a child.

And yet, it would be a while before Livy didn't also see flashes of the dramatic encounter with Claire. The destroyed flowerbeds, broken glass, the struggle in the yard. *Lord, help me to fully forgive Claire. And help Jack.* It was a prayer she'd prayed at least once a day these past few weeks.

The rest of the day Livy unpacked her clothes and found places for the last of her belongings from the inn. She then headed out to the yard and spent a few hours tending to the flowers under the warm late spring sun, which, thanks to the breeze, was quite pleasant. The various blooms still had a bit of growing to do before they would begin to resemble Gram's nurtured, colorful yard. But it was coming along, and Livy intended to enjoy the chance to watch it grow.

The day before, she and Jack had installed a new tree swing for Beth and Noah to play on when they visited with Owen and Jen. Jack had pushed her on it when they were done, just as he had that summer when she was a young girl. Livy took a seat on the wooden plank seat and pushed off the ground, letting the sun wash over her as she glided. From childhood friends to being in love, life with Jack had come full-circle. The new start she'd hoped for in Laurel Cove turned out to be so much more than restoring a run-down home. She'd rebuild her life.

We did it, Gram. We did it.

CHAPTER
Twenty-Eight

*L*ivy blinked awake to a beautiful sunny morning. She'd been up late the night before with Jack and the crew finishing inventory at the store, but had no trouble throwing back the covers. She'd waited for weeks for their drive through the Blue Ridge Parkway. It took her no time at all to get ready. As she left the house, she grabbed her camera, sure there'd be some sights worth capturing today.

At Jack's place, Rex's eager licks and the savory aroma of breakfast greeted Livy.

"Good morning, beautiful." Jack brushed his lips against her cheek, a kitchen towel thrown over his shoulder and a spatula in one hand. He looked handsome and rugged in Army-green hiking pants and a snug gray T-shirt. His red NC State baseball hat was backwards, one of her favorite looks on him.

She peeked around him to the stovetop. "Smells like my favorite!"

"Yep. Blueberry pancakes."

She hugged him from behind as he flipped the last few onto a plate. "How'd I get so lucky?"

He turned with the plate of hotcakes and leaned close. "I think I'm the lucky one." His voice was low and tender in her ear.

They enjoyed breakfast overlooking the mountains then packed a few snacks and some water before heading out. Rex had always accompanied them on hikes, so when Jack patted him on the head and said, "See you later, buddy," it surprised Livy.

The entrance to the Parkway was only a few miles south of Jack's property. Once they turned onto it, the scenery took on a different feel. Laurel Cove was a small town and fairly remote compared to Asheville. But on the Parkway, it was as if nothing had been touched, save the narrow, paved two-lane road. Jack drove them around winding roads, some fairly steep, the truck hugging the side of the mountain. Looking too far over the edge made Livy dizzy, so she focused her gaze across the valleys to far-off ridges and peaks.

They pulled off at several lookouts and took pictures of grand views and even a few small waterfalls. They took time for Livy to read all of the signage that told about historic spots and little-known facts. She even got to see one of the famous aqueducts, an impressive feat of engineering.

When the sun, hanging high above their heads, warmed the pavement and rocks, they retreated to the shade of some trees for a picnic lunch. Patches of purple and red wildflowers danced in the wind. Everything was so lovely. After eating, they lay on the quilt they'd packed and watched the clouds pass through the bright blue sky, fingers intertwined. After a while, Jack looked at his watch and suggested they pack up and head down the road a little farther.

"There's a spot you've got to see before we head back," he said. "It's just above the tree line, where the air is thin enough that only a few plants grow there. It's really different from all of this. Worth seeing for sure."

"That sounds really neat. How much farther?" Livy had heard of the different environment past the tree line, but had never seen it for herself. It was definitely something to check off her list.

"Just about ten minutes, I think."

A few miles down the road, Jack maneuvered the truck up a steep incline. All of a sudden, the tall pine trees thinned out. Some only had needles on the very top points of their trunks. Other shorter plants had thicker, heartier leaves that reminded her of the desert. Jack was right. It was very different, but breathtaking in its own right.

Jack parked in a small lot for an overlook where only a few other cars were parked. Livy didn't see any other sightseers, so they were probably the cars of hikers who'd gone into the woods on the other side of the road. The view was magnificent. They stood there for a moment, breathing in the thin air, taking in the 180-degree view of the Blue Ridge.

"Let's go on an adventure." Jack took Livy's hand.

The phrase he used made her shiver and turn to look up at him. She'd asked him to take her on an adventure back when they decided to begin their relationship. It was what she'd ask him to do as children. She smiled and followed him across the road to a trailhead. They walked into the woods a short distance before coming upon a clearing framed by an impressive view of a larger mountain ridge to the north.

Then Livy saw it—an artist's easel in the middle of the clearing. The beautiful old easel they'd seen in the antique store the first week she was in town. It held what appeared to be a canvas covered with a white cloth.

What was going on? She didn't see any other hikers. She looked up at Jack with questioning eyes. He smiled and led her to the easel. So, he was the one who'd bought it—and she'd been so disappointed to see it gone.

"Jack..." Livy placed a hand over her heart, fingers shaking.

"Livy, darling." He paused and took a few deep breaths. She grabbed both of his hands, encouraging him. He smiled gratefully. "I've brought you here for more than just admiring the scenery. Way up here, above the tree line, only the strongest plants survive. They can't rely on the water that runs down the mountain after a rain or snowfall. They can't hide under the protection of bigger, stronger trees. Instead, they rely on their deep, strong roots, trusting that their

Creator has made them to not only survive, but to thrive in the conditions in which He's placed them."

Livy wiped at a tear escaping down her cheek, then reclaimed his hand. It shook, too, as she squeezed it.

"I believe God has placed us together to thrive. In our own ways, we've tried hiding under circumstances that were maybe holding us back. But with you, up where the air is thin and the view is so spectacular, I am not just surviving, I am thriving."

Jack removed the cover from the canvas and knelt on one knee. From his back pocket came a black velvet box. He opened it, presenting a diamond ring more breathtaking than the scenery. Livy's heart soared as she read the words painted on the canvas: "Be my adventure. Marry me?"

Livy let out a laugh mixed with happy tears. "Yes, Jack. Yes!" She lowered to her own knees, throwing her arms around his neck—the man she would soon call her husband.

He pulled back, taking her face in his hands. She watched his eyes brim with tears and mouth quiver. "You've made me the happiest man. I love you, Olivia." They then shared a long kiss—one whose passion matched the grandeur of the Blue Ridge itself.

Livy stared at the gorgeous ring sparkling on her finger as they sat in the grass savoring the moment. "So, how did you do this?" The thought and detail that went into this perfect proposal could not have been easy.

"When we were at your mom's, I spoke to her about my plans, asking her permission. She was so wonderful and asked me if I'd like to have Gram's ring. It was unexpected, but so perfect."

A gasp escaped Livy. She peered down at the ring he'd placed on her finger. In the excitement of the moment, she hadn't even noticed that the gorgeous, antique, round-cut diamond ring was the very same one she used to admire on Gram's wrinkled hand.

"Oh, Jack." It meant so much that he had included her mom in this moment by talking to her about his intentions first.

Once they had made their way back to the truck and were headed down the mountain, Jack explained how everything had come together. "I went back and bought the easel soon after we saw it that day I took you to breakfast at The Blue Bird, thinking I'd save it for your birthday or Christmas or something. But it came in handy a little sooner." He smiled, looking proud of himself. "I'm no artist, but at least it got the message delivered. Jen and Owen came up here a bit ago and set it up. We probably missed them by just a few minutes." He looked positively giddy, smiling bigger than she could ever remember seeing him smile.

"I love you so much." Livy thought she might burst.

"I love you, too," he said. "You deserve the best, so that's what I tried for."

Livy's thoughts wandered back to Claire's note, telling her that the woman who healed Jack's heart deserved to marry him. *Thank you, God, for making this moment possible.* The good, the bad, and the many moments of grace. She also included Claire in her prayers, asking for God to heal her in ways that only He could.

When they arrived back at Jack's house about an hour later, all of their friends were waiting to celebrate their engagement. The sound of music and aroma of the grill greeted them. When Livy and Jack walked out to the porch, the women screamed with excitement, and everyone rushed over to hug and shake hands. Owen blessed the couple with a celebratory prayer before dinner began a while later. The moment was sweet since Livy knew without even talking to Jack that Owen would be the one to perform their ceremony.

Later in the evening, after everyone had left, Livy sat on the porch looking out at the land. She and Jack had survived these crazy few months to see God's faithfulness prevail. A faithfulness mightier than all the obstacles they'd encountered. This was a story Livy would have never dreamed for herself back in New York City, but one she ultimately came looking for and found. The sliding glass door from the house opened, and Jack walked toward her with a steaming coffee cup. He'd been her happy memory, her someplace familiar. Now, he'd be her future, forever.

Epilogue

"Take a deep breath." Owen's hand rested on Jack's shoulder to still his swaying as they stood at the front of the sanctuary. *Lord, help me be the husband she needs.* His heart thundered in his chest. Jack focused on the impressive orange, yellow, and red hues of fall foliage through the tall windows of the church on this Saturday afternoon in mid-October. Just what Livy had envisioned for their wedding day.

Jack drew in a long breath. He smiled and relaxed as he looked across the congregation of Laurel Cove Fellowship Church and focused on the faces of friends and family who loved him—who had grown to love Livy, too. Lane and Hank fidgeted with their new baby boy. From seats near the middle of the aisle, Meredith gave him a smile and a wink as Greg offered a thumbs-up. Sweet old Mr. Wilson sat in the back row, leaning on his cane with both hands.

Jack found Katherine's eyes, brimming with pride and love for them both. With both of his parents gone, he had asked Aunt Bea to let him walk her down the aisle, arm in arm, and sit at the front to represent his family. She had cried then and was already crying now, wiping happy tears from her eyes with a handkerchief that Livy had given her with *Love J & L* embroidered into the corner.

Standing next to Jack at the front of the church was Jasper, his best man. He had been an invaluable friend and supporter in the very best and worst of times.

As the organ music began to play, Jack's mind flashed with highlights of the last seven months. He had known, in some small way, the moment they'd bumped into each other outside Room 12 that Livy was the one for him. *It hasn't always been easy, Lord, but it sure has been worth it.*

"This is it, buddy," Owen whispered in Jack's ear as the organist began the wedding march. A peaceful calm washed over him as the doors at the back of the church opened. Jen stepped down the aisle in a simple, elegant copper-colored dress. She beamed a bright smile at Jack when their eyes met. Next came Beth as the flower girl and Noah as the ring bearer, both so grown-up in their formal outfits.

Finally, the bridal march began, and the congregation rose, turning to face the back of the church. Jack's eyes fixed on the entrance, waiting for the first glimpse of his bride. He could not wait another moment to make her his wife. Livy stepped out, looking down at her feet. The white dress was stunning, and his emotions brimmed. *Show me those eyes.* She slowly looked up right at him. His breath caught and tears threatened to fall. Her sparkling green eyes never left his the entire time she walked toward him. Nobody else existed in the full church.

Their hands came together as she stood in front of him at the altar.

"You are beautiful." Jack's voice was a whisper, only for her. She answered with a tearful smile.

"We're here today to witness just one step—albeit an important one—of the adventure these two are on together. An adventure can be scary, requiring of us the best we possess. The strongest, most patient, most enduring, and most challenging parts. Sounds a lot like marriage to me." Owen paused as the congregation nodded and laughed.

Jack smiled at Livy, then at his friend for weaving in the language so important to their relationship.

When the time came to exchange vows, Jack held Livy's hands, rubbing his thumbs across her soft skin, and swallowed hard. "Olivia, if someone had told me almost eight months ago that before the end of the year, I'd be marrying the woman of my dreams, I would have laughed. I would have also been a fool for not believing in God's amazing love for me. In you, He's given me a gift." Jack's voice broke. "You are my precious gift. I promise to treasure you, to love you for the many ways you bless me every day, and to encourage you when you forget how marvelous you are. I promise to always see life with you as an adventure, keeping things exciting as well as keeping you safe. I love you."

Jack wiped a tear from Livy's cheek.

I love you, she mouthed. "Jack, darling." The corners of Livy's lips trembled. Jack squeezed her hands and smiled. "My entire life changed the day I decided to move here. I see now that God was setting my feet on a path—a path to you. And there's no place I'd rather be. I promise that I will love you fiercely for the caring, tender, thoughtful man you are. I will remind you when you forget the ways you are so wonderful and encourage you when you need a helping hand. I love you."

Jack's heart swelled listening to the words of his bride.

After exchanging rings, Owen prayed over the couple then turned to the congregation. "I am now overjoyed to introduce you all to Mr. and Mrs. Jack Bowdon."

Before Owen could say, "You may kiss your bride," Jack reached for Livy's face with both hands, unable to contain his excitement and enthusiasm that this woman was his wife. Just like when Livy walked down the aisle to meet him, it was as if everyone and everything faded away in that moment. Jack felt Livy melt into his embrace as he whispered in her ear, "I love you, Mrs. Bowdon."

"I love you, too, sweetheart. So very much." Livy threw her arms around his neck and kissed him again to the applause of the full church.

The inn was simply stunning decorated for the reception, just how Livy envisioned. Hors d'oeuvres, cocktails, and cake adorned tables draped in white linens under trees lit with strands of twinkling lights. The early evening sky gave a cozy glow to the celebration. The band that had played at The Garage the first night Livy and Jack danced together now played acoustic sets of their folksy tunes.

"I can't wait to take you home." Jack whispered the flirty line into her ear during their first dance.

"So you've said." Livy blushed like she had every other time he'd said as much. "It's been a perfect day, hasn't it?"

"It sure has." Jack dipped her then, and she let out a loud squeal that earned a laugh from the crowd.

"Hey, you two. Time to cut the cake." Meredith beckoned to them from a table near the dance floor with the ivory three-tiered cake that Greg had insisted on gifting them.

Livy savored the playfulness in Jack's wide eyes as he held out a piece of cake for her to taste. "Don't even think about it." She pointed a finger as onlookers encouraged him to shove it in her face.

"Don't you dare waste that cake!" Greg's voice bellowed from somewhere deep in the crowd, sending a song of laughter into the breezy evening sky.

"I wouldn't dream of it." Jack gingerly placed the sweet, soft cake in Livy's mouth then grazed her lips with his.

She returned the favor with a forkful of cake and a sweet kiss of her own.

The evening wound down with pats on the back, hugs, and the clinking of a few glasses full of the night's last champagne. With her husband's help, Livy settled into the truck and waved to the remaining guests. "Let's go home, Jack."

"You got it." Jack drove out of town with a few toots of the horn to his house—now *their* house—to spend their first night together as husband and wife.

Livy kicked her shoes off inside the truck and propped her legs on Jack's lap, leaning against the passenger door so she could look at her husband while they drove. He reached down and rubbed her feet, then an ankle, then a calf, then leaned further up her dress to reach for her knee.

"You're teasing me, Mr. Bowdon." Livy giggled and squirmed a little.

"Call me Mr. Bowdon again and see what happens." He flashed her a frisky smile, but his tone was deep and serious. Even after seven months together, she was still taken by his ability to be both sweet and incredibly sexy all at the same time.

"Mr. Bowdon." Her whisper was slow and deliberate.

They had just turned onto the long driveway. Jack pulled the truck to a slow stop on the shoulder of the road, parked, and climbed toward Livy before she could realize what was happening. The weight of his body pressed her against the door. He held the back of her neck with one hand and kissed her with the passion of a man who couldn't wait any longer to be with the woman he loved. Her body arched toward him, meeting his passion with her own. Then he pulled away, just an inch from her face, and smiled. "That'll teach you to tease me." He sat up, put the truck back in drive, and headed up the driveway, leaving Livy out of breath and speechless. Being husband and wife wasn't going to disappoint, of that she was more than certain.

"I'm off. See you in a few hours." Livy's lips were warm against his face as she leaned over the back of the couch where Jack watching a football game. She was off to teach a painting class at the cottage, which Jack had helped her convert to Art at Audria's, a studio space named after Livy's grandma. Since they were living at Jack's place—now *their* home—it was the perfect solution to requests for lessons Livy had received in the past several weeks. In every other way, too, life had just fallen into place with her, and Jack had never been happier.

After the game ended, Jack turned to putting away the laundry Livy folded that morning. As he reached into Livy's top drawer with some socks, he noticed what appeared to be a stack of envelopes sticking out from underneath a folded scarf. His curiosity got the best of him and he pulled them out. He instantly recognized Claire's unique handwriting on the outside of the eight notes addressed to Livy. He opened the one on top and began to read. It was dated only two weeks prior.

> *Dear Livy,*
>
> *I'm so glad to hear that the classes at the studio are going well. I knew you'd have a lot of success. Thank you for your offer to come and take a class, but I still don't think I'm quite ready.*

I've started seeing someone. We've only been on two dates, but he's very nice and polite and seems interested in what I have to say. I would appreciate your prayers as I see where it goes.

I know I say this every time, but your encouragement has made such a difference. I still can't believe you have forgiven me for what I did to you. I've been talking to my pastor about accepting forgiveness from God, but it's a slow process. Thank you.

I hope you and Jack are well.

My best,

Claire

Jack stared out the window. Livy and Claire had been in communication with one another? He pulled out the note on the bottom of the stack, probably the earliest. Sure enough, it was dated May 25, just a few weeks after the incident with Claire at Livy's house.

Olivia,

I'm sure you can imagine my surprise when I received your letter here at the clinic. I guess the whole town is probably talking about what I did and where I am.

Did you really mean it when you said you forgive me? I don't know how that is possible after what I did to you and Jack. People don't just forgive terrible things like this. But I am glad you found my note. Yes, I wrote that after I realized what I had done, how far I had let this go. I was—I am—so consumed by the shame and guilt about what I did to Jack. How I ruined everything.

Just before you and Jack arrived, I had decided it was better for everyone that I was gone. I got the gun from my truck and something to write on to leave you a note telling you that you deserved Jack.

And after receiving your letter, I know I'm right. Not only do you deserve him, he deserves you. Jack deserves someone good, someone who cares for others more than they care for themselves. Like he does. I'm working on it. I don't want to live like this, but I do want to live. They tell me it will be a long road.

Thank you for the Bible. I've not read one in quite some time. I don't think I'm ready for you to visit, but maybe one day.

Sincerely,

Claire

His wife amazed him. Jack wasn't sure what letter Claire was speaking of that she had found, but it seemed Livy had reached out to Claire to offer her forgiveness. Jack still struggled with anger toward Claire off and on.

Livy was encouraging him and praying with him about that. On more than one occasion she had said, "It's got to be in *your* own time." Now he understood that actually meant, "I may have forgiven her, but you have to do it in your own time." She didn't want to get in the way of his healing process.

Jack replaced the letters in Livy's drawer and stood at the window, grateful for his wife's forgiving heart. The pain and anguish they had all experienced in the last few years had been so tough. Claire's suffocating guilt. Livy's damaged confidence. Jack's own heartbreak.

Looking out at the mountains growing darker in the shadow of another brilliant setting sun over Laurel Cove, Jack was overcome with gratefulness and awe at God's faithful, endless, redeeming grace.

ACKNOWLEDGEMENTS

As the saying goes, it takes a village to raise a child—the same can be said for publishing a book. I would not have arrived at this point without the help of several special villagers.

I've been a writer for longer than I can remember. But thanks to the most loving and no-nonsense friend who refused to entertain my excuses, I sat down and wrote the first draft of this novel in November 2013. Indi, you made me believe I could do it. So, I did.

To my family and friends, you've been there the longest and cheered the loudest. Thank you for listening to my whining when things were hard, for your steadfast encouragement, and being genuinely interested in what I've chosen to do with so much of my time. Thank you.

To my critique partners who knew and loved this story in its earliest stages. Mikal, Shawna, and Holly—you three were there at the start and have taught me so much about the process of writing. Angela and Amy, so thankful to have you join our team! I can never repay you all for the time and thoughtfulness you've put into the book.

To Mikal, Jaime, Meghan, and Laurie. The four of you have become more dear to me than you will ever know. God brought us together over a shared interest and you've all taught me priceless lessons in the business of writing—but the friendships formed with you will far outlive any book success I could ever dream of having. Thank you for being my champions and loving me so well.

And, finally, to my great grandmother, Audria Bowdon. My vivid memories of childhood visits to her charming bungalow home in West Palm Beach inspired the cottage of Livy's Gram in this story. Playing in her gardens, picking vegetables and fruits, and watching her hang clothes on the line to dry—these are magical, cherished memories. It's my honor to introduce you to her gentle spirit and enduring faith in *Someplace Familiar*.

TERESA TYSINGER is a wife and mother transplanted from North Carolina to North Texas. When not writing charming southern fiction inspired by grace, she works as the Director of Communications for a large church. A member of American Christian Fiction Writers, the Religious Communicators Council, and the Association for Women in Communications, Teresa has spent over a decade committed to telling stories of faith through written word. She also enjoys offering graphic design services to other authors through her business, Good Day Publishing. She loves coffee, caramel, and happy endings.

CONNECT WITH TERESA

TeresaTysinger.com
and on Facebook, Twitter, Instagram, and Pinterest

Join Teresa's Newsletter Community for special
updates and exclusive offers at
TeresaTysinger.com/newsletter

Made in the USA
Middletown, DE
02 December 2017